TRIPLE POWER PLAY 3

JESSICA LYN

Copyright © 2025 by Jessica Lyn

authorjessicalyn.com

All rights reserved. No part of this book may be reproduced in any form or by any electronic or mechanical means, including information storage and retrieval systems, without written permission from the author, except for the use of brief quotations in a book review.

This book was not created with AI. This is a work of fiction. Names, characters, businesses, places, events, and incidents are used in a fictitious manner and are a product of the author's imagination. Any resemblance to actual persons, living or dead, or actual events is purely coincidental.

This book series was originally published in September 2023 on Kindle Vella.

Edited by Studio ENP

Copyediting and Proofreading: The Fiction Fix

Cover photo by Wander Aguiar

Cover design by Lori Jackson @lorilovesbookjackson

Formatting by Prince Finnick @princefinnickreads

WARNING: PLEASE READ!

First and foremost, your mental health is important.

This book series is a dark romance.
It contains themes related to mental illness and addiction,
including intrusive thoughts and ideations,
flashbacks and hallucinations,
past trauma/abuse, PTSD,
obsession, manipulation,
and substance use.

Please understand everyone's journey and experience with mental illness, trauma, addiction, and pregnancy are different.

Visit authorjessicalyn.com for a full list of content and trigger warnings.

This is a work of fiction.
The characters in this series are imperfect

but no less deserving of love.
'Fixing' them is not within the plot.

This book series was originally published in September 2023 on Kindle Vella. Current events and other similarities are purely coincidental.

For those who dream of a villain to chase away their nightmares, I give you Ethan Blackwood... and a tattooed, pierced Viking... and a baseball bat.

1
REECE

Fentanyl. The determining factor in Kyle's death. *Fentanyl.*

Charlie tosses a photo of a bloated and deceased Kyle onto the gleaming dining room table. "He wouldn't go out like that."

"Report says no one else entered the house." My voice is monotone, lifeless, my heart no longer in this. *Just bury the fucker and let me return to New York.*

"Except for Jackson, who knew how to evade you, me, and surveillance."

Kyle's Bel Air home is secluded, impossible to monitor. Nestled in the foothills of the Santa Monica Mountains, it's surrounded by dense trees and thick landscaping. Forest and shrubbery conceal trails leading to the garage, pool house, and off the property.

Any visitor could've easily gone unnoticed. We couldn't exactly park a surveillance van outside Kyle's gated estate—he would've spotted us instantly.

"Jax has been in New York and wasn't carrying drugs. He wouldn't be that stupid, not with Aurora, and not with fentanyl."

Everyone is pointing the finger at Jackson. Is it possible he tampered with his father's supply? Sure, but it's more suspicious Ethan met with the head of the Rossi family the day before Kyle's death.

Honestly, though, who gives a fuck? No one—and I mean absolutely *no one*—is crying over Kyle's death, not even the 'maid' who found him.

I shuffle through crime scene photos absentmindedly, processing nothing. I'm in a haze of shock and denial. I can't accept that my time with Aurora has ended. One moment, I'm on a bench with her in Bryant Park, wondering if I have a pregnancy kink. Next, I'm at Jackson's childhood home, fantasizing about taking my anger out on a corpse.

No pregnancy kink, by the way, just an Aurora kink.

My partner nails me in the forehead with a pencil. "Please, for the love of Yoda, stop moping. Get laid. Meet someone on Tinder. Go to a bar."

I cringe at the thought of touching anyone else, my stomach curling in on itself. "Not happening."

"I'm your closest friend, your *only* friend, and I'm telling you, she was using you to save her boyfriend's ass."

Aurora's loyalty to Jax is unshakable, but I had a close relationship with her before she learned I was an agent. We have a connection, one rooted in friendship, though it sure as hell doesn't feel platonic.

She didn't ask me to stay in New York, nor would she. Her attention was on Jackson, fear in her eyes whenever she glanced my way, a silent plea begging me not to take him from her.

Ethan gave me an entirely different look, one that threatened to dump my body in the Hudson River if I dared to arrest his bestie.

"She's not like that." Even if she were deceiving me, I'd

lay her fiancé's freedom at her feet. At my core, I'm her bodyguard, *her* soldier. "Let's keep searching."

Kyle was found in bed, an open bottle of laced Percocet on the nightstand—an easy kill or overdose. Possibly self-inflicted, but I highly doubt it.

As Charlie combs through the security footage, I explore the mansion. Following Jackson's disappearance from the arena, while Aurora was with Ethan, Kyle went silent. He seldom left the house, but there's no trash or clutter.

I wander through each room, scanning for anything notable before we ransack the place. After that, everything becomes disordered, and significant details can get lost in the chaos.

The interior is meticulous—too meticulous. No family photos. No pictures of a younger Jackson. No hockey memorabilia...

Kyle wasn't the proud father he wanted everyone to believe.

All the bedrooms resemble generic guest rooms. If any were Jackson's, you'd never know it. His belongings are gone, along with his mother's.

Except for the kitchen. Above the stove, I find a shelf of cookbooks, the only thing personable in the entire house. I remove one that appears well-loved, the spine worn and cracked, and set it on the marble counter. Flipping through, I spot notes in the margin in delicate, feminine handwriting.

His mother's cookbooks. It's a punch to the gut, and I feel for Jax harder than I expected.

Tucked within a dog-eared recipe for chocolate-chip cookies is a folded sheet of paper—a birth certificate with the name Thad Jackson Vaughn. The mother is listed as Jacqueline Monroe Vaughn, no father. The document matches Jackson's date of birth—May 12th—and my palms turn sweaty.

I wipe my hands on my pants and pull out another cookbook, where I discover a matching Social Security card. Holy shit. This is no accident.

Did his mother want him to find these? She must have. Why? Fake documents to run? Did she suspect their lives were in danger? Was she preparing to escape the house of horrors? To save Jax from Kyle's grooming?

Unbeknownst to her, her son never returned. He was abandoned at a boarding school in Canada and became a professional hockey player at eighteen.

A close-up photo of a pretty blonde and a green-eyed boy falls from the last book. He appears to be about four, missing the scar in his brow. They're at the beach, wearing identical smiles, his arms wrapped around her neck.

A shudder runs through me. It's like seeing an altogether different person, his eyes bright and full of life.

I put everything back, my intuition urging me to keep the books and documents for Jax. They belong to him, his story to unfold if he wishes.

Every day, I drift farther from what's *right*, no longer a mindless robot. It used to torment me not to follow orders. Now, I just want my heart to beat again, want the light to return to my own eyes.

One of my team members enters the kitchen. "Hey, you gotta check out the pool house."

I nonchalantly slide the cookbooks back onto the shelf the way I found them. I'll come back for them later.

* * *

Why would someone build a pool so far from their house? What fun is hanging out at the remote end of your property? No BBQ or grill—what's the point?

The pool house resembles a modest one-bedroom cottage. It's where Jackson attempted suicide about six months ago, and, judging by the dust and debris, nobody has been here since.

Scattered about are liquor bottles, pizza boxes, and drug paraphernalia. The bed is torn apart, clothes strewn across the floor, the bathroom mirror smashed.

By the looks of it, he spent his time getting high and playing video games.

One of the crime scene investigators, Shandra, dons gloves. "Should I bag and tag these pills?"

"Yeah, sure." They won't find anything connecting Jackson to Kyle's death. If Jax were messing with fentanyl, he'd be dead. "Hand me a pair, will ya?"

She tosses me some gloves, and I squeeze into them, barely. I check the pockets of the jeans lying beside the bed, finding empty baggies and a wad of cash. On the nightstand: weed, cocaine, pills, a half-full bottle of vodka, and a Ducati key fob.

Only Jackson would leave behind a fucking Ducati.

Shandra drops a yellow evidence marker and snaps a photo. "Why wasn't this place cleaned? Makes little sense compared to the main house."

"My guess is, whoever killed Kyle wasn't aware of Jackson's hideout."

She raises a brow. "You don't think it was him?"

"No. He would've done it long before now." I believe the words, but I also don't. I pushed him too far with my suggestion to use Aurora as bait. She was willing to do it, and it drove a wedge between her and Ethan. Jax was facing not only danger to Aurora but the loss of his best friend.

I didn't fully understand their dynamic then, but after spending time in New York, it's clear Ethan is important to Jax and essential to keeping the three of them together.

If Jackson killed his father, it wasn't solely for Aurora.

The rest of my search is dull—a baseball bat, surfboard, and wetsuit in the closet, a hoodie tossed on a chair. Half under the bed is a pair of sneakers; crouching, I note the size: fourteen.

Nothing remarkable until I catch a glint of light between the headboard and the nightstand. I glance over my shoulder. Shandra is at the bathroom vanity, tweezers in hand, examining potential evidence.

Reaching between the two pieces of furniture, my fingers connect with a cell phone. It has to be Jackson's; it probably fell when he was fighting EMS.

I slide it into my front pocket to scrub before turning it over and stand to my full height. "I'm headed out to the van. You need anything?"

"No, I'm good. Just finishing up. What's for dinner tonight?"

"Charlie's choice, so Chinese."

"Again?" she groans.

I force a chuckle and step out into the chilly night air. Lanterns cast deep shadows along the tree-lined trails and stone walkways. It reminds me of the parks and gardens I grew up with in the Carolinas, not a neighborhood in West LA.

In the van, I connect the iPhone and wait impatiently for the Apple icon to light up on the screen. It only takes one guess to crack his password—Aurora's birthday. I shake my head. And he thinks *I'm* the idiot?

Aurora blowing a kiss is his background picture. Sunlight catching her eyes highlights flecks of gold, giving her an ethereal glow. I take a moment to stare at it, wishing it were me on the receiving end, then force myself to move on.

No hidden apps or files. No email. I refrain from gawking at any more of Aurora's photos, no matter how much I really, *really* want to. I tell myself it's wrong to look at pictures not intended for me—damn morals.

Open in the browser is a home security website. Of course, the password is stored on his phone, and in seconds, I'm connected to cameras inside his downtown penthouse. The entranceway, kitchen, balcony, living room, and primary bedroom—all monitored.

He lived there with Aurora. Was he sitting here watching her?

Worse, he saved videos of them together—intimately— and a few of her alone. My stomach churns. He recorded and watched her, and I doubt she knows.

He can access this website anytime, anywhere, along with any hacker with half a brain. What a moron.

My emotions do a complete one-eighty when I find a recording of Kyle and two other men. I blink in disbelief. The tiny screen limits my view, but a quick scan of the video shows girls dancing and couples coming and going from the living room.

It's not the only one. Kyle frequently used Jax's penthouse. My mind races, considering who we might identify, only to realize if I hand this over, my team will have compromising videos of Aurora. I'm sure Jax reached the same conclusion.

Even if he removed Kyle's videos and deleted the others, he'd still have to explain the source. We could subpoena the website and recover the archived footage, and Aurora might find out the downtown penthouse had cameras the entire time she lived there.

He withheld evidence so his fiancée wouldn't discover he was a full-on stalker.

I'm so ingrained in my thoughts, I jump when Charlie opens the door.

He peeks his head in. "Hey, man. We got a problem."

"What is it?" I snap, trying—badly—to sound casual.

He narrows his eyes in suspicion but doesn't call me out. "I found something on Kyle's phone." He hands it over. "You recognize this address?"

"Fuck!" In the message is Aurora's new address, sent to some unknown perp, along with pictures of all of us, including me. "Did he send these, or did someone else, after his death?"

"Good question."

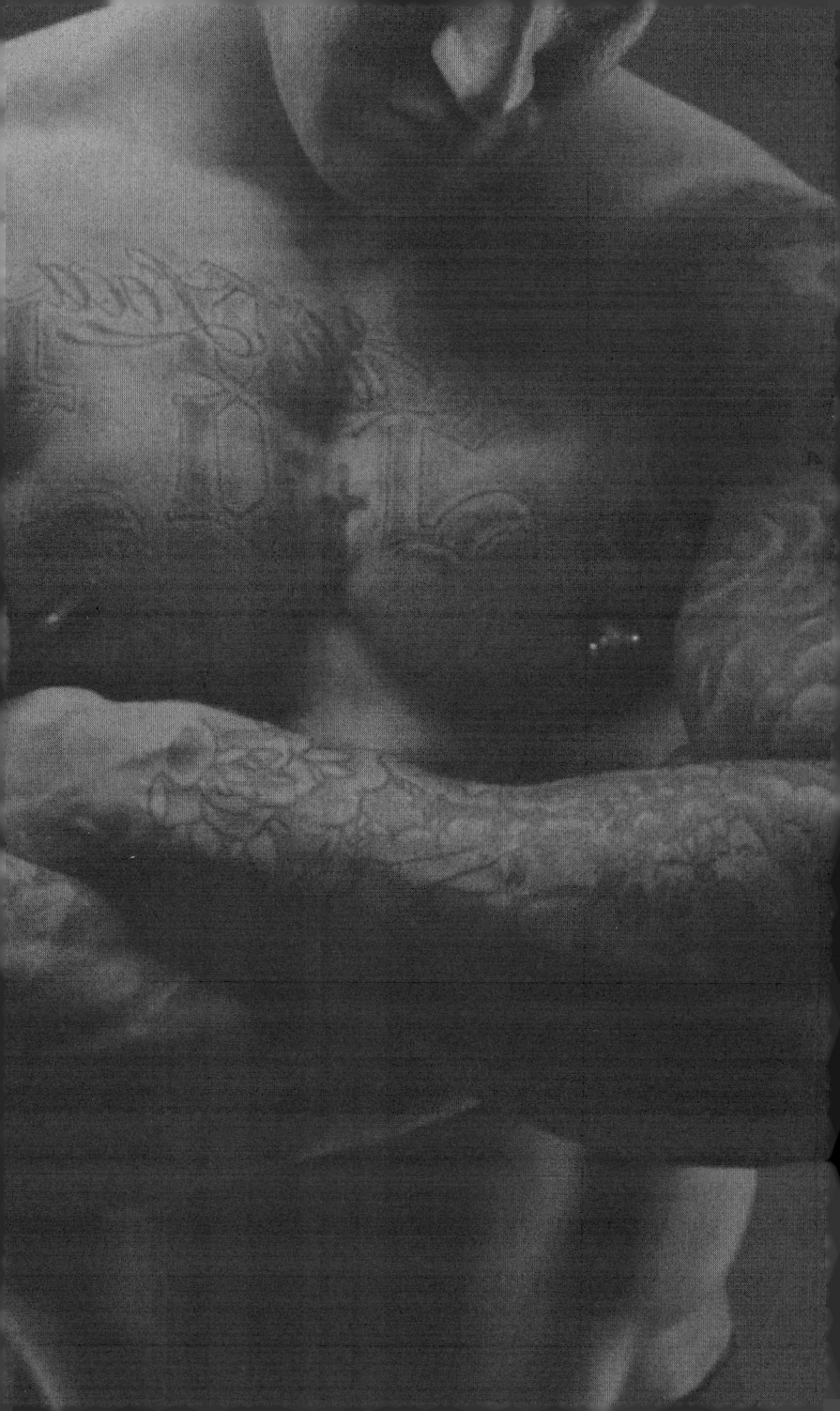

2
REECE

"So Kyle was still keeping track of his son," Charlie says around a mouthful of shrimp fried rice. He's the sloppiest eater, worse than Jax, who at least tries to be polite while stuffing his face.

It's just the two of us in this creepy house, using Kyle's dining room table probably more than he ever did. The rest of the team bailed on another takeout dinner.

"How'd he even find the address?" I push the Styrofoam container of General Tso's chicken away. I can't stomach it with this conversation and the dread swirling in my gut. "And why would anyone else need it? Who?"

He sweeps his shaggy hair from his eyes with the back of his hand. "Doesn't mean Aurora is in danger. I know that's what you're thinking."

I clench my jaw, exacerbating the headache coming on. With Kyle dead, Aurora should be safe. *Should be.* Doesn't guarantee she is. "What if they're aware of the investigation and believe Jackson has evidence? They'll go after him."

Charlie arches a brow and holds my gaze. "Does he?"

I trust my partner explicitly. We were deployed together

before joining the Department of Homeland Security. Whatever lies ahead in life, he'll follow me. "I'm not protecting him, if that's what you're asking."

He cocks his head and purses his lips.

"I'm not," I insist. "I'm protecting Aurora. I have something, but I need your help."

Hours later, after painstakingly going over the evidence, I'm staring at the ceiling of my hotel room. Unable to sleep, I check Aurora's location—she's in New York. She has the guys with her, including the twins, but it still weighs on me. I should be there to protect her.

I flip the phone over in my hand, wanting to call, but it's past midnight on the East Coast. I'll message her. If she's awake and replies, maybe I can relax and get a few hours' sleep.

> I need you to be safe for me, princess.

Three dots pop up, and a smile replaces my unease. It's not normal—or helpful—to be this excited over a simple text.

ANGEL
Everything okay?

> It will be. Be good and stay with the guys.

ANGEL
I'm always good 😇

I might be imagining things, but that response feels a little flirty.

> Liar. Why are you awake?

> ANGEL
>
> I haven't been feeling well. Spent most of the day in bed.

It's likely anxiety, her worrying about Jax, but her being sick only adds to my misery. They're too preoccupied to care for her properly. I bet they didn't even check her blood pressure.

> Where's your harem?
>
> ANGEL
>
> ☺ Sleeping. We have an early flight tomorrow.
>
> You need me to take care of you? Say the word, and I'll be there.
>
> ANGEL
>
> Go to sleep, Viking.

Nope. Not flirting. Damn.

> Yes, princess.

I fall asleep with a stupid grin.

Her scream echoes in my skull. I bolt upright and grab my pistol from the nightstand. I'm shirtless, only in a pair of black boxer briefs. My weapon out in front of me, my heart pounding, I navigate through the suite, finding it empty.

I spin in circles as flashes of lightning fracture the darkness. Only Aurora is here, shaking and frightened. I place my gun down and draw her into my arms. "It's just a storm, angel. You're safe."

She peers up at me, her expression full of fear. "Can I stay with you?"

I hesitate, knowing she's too much temptation to have in my bed.

Her eyes turn pleading. "Please, Reece."

My name escapes her lips, and steals my restraint. I lift her, carrying her to the sofa, her soft, silky legs encircling my waist. She straddles me and lays her head on my shoulder. Thunder crashes, and she shivers in my arms.

"Shh. I got you. I'm here." I grab a blanket from the back of the couch and wrap it around her.

"You can't want this."

Why does that sound familiar? And why can't I want this? I do. I want her so fucking bad. My erection is harder than it's ever been, throbbing underneath the weight of her perfect ass. "I want this. You know I do."

She sits up, and the blanket falls. Like the day in the kitchen, she only wears a T-shirt, but tonight, her nipples are pebbled, her bare thighs pressed to my waist. I clench my fists to stop from touching her.

"Why?" she asks. "Tell me."

I'm in love with you. It physically hurts me to stay away. *Yet, the words remain stuck in my throat. "Just sleep. Okay?"*

She releases a frustrated sigh and lies back down. Her disappointment is a deep ache in my chest. I'm fucking this up, again and again.

"Aurora—"

I tilt my head, and she's right there. Our lips brush, and I feel it throughout my entire body, every cell awakening.

Her fingers weave through my hair, and she grinds against my erection. "Please."

My hands come to her waist. "Angel..." My voice is rough, my resolve hanging on by a thread.

She trails kisses along my jawline and rocks her hips.

I release a throaty groan and grip her ass, guiding her over my length. "What do you need? Say the words, Aurora, and everything changes. You just better mean them."

"Make me yours," *she breathes.*

Three words I never thought I'd hear. Three words I never knew I needed. Three words that turn my entire world upside down.

A whimper breaks through the sounds of the raging storm as she becomes mine, one thick inch at a time.

A sharp gasp, my piercings hitting the right spot.

Her ass meets my thighs, my cock buried deep, her tight walls gripping me like the sweetest oblivion.

I clutch her to me, afraid to let go, afraid she'll slip through my fingers.

Her lips find mine, an our tongues intertwine. She lifts her hips, taking her pleasure and my heart.

She's greedy. Her tanned thighs widen, her bare, smooth pussy stretching to fit every inch of me. She takes it all—my skin between her teeth, my cock until my piercings hit deep and she's crying out, my sanity when she shatters with my name on her tongue...

She's simultaneously destroying me and piecing me back together.

I surrender to the madness, pounding months of resentment, desperation, love, and lust into her. I memorize every detail, never wanting this to end. The way her breath hitches and her legs tremble. Her seductive scent. Her moans as she begs for more. The powerful wave of her cunt milking me for what belongs to her.

My balls hug my shaft. I grow impossibly hard, and her body tenses with the realization of what's coming.

She's not escaping me. She said the words, and I'll never let go. "Don't you dare fucking stop now. You're mine, and you're taking all of me."

Ecstasy dances in her half-lidded eyes. "Say it again."

"You're mine." I slam into her. "Mine to touch." Thrust. "Mine to please." Thrust. "Mine to care for." Thrust. "Mine to protect." Thrust. "And mine to fill."

Reality pushes in, and I shove it away, holding tight to the dream...and my throbbing cock. I still feel the ghost of her—her heartbeat beneath my palm, her lips on my skin, the weight of her on my thighs, the taste of her on my tongue.

I stroke harder, faster, the fantasy of her cries of pleasure sending me over the edge.

"Fuuuck, fuck, fuck. Shit." I come so hard, the air freezes in my lungs, my cock jerking, shooting cum over my chest and stomach.

When I'm finished, I collapse into the pillow, gasping for breath, my body tingling from head to toe. My eyelids fall shut, and I see her, those golden, lustful eyes piercing my soul, and I crave her worse than ever.

3
ETHAN

Once we're settled into our seats, I clear my throat. "We only have a thirty-minute flight and a lot to discuss."

I'm behind schedule getting to Montreal. I wasn't leaving Jackson—even though he seems unconcerned about Kyle's death—and he needed to meet with Rocco to straighten out his father's affairs. Rocco feared Kyle's sleazy lawyers would take advantage of Jax without *persuasive oversight and a unified front*—his exact words.

Aurora leans over the armrest and kisses my cheek. "We can talk about everything later. Just relax."

Worried about her stomach and wanting her to be comfortable, I raise the divider.

Jax huffs. "Seriously, dude. You're freaking out. I feel it from over here. Take a nap. If I have to listen to you snore again tonight..."

"First, *dude*, I don't snore. Second, we won't be sleeping in the same bed tonight." My gaze connects with Aurora's. "You'll stay with Jax while we're with the team."

Her jaw drops, and she spins to face her fiancé. They do

that silent communication thing. He quirks a brow, and cocks his head as if to say, *I told you*.

I have no idea what they're debating—I don't speak *Jauroran*. "You two wanna share with everyone?"

She picks at her fingernail polish. "Are you sick of us, or are we back to pretending we're not together?"

"He's dumping us." Jackson's shoulders sag, and his tone is so grave, it's almost convincing. "Bastard."

"I'm not dumping you." Why am I even answering him? Entertaining his foolishness? "Just listen for ten seconds."

He wraps an arm around her baby bump and kisses her temple. "You and the baby will always have me. We don't need him. Sex is better without him anyhow."

His diabolical eyes meet mine, and my lips tug into a smirk. He's a damn liar. Sex with us is phenomenal, and he knows it.

"Set aside the fact that I make sex spectacular"—Aurora giggles, and he scoffs—"this is the calm before the storm. All we know is Kyle was found dead by the cleaning lady."

"So cliché." He releases a dramatic sigh. "I was really hoping for a beheading or dismemberment."

I ignore his theatrics. "When the media finds out, it'll be chaos. Add your return and our unorthodox relationship, and that's a lot of interference for one team."

Our girl hangs her head, and silence falls between us.

It's not my intention to hurt her. I have to focus. They're a distraction, but if I leave them to their own devices, there's no telling the mayhem they'll cause.

I tilt her chin and lift her gaze to mine. "I'll prioritize alone time, but if we want this to work, there needs to be boundaries."

Her stomach rumbles, and my mood plummets.

"You didn't eat?"

"When was I supposed to eat? You rushed us out the door this morning, and I forgot."

Jackson throws off his seat belt. "I'll find something."

I pinch the bridge of my nose. How does someone forget to eat—and their prenatal vitamins, requiring a return to the loft, and where they crammed their ID in their bag, *and* that their tickets were on their phone, also lost in their bag?

My limited patience snaps. "Do you want to be with me?"

She recoils but recovers quickly. "Are we back to this, Blackwood? Are my imperfections too much for you? You know what Reece does when we travel? He—"

"No," I cut her off, "and I don't care. This is how it's going to be. I'll give you everything—my time, attention, love, money, protection... In return, you'll shut off that overworked brain and give *me* everything—your time, attention, worries, trust, love, body. Your complete submission."

A scowl twists her pretty face. "That's not a relationship. That's you telling me what to do."

I grin, a slow, satisfying smile spreading across my lips. "You're getting this already."

Her glower intensifies. "Why do you get my body but I don't get yours?"

"That's what you focus on?"

"Yeah, it sounds suspicious."

She never ceases to amaze me. "No one gets my body but you, baby girl. Is that better?"

"Yes. Go on." She gestures with her hand.

"You marry Jax, but you give yourself to me. You wear his ring, but *I* have control. I ensure you have everything your heart desires, and you focus on you and the baby—nothing more. Not work. Not the case."

She blinks, blinks again. "Okay."

That's it? No smart-ass comments?

My knuckles ghost over her cheekbone. "That's my girl. Email me your expenses. Send Felicity your notice. Understand?"

Her head bobs gently, a faint smile playing on her lips. "You said everything my heart desires?"

I nod.

"Well, I have a list of stipulations."

There it is. I trace my thumb over my bottom lip to hide my amusement. "Do your worst, love. Let me hear it."

Chin held high, she projects an air of superiority. "I'd like the loft studio—if the twins aren't using it—for my own clothing line."

"Easy. Done." I'm one thousand percent certain they bought it for her anyway.

"I walk the runway next year."

"Not if you're pregnant—talk to your fiancé about that."

She drops her chin, her gaze unwavering. "I want my bodyguard reinstated. Make it happen, Blackwood, and you can have whatever you want."

Now, it's my turn to blink in astonishment. When the shock wears off, I toss my head back, laughter bursting from my chest and reverberating through the cabin as tears leak from the corners of my eyes.

This fucking girl.

* * *

Avoiding Aurora proves to be harder than expected. I finally have her with me, and I devise a plan to keep her away. What is wrong with me? Sometimes, the part of my brain that demands control is an uncompromising and jaded asshole.

I settle into my room and force myself to focus on preparing for tonight's game. I'm already behind schedule, and I missed morning skate.

Only for them do I neglect my responsibilities—or perhaps I'm choosing my priorities.

Jackson's suspension prevents him from being with the team, which is helpful. I don't feel guilty about leaving Aurora alone, but I constantly wonder what they're doing.

They mentioned exploring the European-style city, and my mind plagues me with worries. I haven't discussed the bodyguard situation with Jax. I doubt it'll go over well.

Instead of paying attention in meetings, I find myself texting him to be sure Aurora dresses warm, eats a solid meal, and doesn't leave his side. He replies with his usual snarky '*Yes, Dad,*' but he doesn't send me any pictures—not that I asked. Still, it's disappointing.

The team gathers in the lobby before the game, security present, fans snapping photos, a few players signing autographs. My coaching staff and I are the last to arrive. The excitement is palpable; smiles abound, and conversations are filled with laughter. The team hasn't been this animated all season.

Then I see why.

My assistant coach slows his steps beside me. "Wow... she's..."

"Mine," I blurt, a stony glare solidifying my absurd possessiveness.

He shoots me a sidelong glance, an amused glint in his eyes, a smirk on his lips. "Damn, I was about to say...here. She's *here*...with O'Reilly."

My gaze returns to the most stunning woman. In the middle of the crowd, Aurora charms those around her and doesn't even know it.

A low growl rumbles in my throat. She's terribly underdressed for the snow, wearing a peacoat undone to reveal a sweater dress that hugs her curves, a stretch of thigh exposed above her high-heeled boots. How will she walk in those things? It's winter and slippery.

My mind journeys to a time of loincloths and chest-thumping, my inner caveman urging me to knock her up with twins next so she can't easily hide the evidence of my claiming. Perhaps Jackson was onto something with the hockey team of kids.

She stands beside my captain, players sneaking peeks at her while they joke around with him. Her long, dark hair is loose and wavy, and as she chats with Grant, she runs her fingers through it seductively. Jealousy curls tight in my gut. Why does Jax have her out here? Grant is the biggest playboy.

Before I can stop myself, I'm stalking over. "What are you two doing here?" The words come out as hard as intended, catching everyone's attention.

Jackson gives me a knowing, taunting grin. "Chill, Coach. We're just leaving."

My little brat extends her hand. "Hi. I'm Aurora, Jackson's fiancée."

My star player snorts, and Grant coughs, but her polite smile never wavers.

She's letting me define our relationship in front of the team. Whatever I choose, she'll follow to a tee, and it'll drive me fucking mad. If I pretend not to know her, she'll do the same, icing me out.

A pang of *something* strikes me in the chest. Regret? Dread? Whatever it is, I don't enjoy it.

I take her hand and pull her to me. Releasing her, I zip her jacket and thread the buckles through the leather loops. "Stop showing off what's mine," I grumble, my tone low.

"Just making sure you don't forget." Her voice is flirtatious, barely above a whisper.

"Never. I'll be thinking about you all night. Now, behave. Go play with my money, not my emotions."

Her pouty red lips curve into a pleased smile. "Yes, sir."

"Jackson—hat and gloves, a full meal."

He gives me a sarcastic salute and laces his fingers through hers.

Later, after that buzzing energy carried us to victory, I lie in bed, craving my girl. I consider going downstairs to have a drink with the team, but a sharp feeling of betrayal has me dismissing the thought.

I only want Aurora and Jackson's company. I want to know about their day, what she bought, what she ate. I want to watch Jax braid her hair while she chatters about her newest infatuation.

I climb out of bed. Yeah, I'm fucked.

Jackson opens the door, a smug grin plastered on his face. "Couldn't stay away, could you?"

"What can I say? You're just too pretty."

His smile fades, his eyes harden, and he spins on his heel, jaw clenched.

I step inside the entryway, kick the door shut behind me, and fist his shirt.

"Hey." Risking it all, I yank him to me. His back collides with my chest, and I wrap my arms around his front. "I'm sorry."

He grips my forearms but doesn't throw me off him. "I'm fine."

"You sound like Aurora." I inhale deeply. "Smell like her too."

A shudder racks his body, his shoulders bunching up to his ears. "Don't sniff me, you creep!" He elbows me in the ribs and shoves me away, his voice laced with laughter. "God, I hate you."

My shit-eating grin is impossible to hide. "Is that why you have goosebumps?"

"Fuck off."

He strides into the bedroom, and I follow.

"It's your baby daddy," he tells Aurora then plops his ass in a leather chair in front of the fireplace.

"Hey, what are you doing here?" She beams at me from the floor, folding and packing newly bought clothes.

She's like a kid at Christmas, and I love it.

Bending down, I cup her face and kiss her lips. "Visiting my favorite person."

"I hear we have a new place." Jax fixes me a halfhearted glare. "I thought we weren't buying any more property?"

I settle into the chair across from him, Aurora between us. "It was already hers. I'm just encouraging her creativity."

He stretches out his legs. "She has a whole Pinterest board of design ideas. Be prepared."

"Come show me, baby girl."

She grabs her iPad and climbs onto my lap, wearing an oversized T-shirt, tiny shorts, and those tall socks that drive me crazy. Relaxing into me, she flips through pictures. "I wanna stick with the industrial aesthetic. I like the exposed brick and wooden beams."

"Me too." I point to a picture of a bathtub facing a city skyline. "What's this?"

Mischief dances in her eyes. "For us. Much bigger, obviously."

Now I look at Pinterest and take bubble baths. Jesus, fuck, what have they done to me?

Aurora reads on my lap while Jax and I discuss the game and upcoming schedule.

My body, heavy with exhaustion from the day, sinks into the chair. Why am I always tired around them—so bone-tired, maybe I *do* snore—but can't sleep alone? It's as if my brain instinctively knows this is home. I can relax.

"Your suspension ends soon," I tell Jax. "After this weekend, we'll be flying with the team." I don't have to remind him this leaves our girl with no protection or support.

She catches on quickly. "I can fly solo."

"Absolutely not." I smother a yawn with the back of my hand. "We could hire—"

"No." He cuts me off, firm and nonnegotiable, before I even say Reece's name.

"What's your plan then? You know how chaotic traveling can be. Media, ice time, team meetings…"

Shy whiskey eyes peer up at me. "You don't want me to go?"

"No, I do. If I had a choice, you'd be waiting for me in my hotel room, but I need you to be safe and for Jax to acknowledge my expectations. You can't travel with him."

He leans forward, eyes narrowed. "That needs to fucking change."

I tell it to him straight, knowing if I give him an inch, he'll take a mile. "If I made an exception for our girlfriend, I'd have to make an exception for the entire team. We'd have a plane full of family. It's a logistical nightmare. She can't go."

A threat burns in his gaze, gripping me. His distress is palpable, and my chest tightens—not out of fear of him, but of my intense feelings *for* him. His anguish is my anguish.

Before I can make sense of it, he's hitting me with another blow.

"And if we hire your *boy toy*?" he sneers, jaw set.

I don't understand his jealousy toward Reece, at least not where I'm concerned. The bodyguard follows Aurora's wishes, not mine. Like everyone else, he's wrapped around *her* finger. Reece listens to me and protects Jax because it serves Aurora—that's the only reason.

She straightens in my lap at Jackson's harsh tone. "I'll stay home. It's not a big deal."

It's a tremendous deal. His sanity depends on her. He plays better with her in attendance; therefore, someone must accompany her. "He's not my boy toy. Don't start. He'll fly with her to games, sit with her in the crowd, and she'll sleep with you at night. We've done this before."

A spiteful, tight-lipped grin stretches across his face. "Too bad he's a little busy right now."

"He'll return." Aurora picks at her nails. "If I ask him to."

Despite knowing the truth of her words, my hackles rise. "How do you know that?

Her gaze meet mine, hesitant but unwavering. "He told me."

Jax scoffs. "Of course he did."

I grip her chin. "When? Since he's been gone?"

She twists the hem of her shirt around her finger. "Yes. In a text. It's not what you think. He was worried."

Nothing is easy with these two—well, except sex and affection. Aurora's attachment to her bodyguard directly opposes Jax's desire to have her to ourselves and never see Reece again. Unfortunately, we need him. Still... "No texting. If he's concerned, tell him to contact me. Understand? Don't keep shit from me."

"Oh-kay." She rolls her eyes.

I scoop her into my arms, bridal style, and stand. "Are

you giving me sass?" I drop her onto the mattress unceremoniously. "You ready for bed?"

"Yeah." She glances between Jax and me. "Are we...are you spending the night?"

"Maybe. Get undressed so I can remind you who you belong to."

Jax remains seated, his legs spread, his arms crossed.

Ignoring his tantrum, I switch off the lights, leaving the fire burning low. I yank my shirt over my head and toss it at him.

"Fucker." He snatches it, but not before it hits him in the face. "You're not persuading me with sex."

"Wouldn't dream of it." I strip to my boxer briefs. "You can sit there and watch."

4
JACKSON

I'd enjoy watching Aurora and Ethan fuck, but you know what I'd love more? Being inside her with him.

And the asshole knows it.

There's nothing greater in this world—no drug, no high, no accomplishment—than having sex with my two favorite people, Aurora's pussy tight around me, Ethan's cock sliding against mine, only a thin layer separating us, his dirty mouth... Fucking heaven.

I'd give anything to have this the rest of my life, kill anyone who came between us. We're the perfect trio. Why chance screwing it up?

The warm glow of the fireplace casts long, flickering shadows, leaving the bed in muted darkness. Aurora moans, and like a siren's call, I head to the bathroom for the pure body oil she uses, the only thing we have for lube. I set the bottle on the nightstand and strip naked. My cock springs from my boxer briefs and smacks me in the stomach, furious and ready.

I climb into bed next to her, Ethan on the other side. They're kissing, passionate and lazy, tongues intertwining.

My gaze lowers, tracing the rippling muscles in his arm as his fingers fuck in and out of her, and my dick twitches.

Her legs spread wider, inviting me in. I reach back to grab the oil and drizzle some over her pussy.

Ethan lifts his head, his hair tousled, lips swollen, eyes half-lidded. "You done being a brat?"

I hand him the bottle. "Here. You're welcome. Now, fuck off." I ignore his smug grin by kissing Aurora.

The three of us come together effortlessly—no awkwardness, only unadulterated pleasure.

She fists my cock and moans in my mouth while he stretches her ass, and I alternate between fingering her cunt and circling her clit. His hand brushes mine, and I feel him moving inside her, only adding to my already rapidly-building climax.

Aurora breaks our kiss, writhing and whimpering, fingernails digging into my wrist. "You're going to make me come."

"Fuck," he mutters low. "You like getting both your holes filled, don't you, baby? Our perfect fucking girl."

Our girl. No one else's. There's no room for another. I'm not at all attracted to Reece, and the thought of him sharing this with Ethan ignites a white-hot rage within me.

Her head tilts back, and her hips rock, begging for more. "Ethan, please."

He withdraws his fingers and slaps her ass. "Be a good girl and ride Jax for me. I want to fuck you from behind."

She rolls toward me, my shoulders hit the mattress, she lines us up, and her wet heat swallows my cock. Hands splayed over my pecs, she raises and lowers herself, eager to be fucked.

"So beautiful." I flex my hips and give her what she needs.

I caress her belly, in awe at the life she's gifting us. I never thought about it before she became pregnant, but her growing our baby is pretty fucking incredible.

My heart rate skyrockets, and my stomach tenses when he gets into position behind her. This is new. I don't know what I was expecting, but it wasn't him between my legs.

He clasps a hand around her throat and brings her in for a kiss. "Lean forward. Make sure you're comfortable, and don't come until I tell you to."

She drops to her elbows, tangles her fingers in my hair, and trails kisses along my jawline. I wrap my arms around her and grip her nape. I have nowhere to look but at Ethan, his hands clutching her ass, his eyes lowered.

Her breath hitches, and the mind-blowing pressure on my dick intensifies.

"Fuck," I curse and thrust up into her. "So damn tight."

He enters her, inch by slow inch, his gaze never wavering from our joined bodies. "That feel good, baby? My cock stretching your ass while Jax stuffs your pussy?"

Fuck. Me.

"Yes," she whimpers, her mouth on my throat, her fingers in my hair.

"You like being our fuck-toy?" His hips meet her ass with a jolt. "Letting us fuck and fill you?"

My God, he's going to make me come. I tuck my face into Aurora's shoulder and squeeze my eyes shut. I can't stare at him while he watches us—*me*—fuck her. It's too much combined with his filthy words.

I swear, he grinds on my cock harder. He has to be angling his hips on purpose to mess with me. He's fucking us both, and it's like nothing I've ever felt before, driving me feral.

We fall into a pounding rhythm, the three of us desperate, the room a symphony of erotic sounds and heavy breaths.

"Ethan," she pleads. "Let me come."

"You wanna come, baby girl? Beg Jax to fill your pussy. You can come when he does."

Fucker. Now he's controlling my orgasm too?

"Please, Jax," she whines so sweetly. "Come inside me. Fill my pussy with your cum."

Jesus Christ. I'm close, my body on fire, my head hazy with lust.

"Good girl." That fucking deep rumble. "Can I fill your ass full of cum, baby? I wanna see you dripping from both holes."

That does it. My balls draw up, my muscles tense, and I piston in and out of her. "Soak my cock, Aurora. Fuck."

"Yes," she cries, her legs trembling around me. "Fuck me. Fill me. I'm going to come."

Her cunt pulses, and a wet warmth spreads over my shaft, triggering my own explosive orgasm. Ethan slams into her, his dick jerking with mine, and the three of us flood the room with moans and curses.

I was certain I'd die without Aurora. Now, I'm convinced I'd die without *this*, without *them*.

After a shower, Coach falls fast asleep beside our girl, snoring softly—not a single night away from us. We'll see how traveling goes when he's just as addicted as I am.

5
AURORA

It's not even nine a.m., and already, it's a rough day. First, the baby kept me up all night practicing gymnastics in my uterus. Then, I woke after a few blessed hours of sleep nauseated. This freaks Jax out, and despite my arguments, he texts Ethan, who returns from an early morning meeting.

Now, he kneels next to me in his slacks and button-up, sleeves rolled, holding my hair and rubbing my back.

"Please go away," I groan, wanting to be alone in my misery. "I don't need an audience."

"Like I care."

His voice is growly, and usually, I love him taking that tone with me, but right now, it feels as if he's annoyed.

Nausea rolls through me once more, and my stomach turns over. Ethan gags, hiding his face in the crook of his elbow, and I want to die of embarrassment. I prefer Reece. At least he was a medic, trained not to express his displeasure.

Dizzy, I hug the porcelain, lay my head on my forearm, and concentrate on drawing slow, steady breaths.

Icy fingers press against my feverish cheeks. "Jackson, call room service for food."

"Already done." Jax wets a washcloth and hands it to him. "When does this end?"

The question is rhetorical, a thought spoken out loud, but Ethan isn't in the mood.

"How the fuck would I know?" He places the cold compress on the back of my neck. "I don't have other children."

He's agitated, and I feel like a burden. "Am I inconveniencing you?"

My whispered, strained words are swallowed by Jackson's louder voice, now equally irritated. "You sure about that?"

Ethan turns to Jax, and the washcloth falls to the floor. "Yes, asshole. Are you?"

"Yeah, dickhead. I'm demisexual, obsessive, and paranoid. I know exactly who I've nutted in, and she's in this room."

"Stop—both of you. You're not helping. Being pregnant sucks. Period." I sit back and face Ethan. "If you have somewhere to be, go. I'm fine. I've been sick most of this pregnancy. I can handle it."

He gives me a steely glare. "That doesn't make me feel any fucking better. *You* are my priority. I'm pissed at—" He stops short and massages his nape. "Not at you."

I stand, closing my eyes for a moment to let the vertigo subside. "Go. It's just morning sickness. I'll survive."

"I got it." Jax wraps an arm around my shoulders. "Sorry I bothered you."

Conflict rages in Ethan's gaze, but with a reluctant sigh, he kisses my clammy forehead and promises to fly back with us.

* * *

I nibble on some toast and sip coffee, which I'm positive is decaf, until it's time to catch a car to the airport. On the private jet, while waiting for Ethan and able to hold my head up, I make a list of my expenses for him, knowing it'll ease his guilt to help me financially.

But when I log in to my bank account and the number is much lower than expected, fear grips me. A cold sweat breaks out along my heated skin. The pounding of my heart echoes in my ears, and the cabin is suddenly suffocating.

My fingertips tingle, and I shake my hands to ward off the impending sense of doom.

Jackson leans over and grabs my wrists. "What's wrong?"

"I…" My mind goes blank. "My. Expenses." My words are choppy. I'm on the verge of a panic attack.

I have no issues with Jax buying designer clothes and adorable baby outfits—he loves to spoil us—but relying on others entirely? That's terrifying.

It hits me all at once. I don't belong with these two. I'm still paying medical bills from years ago and have a child on the way. I can't manage this lifestyle, can't take time off work, can't expect someone else to pay for my grandmother.

"Okay…?" He stretches out the word, brows furrowed.

"I can't do this."

"Oh, no." His shoulders slump. "It's house shopping all over again."

"Fuck!" Yet another realization strikes me, and my head swims.

How am I supposed to afford a house? At this rate, I won't be able to afford groceries.

"Stop." He cups my face in his hands, his thumb

ghosting over my cheekbone. "It's already paid for. Don't think about it."

I lean into his touch. It's almost enough to quell the dread kicking at my chest, but he doesn't understand. His account has many, *many* more zeros than mine. He has a career and a trust fund. He's never panicked about his bank balance or gone hungry or lost a childhood home.

My lips tremble. "I can't walk the runway."

The crease between his brows deepens. "You have in the past. You can in the future."

"That's where I earn the most money. The rest is only a daily stipend to wear the brand."

"And?"

He's trying hard to be supportive, but I'm an anxious, hormonal mess.

"I have shit to pay, Jax."

"Just breathe. What's your biggest concern?" He gives me that boyish smile, confident and determined to get me through this freakout.

I take a deep, quivering inhale. "The nursing home."

"Okay, good. How much is it?"

"Seven thousand a month."

His jaw drops. "Seven thousand a month?" His voice rises, green eyes widening in utter disbelief. "That's criminal."

"Don't I fucking know?" My throat constricts, and my vision blurs with tears. I have no chance with Ethan if *Jackson* thinks it's excessive.

"Oh, shit. Please don't cry, babe. I'll give you anything. You have nothing to worry about." He frets over me, wiping away my tears with his knuckles and peppering my face with kisses.

"What the hell happened now?" demands a deep, familiar voice.

I sob harder, not wanting to upset him further.

"Thank fuck you're here. She's having a panic attack about paying for her grandmother's nursing home."

Ethan takes a seat across from us in one of the captain's chairs, an unraised table in between. "Come here."

Unable to speak, I shake my head. He's dealt with me enough today.

He cocks his head and quirks a brow. "Who's in charge here, Aurora?"

I rub at the ache in my sternum and climb onto his lap. Tears stream down my cheeks, my chest tightening at an alarming rate.

His large hand covers mine. "Jesus, your heart is pounding. Look at me." Gray eyes bore into my soul. "I promise you, baby girl, I won't let anything happen to your grandmother. Trust me. I know what it's like to feel helpless when someone you love is sick. That must have been scary for you all alone."

The fist gripping my chest loosens, and I nod.

He tucks a strand of hair behind my ear. "Whatever she needs, we'll get."

I swallow the painful lump in my throat, nodding again.

He clasps the back of my neck in that possessive way of his. "Lie down and let me hold you. You're exhausted. Did you sleep much last night?"

"No." Sitting sideways, my knees bent in his lap, I snuggle into him. His muscular arms wrap around me, providing the safety I need, and my breath gradually slows, my pulse no longer slamming against my rib cage.

Jax unbuckles his seat belt, sits next to us, stretches my

legs over his, and rests his head on Ethan's opposite shoulder.

He mouths, "Love you," and I mouth it back.

Ethan reclines in his seat. "This is the last time we can stay together, fly together. I mean it."

Jackson and I exchange a glance, neither one of us believing him.

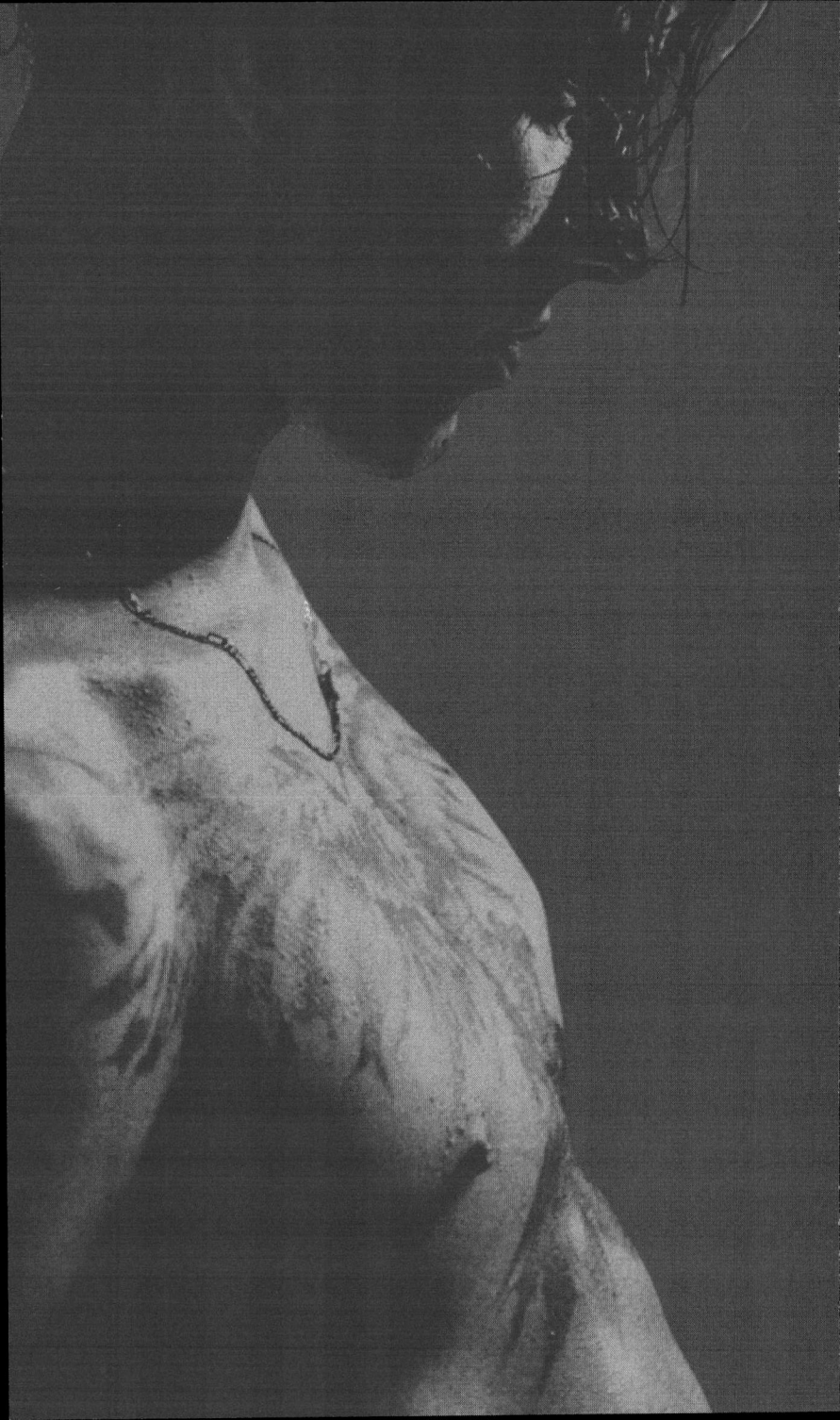

6
JACKSON

"You shouldn't be playing." Doc gives me a hard stare before continuing to wrap my right hand.

The visitor's accommodations are deplorable, with peeling blue paint and outdated equipment. I'm sitting in a worn chair, its stiff cushions cracked, yellow stuffing peeking through. I bet their facilities are lavish—cheap bastards—but I'm too high on life and adrenaline to let this depressing training room or Doc's scowl kill my vibe.

My knee bounces with anticipation and boundless energy. "It's not my first time playing with a broken hand."

"That's the problem." Silence hangs between us, and I sense him holding back. "Your drug test was negative."

"Never doubted it."

His focus remains on my knuckles. "Did you complete the league's therapy requirement?"

What do I need a therapist for? "I have Coach."

Skeptical eyes surrounded by deep wrinkles lock with mine.

"Seriously, I'm fine. Coach takes good care of me." Why

would I turn to drugs or alcohol? My life is better than ever. I have everything I desire.

Doc snips the tape, and I flex my fist a few times. The pain is minimal, and my glove will add an extra layer of protection.

He straightens and pushes his glasses higher on his nose. "Want me to bind your ribs?"

"No, it's annoying as fuck."

An exasperated sigh escapes him, and he crosses his arms over his chest. "It'll be a tough night. You know that, right?"

"Better than anyone." There'll be constant shit-talking. Players will be gunning for me, and then there's Carmichael, their seven-foot enforcer. "Besides, what good is tape gonna be if I get hit?"

"Avoid fighting. Think about that pretty girl of yours and how far you've come. If you're struggling, I'm telling Coach to pull you."

Everyone suspects I've been doping. Everyone assumes without drugs, I can't perform. Only a handful of people have faith in me—Aurora, Ethan, Grant, and Kill.

The latter two knew me before my addiction. Ethan believed in me, protected me, even when he hated me, and Aurora is my ride or die. For them, I'll prove every doubter wrong.

"Doc, this'll be my greatest game yet. Just watch."

I haven't played for me—for the thrill, for the challenge—since my rookie year. I dreaded playing once it became a job, a requirement for someone else, but that asshole won't be looking down on me tonight or ever again.

Despite my setbacks, hockey is still the best thing for me, besides Aurora and Ethan. When my skates hit the ice, everything disappears. The harder I play, the faster I skate, the calmer I feel.

Not even Carmichael's taunts provoke me.

He glides past me backward and juts his chin. "Your girl like my gift?"

The jersey in her dressing room. I fucking knew it.

"Yeah, thanks. I used it to wipe my dick after we fucked."

I steal a breakaway, my second goal already in the bag and a third on the way. Carmichael is bearing down on me, a runaway freight train. His stick is useless—he's only scored once all season. His only objective is to stop me, injuring me the ultimate payoff. His size is his strength, but it also makes him much slower than I am.

He's almost on me, but I keep my focus on the goal, let Carmichael think I don't see him. I know exactly what the big fucker is plotting. He's not aiming to check me into the boards. Stopping this play is not enough—he needs to lay me out. Their only chance of winning is by impairing me or getting me ejected, but fuck them. I've got shit to prove.

On a side note, or funny coincidence, Carmichael plays Coach's old position—enforcer for the New York Stars. It gives me an odd sense of projected gratification to blow this guy away.

Sweat drips down my neck, my thighs on fire. I'm still sore from yesterday's practice, my punishment for stuffing my face with donuts and not going to the gym over the past few weeks. I don't let it slow me down, though. I live for the burn, the ache. I crave the pain.

Just before the enforcer reaches me, flying like a bat out of hell, he leaps. I drop low and propel forward, the puck sliding underneath me.

His jersey brushes mine, his chest over my shoulders,

and he crashes into the boards head-first. It's a nasty hit, and I'm damn glad I'm not between him and that wall.

At my back, the over-muscled boulder falls to the ice. I boot the puck from my skate to my stick, never once losing control.

I pass to Grant. He takes it behind the net, and I get into position. He gets fancy with the extra moves—going left, right, and kicking up ice before he taps it to me, and I knock it in. It all happens so fast, the goalie doesn't have time to react.

Arms raised in celebration, Grant jumps on me. "That was sick!"

"Ribs, motherfucker," I laugh.

More bodies smash into me, one after another. We're a pile of limbs and excitement, my hat trick putting us ahead by two, and it's not even the third period.

After the celly, my gaze searches for my girl. She's cheering a few rows above the bench. I point my stick at her, and she gives me the biggest, proudest smile. I live for that smile.

I spend the rest of the game teasing Ethan. He's been on edge about my return, a mother hen. He needs some comic relief.

It's the start of the last period, and I'm sitting on the bench. He cuffs my shoulder and bends down behind me. Their goalie is figuring us out, and Ethan wants me to shoot for goal number four.

His advice: "Go for the smallest hole."

I'd be crazy to let this opportunity pass by. "I think that's more your thing, Coach." I wink.

He walks away from me real quick.

Another break in shifts, and I'm getting slammed with chirps and penalties.

He glowers at me over his shoulder, that perma-scowl firmly in place. "Pretend you're deaf, like you do anytime I talk to you."

I furrow my brows and cup my ear but can't hide my smirk. "What? What'd you say?"

He grinds his teeth so hard, I'm surprised he doesn't crack a molar. "If you get another penalty, I swear, I'll kill you in your sleep."

My smirk stretches into a full-blown grin. "Is that because you can't kill me while I'm awake?"

"It's because I don't wanna listen to your fucking mouth."

Giddiness erupts in my gut. I love it when he's pissed. I see why Aurora enjoys revving him up. He gets all growly, and a vein protrudes in his neck.

"So abusive, Coach. If you keep threatening me, I'll be forced to stop sleeping with you."

His face and ears flush a deep shade of red, and he skewers me with his signature death glare. If I wasn't his favorite player and Aurora didn't love me, he'd probably follow through with his threats. Right now, though, he's speechless. I tend to have that effect on people.

"Don't give me those smoldering eyes, big guy. You know what they do to me."

Finally, the tiniest of smiles tugs at the corner of his lip. "Fucker, you're going to get me fired."

I place a hand over my heart. "If you go, I go." I mean every word. I wouldn't be here, sober, sitting on this bench, if it wasn't for him, and I don't plan on playing for anyone else.

7
AURORA

Right before the game ends, the twins lead me out of the club section, down a few private hallways, and into the players' tunnel. They fist-bump a few security guards along the way. Apparently, they 'know a guy.'

Jax enters the exclusive area, and I grab his beaming face and kiss him.

"That was amazing!"

Sweaty tendrils of hair are plastered to his forehead, but I don't mind. It only makes him hotter.

"I missed watching you play."

Stick and helmet in one hand, he bends down and scoops me up with an arm under my ass.

I encircle his neck and hold on, my legs dangling, unable to fit around his waist with my belly and his full gear. "You can't carry me." My voice is bubbling with laughter, and I try to wriggle free. Soon enough, I'll be too big for him to manhandle easily.

He gives his equipment to a staff member and readjusts me in his arms. "I sure as fuck can. Who's gonna stop me?" He nuzzles my neck, his wet hair dripping all over me.

I shriek and push him away, but he only tightens his grip.

There's media present and a setup for after-game interviews. Cameras trail us as we make our way toward the locker room, capturing every kiss and lighthearted moment.

Jackson's agent advised him not to discuss anything with reporters outside of press conferences cleared by the team, but when someone asks when I'm due, he proudly announces March. This sets off a flurry of questions concerning our relationship.

Are you reuniting because of the baby? Did you go to rehab? Are you really engaged? Have you set a date?

We ignore it all. Then comes the question I've been dreading. My brain doesn't even fully process it. I hear the words 'pics with other women,' and my mind goes into panic mode, my body stiffening.

Jax stops, carefully places me on my feet, and faces the reporter. Players and staff gawk as they move around us, but no one intervenes.

Shit. Shit. Shit. A tussle with the media is the last thing he needs after his suspension.

With trembling hands, I reach for him and snag his jersey. He crowds a short, stocky man against the wall, a deranged grin twisting his sharp features into a mask of madness. Jax, almost seven feet tall in skates, dwarfs the guy, who barely reaches six.

"I wish I could bounce your head off the cement—watch it split open like a fucking melon." His voice is sinister, a low rasp, far more chilling than a threat. "Hear the clink, clink, clink of your chiclets as they hit the floor."

Who thinks about the sound of someone's teeth hitting the floor? Fortunately, there are these pesky things called laws. Without them, I worry Jackson might act on some of the wild thoughts he voices.

"Jax—"

"No killing tonight," Ethan cuts me off, throwing an arm around his captain's shoulders and guiding him toward the locker room. Then, he gestures to the photographer or reporter—I'm not sure which, but he has a camera in his hand. "Show some respect or lose your press pass."

My fiancé intertwines our fingers, and our gazes meet, silently communicating. I'm rattled, not so much by the question itself, but by the rudeness of it all, the crowd, the embarrassment amplified by my anxiety. I'm disappointed. This was supposed to be a moment of triumph for him, but my presence ruined it. No one would've asked about *the other women* if I hadn't been here.

He kisses my knuckles and promises, "It'll get better," before Coach drags him away.

I wait outside the locker room, the twins a wall of muscle and expensive cologne in front of me. Dante grumbles about strangling the reporter with the lanyard of his press pass while Desi bobs his head to the music blasting in the arena.

My phone buzzes in my hand, a message from Reece.

VIKING

Give Jax my congrats. That was a great game. Are you doing anything after?

I should tell him to contact Ethan, but since I'm doing nothing but waiting, I see no harm in chatting.

> We have a charity dinner tonight. Or they do. Not sure I'm going. Why? What's up?

I've had enough stimulation for the day. I just want to go home.

> **VIKING**
> Missing my princess.

How am I supposed to respond to that? I'll admit, I miss my bodyguard—or who he was when he pretended to be my bodyguard. Kind and caring, a big, protective teddy bear.

It doesn't matter. I *shouldn't* respond to that. I'm only asking for trouble...and maybe a spanking, which doesn't sound bad. Still...

> Ethan told me to tell you to text him.

> **VIKING**
> Why? Did something happen?

> No. He said if you're worried about me, contact him.

> **VIKING**
> Oh yeah? Tell your daddy I adore you, and you're all I think about.

My stomach flip-flops. I am *not* telling Ethan that.

> Have you lost your mind? Did you forget I already have two men?

> **VIKING**
> Did you forget I don't care?

I don't answer. I'm tempted to erase the entire conversation, but that feels even more dishonest.

> **VIKING**

> I bet you're alone right now. I bet they can't take care of you. I bet you need me.

>> What is up with you? Friends, remember? And I'm not alone.

VIKING
> I miss you. I'm going crazy. And the Mafia twins don't count.

I ignore the first part, my fingers flying across the screen.

>> Why don't they count?

VIKING
> Because they don't comfort you. You don't see them that way.

>> And what makes you think I see you that way?

VIKING
> To begin with, my voice breaks through your panic attacks.

>> So does Ethan's.

VIKING
> Exactly.

I walked into that one, but at the time, I trusted Reece, trusted him to protect and care for me. I still do, but again, it doesn't matter. Despite what he says, he wants more than friendship, and beyond that isn't possible.

>> To you, this is a fantasy. To us, it's family. Ethan builds Jax up. He believes in him. You put him down and talk to him like he's a failure. I can't live with that.

> **VIKING**
> He hurt you. That's hard for ME to live with. I get it. They're besties. I wanna be YOUR bestie. Now, tell me what's wrong.

Ethan is busy, and discussing this with Jackson will only worsen his guilt. I've accepted his relapse and moved on, but that doesn't mean it's not gut-wrenching to remember for both of us.

> A reporter mentioned the pictures of Jax with other women.

> **VIKING**
> Where do I bail out your fiancé? I hope he throat-punched the asshole.

> Chin up. Straighten your crown, princess. Those vultures are nothing but dirt under your pretty little heels.

His words bring a smile to my face, melting away the tension in my shoulders—until he writes:

> **VIKING**
> Wouldn't have happened on my watch.

8
ETHAN

Aurora wraps her arms around my waist. "Will you come home with us tonight? It's been several days." She pouts her bottom lip dramatically.

I freeze, fighting the urge to pull away. The last thing we need is more publicity. We're in the back parking lot—for players only, but it's hardly secluded—waiting for the twins to fetch the car.

Jax is currently getting an earful from the PR team and his agent. After that, he has to see Doc. Then, we head to this dreaded 'Unity' event with more fucking media.

Forcing aside my anxieties, I brush my knuckles over her cheekbone. "I have to attend this dinner, baby. After that, it'll be late, and we leave early tomorrow."

We're only traveling to Long Island, just outside the city, but if I go home with them, we'll be up half the night. Alone, I won't keep my hands off her, not with the way she's dressed —tall suede boots with fuck-me heels, Jackson's jersey fashioned into a dress, and her leather jacket. Her hair is up in a high ponytail I'd love to wrap around my fist.

God, have mercy on me. I'm trying to be professional here.

"Can I stay with you?" She gives a teasing smile at odds with her apprehensive eyes. "Just sleep, nothing nefarious."

I clench and unclench my jaw. "Go to dinner with Jax. I'll see you there."

Her face hardens, and she lets her arms fall. I hate it. I crave her touch. I miss her clingy affection.

I'm pushing her away. It shouldn't be like this, but I'm under a lot of pressure. I don't want her to become team gossip. The media is focused on her and Jackson, and I'd prefer it stay that way. His inappropriate comments and behavior are enough of a distraction.

Then, there's the morning sickness. It stirs up a deep, uncontrollable rage within me, rooted in my childhood. It has nothing to do with Aurora, but it keeps me from caring for her.

It's been three days since I stayed with them, since she was vomiting and I acted like a coward. I made promises I didn't keep. I haven't communicated. I'm not there for her...

"You know what?" Her words drag me from my downward spiral, her tone laced with irritation. "Never mind."

I'm torn. Does it matter if she's in my arms tonight? Is it worth upsetting her over what others might think? When I leave tomorrow, she can sleep in. No one will know...except the team, and with Jackson's suggestive comments, people are bound to start gossiping if we share a room.

Just as I'm about to speak, to explain myself, she turns and rushes toward the arriving car. I hurry after her, grabbing her wrist to prevent her from opening the door. She yanks her arm away, not even bothering to look at me.

My little brat is pissed.

"Aurora—"

She spins around. "Your ex will be at the dinner tonight, right? She's in town?"

Caught off guard, I don't answer.

"Having regrets, Ethan? Don't wanna be seen together? Thinking of meeting with her? Or *have* you been?"

My face and ears catch fire. "Where the fuck did that come from?" I step forward into her space. "You're lucky—" I ball my fists to stop from saying something I'll regret, because she's right. My ex will be there, but I'd never fucking meet with her.

"Am I?" she asks sarcastically. "Lucky to be pregnant by a man who can't decide if he wants us? Can't wait to explain your abandonment to your so—"

My hand shoots out, clamping around her throat and cutting her off. "Let me help you *not* finish that sentence," I growl and tighten my grip. "Because if you do, you won't sit for a week." I release her and back away, worried if I don't, I'll go too far, further than I already have. "I'll see you at dinner."

"No," she croaks, her eyes glassy.

"No?" I quirk a brow.

"I'll give you my time and attention," she mimics, her voice dripping with scorn. "No, you won't!" Disgust contorts her pretty features. "So, no. You can fuck off. I'm not attending this party just for you to ignore me."

I reach around her and open the door. "Get in the fucking car."

"What do you think I was trying to do?"

She slides into the back seat. I wait for her to glance back and meet my gaze, and when she doesn't, I slam the door harder than necessary.

At dinner, I'm distracted, constantly watching the entrance and Jackson, who keeps checking his phone. I'm waiting for the moment Aurora tells him she's not coming because I'm a fucking asshole, and he charges over here. I barely register what my colleagues are saying, and frankly, I don't give a damn. The only thing on my mind is the empty chair beside Jax.

He glares at his screen, shoves it in his pocket, and heads for the door.

I toss my napkin on the table and follow. "Where are you going?" I call out once we're out of earshot.

"I've got more important shit to take care of."

"Jackson," I snap when he keeps walking. "You need to be here. You're the captain."

Finally, he faces me. "This is your life, not mine. My life is at home, hurting after being harassed for something I did. I need to be there."

I pinch the bridge of my nose, realizing how epically I fucked up. Aurora was feeling insecure, and I only made it worse. "Why did you bring her down the tunnel? Fuck! I'm trying to protect her from this shit."

He gestures toward the team. "I had a phenomenal night—a hat trick my first game back. We killed a rival we usually struggle against. What's the point if I can't celebrate with my fiancée, the person who supports me most?"

My stomach knots, and I release a heavy breath. "She's mad at me. I fucked up." I massage my temples, warding off the tension headache. "She asked to stay together tonight, and I declined."

He scoffs. "You mean you rejected her. Don't act all professional. You're a dick." He shakes his head in frustration. "You know what? Let's trade places. You deal with the media with your over-the-top work ethic and impeccable control, and I'll have a family with the girl who needs constant devotion and reassurance. How about that?"

Without thinking, I mouth off. "Deal with the media? I wouldn't be caught dead at a party with a bunch of drugs and escorts." Tempers are hot, and I regret the words immediately.

Jackson doesn't miss a beat. He leans in close, a tight, smug smile twisting his lips. "No, you just got one pregnant...minus the drugs. Congrats, Coach." Before he storms out, he glances back, eyes hard. "Maybe you should think about how you're going to do this with a kid." He lifts a hand between us, palm open. "Oh, wait—you're not. I am. So don't get pissed when I leave to take care of shit for you."

9
JACKSON

At the loft, Aurora is already in bed, sitting against the headboard and playing on her phone. She glances at me sheepishly and sets the phone down. I release a relieved breath. She's not having a panic attack, crying, or packing a bag. I can handle her ditching events; I'm not fond of them either.

I kick the bedroom door shut using the heel of my boot and loosen my tie. "The worst person in my life is dead." I shrug off my suit jacket and toss it onto the chair. "I played a hell of a game." I yank off my tie and unbutton my shirt. "We should be happy—ecstatic."

"Sorry," she mumbles, her stare glued to my crotch as I unbuckle my belt and unzip my pants. "It's me. I'll return to LA." Her tone is flat, emotionless.

"Aurora." I snap my fingers. "I'm talking."

Her gaze snaps to mine, eyes ablaze with mischief. "What? You're the one giving a striptease—in a suit. What did you expect?"

I shake my head in amusement, shed my clothes down to my boxers, and get into bed. Settling beside her, I stretch out my legs. "Come here." I guide her between my thighs, her back to my chest, my arms around her. "Last week, you said being with me every day was a dream. Did you mean that?"

She glances up at me, brows pinched. "Why wouldn't I?" Only she'd think I was a dream, not a nightmare.

Her phone vibrates on the nightstand, and I'll bet anything it's Ethan. I'm sure he'll be here any minute.

I take her hand, kiss her palm, then intertwine our fingers. "Good, 'cause I plan on spending the rest of my life with you. Let's figure this out. What's going through your head?"

She traces the tattoo on my ring finger and gathers her thoughts. "Maybe I should return to LA. You'll both be happier without me tagging along. Those comments are gut-wrenching, and they only say them in front of me to rile you up. It's bad enough being pregnant and sick." The mention of the baby prompts her to place my hand on her belly. "And now Ethan is pulling away. I'm just..."

"Hurt?" I finish. "Overwhelmed? People suck, babe. Fuck 'em. They don't matter." I tuck a strand of hair behind her ear that had escaped her braid. "The only thing that matters is us, and Ethan will be here soon. I guarantee it."

"Maybe," she mumbles, her voice distant.

I rack my brain to figure out how to make this easier for her. Perhaps Ethan was right, and we need to hire someone. I kiss her temple and hold her tighter. "It's my first game back. I'll charter a jet—" Her phone buzzes again, and I reach for it. "You'd better answer that before the old man has a stroke." I grab it, intending to hand it to her until I see it's not Ethan—it's Reece, his latest texts visible on the screen.

> **VIKING**
>
> Say the word, and I'll come get you.
>
> I'll stay with you in LA, or you can stay with me.

My vision momentarily blurs, and white-hot fury scorches my skin. Is that why she wants to leave? To be with *him*?

"What are you doing?" Her voice is laced with panic as I enter her passcode.

We've always had access to each other's phones. It's not about control or suspicion—she'll never find another woman texting me, nor do I use social media for anything other than to stalk her. It's about trust, and I never thought I couldn't trust her until now.

"Are you fucking kidding me?" I angle the screen toward her. "Fucking *Reece*?" His name is poison on my tongue. "And here I was, thinking we needed to hire security. Maybe him. Nope." I shake my head vigorously. "Fuck that shit with a spiked baseball bat." My mind jumps to the worst possible conclusion. "Have you slept with him? *Are* you sleeping with him?"

She whirls around, her face twisted in a scowl, eyes ablaze. "Are you serious? Did you forget I've been with you, that I'm pregnant?"

From what I've read, Reece doesn't give a fuck about her being with Ethan and me, and I doubt he cares about the pregnancy either.

I shove the intrusive thoughts aside, proud of myself for remaining relatively calm. I haven't broken anything, and I'm not screaming. My head is surprisingly clear. "Never mind. That was a stupid question."

"Why?"

"He wouldn't be in LA if you were fucking. He'd be right here on his knees, panting for it."

She rolls her eyes. "I *meant* why are you asking?"

Isn't it obvious? "To figure out why my fiancée is texting a man who openly wants her."

"He claims he wants me, but he doesn't want this." She sweeps a hand between us, meaning herself and me, or herself and the baby, or maybe all the above.

Either way, he's not getting any of it. "I wouldn't be so sure." I toss the phone onto the nightstand. "Do you like him?"

"Jackson," she warns, as if the question is absurd.

"Do you? Just answer me."

She cocks her head and narrows her eyes. "There's no reason to do this."

That's what she told me when he was her bodyguard and couldn't keep his hands off her. Shocker: I was right about there being something between them, about him desiring her.

I lose my patience and clench my fists. "Just fucking answer me!"

"What do you want me to say?" She raises her palms, her frustration reflecting mine. "When we were apart, he took care of me. I relied on him. I needed someone, and he was there for me."

"That was his job! To take care of you, not fall in love with you!" I grind my molars. I have the urge to reread the texts, to analyze every detail, but that'll only infuriate me further.

Of course, he wants her. Aurora has a way of making a man feel like a god: her softness, her affection, her vulnerability. He won't go away easily, especially if she refuses to tell him to, and neither will Ethan.

Both of them want Reece here. My gut churns and my head spins. I need some air. I move toward the edge of the bed.

"Please don't leave." She cups my face and slips between my legs to block my path. "I choose you." Her gaze locks with mine. "I love you. I'd do anything to go back." Her lip quivers. "I would have stayed. I never would've left LA." Tears cling to her long lashes. "I should have stayed," she cries. "This never would've happened."

Gutted all over again, I pull her onto my lap and bury my face in her neck. "No, baby. This was all me. All Kyle."

"I'm terrified of losing you," she sobs, her hands gripping my shoulders.

"You won't. It's you and me, always. The world could burn to the fucking ground, and I wouldn't care as long as I had you." I swallow the hard lump in my throat and lift my head. "But I need to know. Do you like him? Do you want him?"

She readjusts in my lap and rests her forehead on mine. "I like him. I enjoy spending time with him, but I don't want to fuck him, if that's what you're asking."

I'm a guy and demisexual. I like *very* few people, none of whom I want to fuck—wait, that's not entirely true. Ethan is confusing, since we technically have sex together. Right? Is that the same? I'm not sure, but it reinforces my point: *I like him, but I don't want to fuck him* to me sounds like *I don't want to fuck him...yet.*

Yup, that's precisely what that means, and Reece knows it.

Sucks to be him. Even if she likes him, even if we need him, she'll always be mine. "What are you doing tomorrow?"

* * *

Ethan didn't come home again. I could tell it bothered Aurora. She went right to sleep after we talked and was quiet all morning. Shit, his absence upset me, and given the Reece situation, I feel it's necessary to take drastic measures. I sure as fuck don't want the Viking replacing Ethan in our bed.

I have a few tricks up my sleeve. Today, I spoiled Aurora, cheered her up and solidified my position. We're staying at the team hotel tonight after the game, where Coach can no longer avoid us, and currently, I'm searching the locker rooms for the missing piece of our throuple.

Practice was brutal. He did *not* go easy on me. Every inch of my body hurts, and I'm slow because of it.

Since being drugged, I've avoided all workout supplements and protein powders. I can't even bring myself to take over-the-counter pain medication. It's foolish, but my stomach clenches whenever I think about it. What if I accidentally trigger a relapse? I won't risk losing Aurora and the baby again.

Three more days on the road, two games remaining—Long Island and Boston. I need something to keep going, or I'll play like shit. Just my luck, I find Doc lounging in the visitor's training room, Coach in a plush chair next to him.

I knock on the open door to get their attention. "Hey, I'm glad I caught you both. I'm not feeling well."

Doc pushes his glasses higher on his nose and rises from his seat. "What's going on?"

"I'm dragging. Everything hurts. I need some hydration."

"Late night?" Ethan asks, his voice flat, laced with annoyance.

I drop into the chair beside him. "Nope, not at all. Just fucking sore."

Sensing the tension, Doc glances between us. "What do you think, Coach?"

"I don't have a problem with it. Stick to the regulations."

The room falls silent as Doc sets up the vitamin drip. Once I'm hooked up and we're alone, I ask Ethan, "Have you talked to her?"

He shoots me a side-eye. "She's been busy with you, remember?"

"Hasn't stopped you any other time. Have you tried? Or are you still running scared?"

A sneer forms on his upper lip. "I'm not running. Things went too far, and I'm giving her space."

These two and their damn space. What's the point? How do you resolve issues apart from each other? Aurora can have space when I'm six feet under.

"What happened?"

He hangs his head and rubs the back of his neck. "I grabbed her while we were arguing."

"How? She didn't say anything."

"By the throat... I just snapped and grabbed her to stop her from talking." He gestures with his hand, staring straight ahead. "I shouldn't have. I should've listened to her."

I lift my chin. "Show me."

His stern gaze meets mine. "What? Why?"

"I wanna know if I need to kill you."

"Jackson." Exasperated, he shakes his head. "No. I'm not grabbing you."

"So, what? You're uncomfortable touching me now? Do I have to remind you where our dicks have been?"

He leans in and lowers his tone. "Shut the fuck up. I'm not uncomfortable touching you. I touch you all the time."

A throat clears in the doorway. "Sorry. Just need to get something real quick." Doc, without a glance in our direction, snatches his bag and rushes from the room.

Ethan's face and ears turn a deep shade of red, and his eyes widen comically. His *oh shit* expression is priceless, and, unable to hold back, I burst into laughter.

"I hate you so fucking much. Why are you like this?"

He doesn't even break a smile. How does he not find this funny? I can't *stop* laughing.

"You're my boyfriend." I suck in a breath to rein myself in. "I'm not ashamed of us."

"Motherfucker, I am *not* your boyfriend."

"Come on, Coach. Think about it. We're together, just not *together*-together. You know?"

"We are not together." He emphasizes each word. "What the hell did Doc put in your IV?"

"Agree to disagree, but you're wrong." I dab at the tears leaking from the corners of my eyes with my shirtsleeve. "I'm sure you didn't hurt Aurora. She'd tell me if you did." Or Reece, which would really piss me off. "Besides, that's your kink."

"Anyhow," he drags out. "She'll text me when she's ready to see me."

I scoff. "No, she won't. That's bullshit and you know it. She didn't contact you when she was pregnant; she won't bother you now."

He rests his head against the leather chair. "What am I supposed to do? I was a complete asshole. There are only so many times she'll forgive my temper."

Luckily, he's talking to the one person Aurora has given a million chances to.

"Take out your phone," I tell him in all seriousness. "Text her you love her, you miss her, and you want her to sit on your face. Guaranteed to work."

He gives me a blank stare. "That's your advice? Sit on my face?"

"My go-to is puppy-dog eyes, taking off my shirt, eating pussy, tattoos, and, if all else fails, refusing to leave." I tick each one off on my fingers.

"Wow. So romantic," he deadpans.

"Whatever." I shrug, feigning nonchalance. "Don't expect her to chase you. She's already moved on."

He recoils. "What?"

"Don't act surprised. That's exactly what happens when you ignore a person—they move on."

"Shut the fuck up."

"You don't believe me? While you were ignoring her, she was chatting with someone else. I thought *I* was the one she was replacing." I pause for dramatic effect. "Nope." I punctuate the end, popping the 'P.'

His chest heaves with rapid breaths. "What are you talking about?"

"I'm talking about a certain someone going from shoulder to cry on to dick to ride on, telling her he *misses his princess*," I mock with a twisted frown. "*He adores her,* and *she's all he thinks about*."

Ethan's jaw ticks, his nostrils flare, and the vein in his neck pulsates. His voice drops an octave. "Who?"

"You know who. Fucking Reece," I grit through my teeth. "And get this: He. Watched. My. Game."

"Jesus Christ, he's desperate."

"He's going in hard is what he's doing. He even offered for her to stay with him in LA."

Ethan nods, his face deadly calm, which is honestly scarier than his perma-scowl. "Is that so?"

"No lie. Check her phone. He was still texting her when I came home from the charity dinner."

He cocks his head and raises his brows. "You read this and didn't murder anyone?"

I place a hand on my chest. "You wound me, Coach. I'm a new man. I asked her about it…" I trail off just to irritate him.

"And?" he snaps, his gray eyes dark and stormy.

"And he's probably texting her right now, telling her to sit on his face."

I grin, and he punches me in the arm—*hard*.

"Fuck! I'm sore, asshole." I rub my bicep. "She told me she likes him but doesn't want to fuck him."

"Yet," he adds.

"Exactly. He's just biding his time, waiting for an opening."

"So, what are you going to do?"

"Me?" I ask, taken aback. "I went and married her. You're the one leaving him an opening."

"Yeah, we'll fucking see about that." He stands and extends his hand, palm open. "Give me your room key."

I honestly don't get enough credit for all the matchmaking shit I do.

10
ETHAN

By the time I reach Aurora's door, I'm vibrating with fury. Giving her space wasn't the best approach, and I knew that, but truthfully, it wasn't for her. I needed to sort myself out, and I can't do that around her and Jax. They're my weakness. I fear I'll give up anything for them, and I don't want to lose myself. I fought hard for who I am.

I'm frightened by my feelings and where this is leading, and I'm frustrated with myself. I'm unable to control the violence and panic in my chest when I smell vomit, and I hate myself because of it. Jax is my player; we can't walk around openly as a triad. People won't accept us, and the attention will make me uncomfortable, as much as I'm ashamed to admit it.

I'm relieved at the thought of Reece joining our little family, but there's no fucking way he's replacing me.

I swipe the key card, the light blinks green, and I push into the room, only to be met with the sheer opposite of the dark storm raging within me.

"Jesus, fuck." I stumble over a pink glitter-filled balloon, then another, as if they're attacking me. "Did he leave any flowers or balloons for the rest of New York? Damn."

Balloons completely cover the ceiling, their strings dangling in my face, while pale-pink roses adorn every surface.

Jackson's over-the-top expression of love is precisely why she's spoiled. They eloped or signed a marriage contract or some shit. I'd expect nothing less from him. If it wasn't for hockey, he'd probably fly her to Paris. All justifiable, but how the fuck am I supposed to be angry in this pink explosion of happiness?

Aurora peeks out of the bathroom wearing an altered version of Jackson's jersey, as always. "Hey, what are you doing here?" She seems excited to see me, with the kindest voice and the cutest smile.

Instead of being relaxed, I'm furious all over again. How dare she try to take her sweetness away from me?

I step around her and into the bathroom, my gaze sweeping the makeup-cluttered counter. "Where's your phone?"

Perfect brows knit together. "Why?"

Her defensive tone irks me further. "I don't have time for games. Get your fucking phone."

With a huff, she removes her phone from her purse and slaps it into my awaiting palm.

"What's the passcode?"

"I'm expecting a text from the twins."

"They're not coming." I lock eyes with her. "Passcode."

"Am I going to the game?"

Her voice is jittery, and I almost feel bad. *Almost*.

"Aurora, don't fuck with me right now. What's the fucking code?"

"My birthday. August twenty-third—"

"I know your birthday," I cut her off.

I punch in the numbers and open the Messages app to find her texts with Reece. He sent her a few today, none of which she's answered. The last one asks if she's okay. I read through them, my heart drumming louder with each word, a frantic whooshing in my ears. His intentions to have her are clear, but I see no evidence she's replacing either of us—fucking Jackson.

"Didn't I tell you to stop texting him?" I pocket her phone. "He wants you, and you're encouraging him." I grab the back of her neck, possessive and firm. "Did you think I was joking?"

Hands on her hips, she stares up at me, her chest rising and falling rapidly. "I was mad."

"You were mad?" I lean in, our noses inches apart. "Let me show you mad."

In a single, fluid movement, I spin us, and careful of her stomach, I bend her over the bathroom counter. She catches herself, bracing with her forearms.

I snag her gaze in the mirror. "Don't move, or I'll bind your wrists with a fucking balloon string."

She rolls her eyes. "That's why you're here? Jealousy?"

"Keep running your mouth, baby. I'll take care of that later." I lift the jersey to find a scrap of black lace. "Unless you're no longer mine, it's not jealousy. Remember?"

"What I remember is you not coming home, so maybe I'm not yours."

I disregard her snide remarks and unbuckle my belt. "You agreed to hand over complete control to me."

"And you agreed to be there."

With a sharp snap, I yank my belt free. "My lack of presence doesn't give you permission to entertain someone else." I make a loop, holding the ends of the leather together.

Her eyes widen, her lips part. "You're not spanking me with your hand? Don't I need a safe word?"

"You don't need a safe word with me. You tell me to stop, I'll stop. It's that simple. Understood?"

"Oh my God. I stopped texting him," she backpedals.

She moves to stand, and I tighten my grip on her nape to hold her in place.

"Understood?"

"I'll talk to whoever I want!"

The leather whistles through the air. *Smack*.

"Ethan!"

It's fast, not cruel, nothing more than a sting on her fine ass, and I'm instantly rock-hard.

I raise a brow, belt poised. "Try again."

"Okay, I understand. I won't text him."

"Pull your underwear down."

She hooks a finger in the waistband and tugs her underwear to her mid-thigh. An unmistakable wet spot darkens the center. "How many?" she whines.

"Do you like Reece paying attention to you?"

"At least someone does," she says under her breath, then adds, "When you're not."

"That fucking mouth. You enjoy pissing me off, don't you?" *Smack*. The leather slaps her ass harder, and her skin blossoms a glorious shade of red that makes my cock throb. "Answer me. Do you like him paying attention to you?"

Her eyes sparkle with mischief, a taunting dare glinting within their depths. "Maybe."

I shake my head. This fucking girl. I slap her other ass cheek, alternating sides, and she bites her bottom lip.

"You wanna repeat that? Do you like him paying attention to you?" Silence. *Smack*. "You gonna tell me?" *Smack*.

"Tell me how much of a spoiled fucking brat you are." *Smack.*

"Yes!" she finally yells, cheeks flushed. "He makes me feel better."

Her answer is no surprise. Reece is yet another man who lives to spoil her. I guess it's my job to add some control and discipline into this dynamic.

I rip her panties down to the floor, helping her step out of them. "Spread your legs." Of course, she refuses. *Smack.* "Goddamn it, Aurora. Spread. Your. Fucking. Legs."

She obeys, and I get a full view of her bare, glistening cunt, wetness slicking her upper thighs. Unable to resist, I drop the belt and slide two fingers through her soaked slit. Her head falls to the counter, and she whimpers.

"Always so wet." I circle her swollen clit. "Do you like being punished by me?"

"No," she replies through clenched teeth.

My stubborn girl.

I flash her a wolfish grin and slap her pussy. "Your dripping cunt says otherwise. Try again. You like it when I redden this ass?" I caress my palm over her heated skin.

She hides her face in the crook of her arm. "Yes," she mutters.

"Look at me." I release her neck to wrap her ponytail around my fist and force her gaze to mine in the mirror. "Do you like it when I redden your ass?"

"Yes, Sir."

Even with her sarcastic tone, my cock is about to burst through my pants.

"Good girl." I return my fingers to tease her clit. "Who's in charge here, Aurora?"

"You." She rocks her hips. "Ethan, please."

I circle her clit faster. "What is it, baby girl? Tell me."

Her breath hitches. "Fuck me."

I can't take much more. My dick is jammed so tight against my zipper, I'll be shocked if it doesn't have teeth marks. I'm tempted to jerk off and come all over her ass, but my inner caveman urges me to fill her pussy and watch it drip out.

"You gonna be a good girl and listen to me?"

"You gonna be a good boyfriend and give me that cock?"

Despite myself, I smile. That fucking mouth, her and Jackson.

"Brace yourself." I'm notched at her entrance before my shirt and pants even hit the floor. "I'm taking you hard and fast, filling you with days' worth of cum, and you're gonna sit in it while you watch your husband play."

She places a hand on the mirror and grips the edge of the counter with the other. "You're nasty."

I slam into her in one, brutal thrust, and her words trail off into a high-pitched moan.

"And you love it." I pound into her, a man possessed. "After the game, I'm fucking the attitude out of that mouth."

"Ethan." She arches her back to take me deeper. "Don't stop."

"No worries, love. I'm filling every hole until you remember who you belong to."

11
AURORA

My ass stings. It's not painful, more like a sunburn, but I'll be feeling it for days. That's fine with me, because Ethan's right: I do love it.

His fingers encircle my throat, his other hand working my clit. The orgasm barrels through me—the type that rocks your entire body and leaves you dick-whipped.

My legs tense, and I pulse around him, mindlessly mumbling, "Oh fuck. Oh fuck. Oh fuck. Oh fuck."

"You're strangling my cock, baby... Damn." His voice is strained, breathy.

His grasp tightens, and his thrusts grow furious, pounding me through one climax and into another.

With a slam of his hips against my ass, he bottoms out and releases a rumbling, "Fuuuuuck" that sends a shiver down my spine.

I watch him in the mirror, his brows pinched, his gaze transfixed on where he slowly pumps in and out of me.

"I love the way you grip me, as if you don't wanna let go."

"I don't." Despite my legs being weak, I meet his lazy thrusts.

He abruptly pulls out. Before I can understand what's happening, he's maneuvering me to sit on the counter's edge, facing him, my weight on my forearms behind me.

"I can't stop. You feel too good." He thumbs his still-hard cock and pushes inside me.

Veins protruding, his large hands grip my hips and ass, lifting me to meet his merciless thrusts. "Play with your clit, baby girl. Show me how you make yourself come."

Desperate for more, I don't hesitate. I hook my legs about his waist and tease my clit, circling and pinching.

Broad shoulders, a sculpted chest, his biceps bulging, abs flexing, his thick cock hitting every sweet spot—and my orgasm comes hard and fast with a shuddering moan.

"That's my girl. Squeeze that tight cunt around me." His fingertips dig into my flesh with bruising strength. "Fuck, baby. You're going to make me come again." His words are raw as his jaw clenches, and he growls low through his teeth.

I slump against the counter and mirror. He leans down, elbows on the surface, and gathers me in his arms, resting his forehead to mine.

Silence stretches between us, broken only by our ragged breaths, and my anxiety returns with a whirlwind of questions. He's here, at least for now, but where has he been the past few nights? "Did you stay with her?"

His head lifts, his brows furrowed. "What?"

"Your ex. Did you stay with her last night?"

Intense gray eyes search mine. "You think I'd actually do that?"

My vision blurs. I swallow hard and blink away the tears. "I don't know. She had what I'll never have with you. That must mean something."

"No." He shakes his head adamantly. "It means nothing.

This," he splays a hand over my swollen stomach, "means something—*everything*—and no one else will ever have this with me. Only you."

"It was a mistake—"

"Stop." He puts a finger to my lips, his face stern. "Never say that again. You want me to fuck a baby into you on purpose? I have no problem with that. But then your husband will insist on having two. You wanna spend your twenties pregnant?"

Do I? Maybe. If I felt secure enough.

He ghosts his thumb over my cheekbone. "Whatever you need, I'll give it to you. All you have to do is ask, remember?"

I scoff. He wasn't too pleased with me the last time we were together. "I'm not bothering you if you're not interested in seeing me."

"So I've been reminded." He releases a heavy sigh. "I'm sorry I was distant. It's not you, and it's definitely not my fucking ex. It's me, and I'll do better." He places a soft kiss on my lips. "I don't want to leave, but I need to feed you before the game. Can we talk while we eat?"

"Sure. I have to finish getting ready."

He withdraws, and I instantly miss the weight of his hard body on mine.

"Stay." He sets me on my feet and pulls up his boxer briefs and pants, but he doesn't buckle them.

I hold the jersey around my hips, and he helps me into my panties, drawing them up my legs.

He pauses halfway. His fingers brush my skin, collecting the cum trickling down my inner thigh. "No cleaning up." He inserts his release back inside me. "I wasn't kidding about sitting in my cum."

"I'm pregnant. I'll need to use the bathroom, silly."

"Fine," he gripes, but it lacks bite. He finishes dressing me, then rubs the center of my panties to ensure they're soaked through.

"You're a caveman," I tease, chuckling.

"You made me this way, baby." He dismisses me with a smack on the ass. "Get ready."

After I finish applying my makeup with careful precision and he rights his clothes, he helps me into a pair of white, knee-high, red-bottomed boots.

"Do you have to be so fucking hot?" He scans my outfit with obvious appreciation, his eyes lingering. "Jesus, I can't walk into a restaurant with you."

"I'm a hockey WAG—wife *and* girlfriend. I have to look twice as hot, especially since I don't meet the standard requirements."

He quirks a brow. "And what are the standard requirements?"

"Blonde, peppy, a name that starts with a 'B'—Brandy, Brittney, Bentley, Blakely—some cheerleader name."

He barks out a laugh, deep and throaty and so freaking sexy. "God, I love you. Where's your coat?"

I grab a large black box from the pile of gifts on the floor and set it on the bed. I flip the top and unfold the tissue paper to reveal the personalized bomber jacket Jax had made. His name and number are on the back—not just his name, but MRS. O'REILLY.

"Fucking Christ," Ethan grumbles. "He *had* to make sure everyone knew, didn't he?"

I take his elbow and give him my most charming smile. "Don't worry, Blackwood. I have something in the works for you."

"That scares me. Are you going to run it by me first?"

I shake my head. "Absolutely not."

12
REECE

A year ago—hell, two months ago—I would've felt like an idiot falling for a woman who was devoted to someone else. I sure as fuck wouldn't have been interested in sharing.

I knew men who were in triads, soldiers on opposite deployment shifts who shared a girl. It worked for them, but in my mind, it was only a convenient arrangement, not love.

Witnessing the dynamic between Aurora, Jackson, and Ethan changed my perspective. Commitment doesn't align with our lifestyles. Relationships have responsibilities, and women have expectations. I considered dating a few times but knew it wouldn't work, not in the military and certainly not while undercover.

If I'm being honest, I wasn't interested in anyone for more than a night. Nobody sparked my fire, not even a flicker. No one awakened the emotions I'd lost during deployment. Before Aurora, I was dead inside, numb and cold, lifeless blue eyes staring back at me in the mirror.

I've struggled to adjust to civilian life. It's disorienting not being in crisis mode, not having a gun at my side and the heavy weight of my gear on my chest. It feels...wrong, exposed, vulnerable.

I rarely sleep uninterrupted, or I sleep too much. To most people, I'm moody, closed off. My point is, I doubt I can function in a healthy, 'normal' relationship.

Jax and Ethan are the same. Without money and hockey, Jackson would likely be in prison. Aurora is the only woman who'd tolerate his erratic behavior and love him unconditionally.

Ethan is a workaholic, which means he's always stressed the fuck out. He has to be in control, and modern women would consider him a chauvinist—except our girl, who seems to like a man who's rough around the edges, who needs someone to take charge.

Even with their shortcomings, or maybe because of them, Jax and Ethan support one another. It's not perfect, but that's where I come in. I'm just foolish—or desperate—enough to believe I can make it work.

From my surveillance and texts with Aurora, they're not a happy trio. As predicted, they can't care for her during the season, no matter how hard they try. Their life is too chaotic.

I watch as Ethan and Aurora have a heated conversation in the hotel restaurant. He leans over the table, says a few words, and she hangs her head. Something is going on between them. He's been staying with the team, and they no longer text or call each other.

I message her again—**Answer me, princess**—unable to resist the urge to soothe her.

Ethan slips a phone from his pocket, glares at it then at her, and I realize why she's not answering: He's taken her phone, which means he's read my texts, and he's not pleased.

He has to know how I feel—it's been clear, even to Jax.

I need to get back to her, and since Ethan's the more level-headed one, I text him directly.

> It's unsafe for her to go without a phone.

He returns her phone to his pocket and takes out his own. He reads my message, and his gaze darts across the restaurant, searching for me, but I remain hidden behind a security camera and a worthless firewall.

Ethan

You playing bodyguard or stalker?

Both.

> Something like that.

ETHAN

You in NYC? She wants you back.

Huh? Not at all what I expected.

> What?

ETHAN

She asked me to get you back in exchange for her not working.

> As her bodyguard?

I haven't a clue why I question it. Wishful thinking? Of course, it's as her bodyguard. What else would it be?

He lifts his head to consider her downcast expression.

ETHAN

You and I both know it's more.

I'm not stupid. I understand she'll never betray them, and I'm okay with that. I simply want to be there—or so I tell myself...repeatedly.

> I'm in NYC. Let's meet.

He rolls his neck and pays the check before answering.

ETHAN

> You try to take her from us or harm Jackson, and you'll never see her again.

* * *

We meet at the hotel restaurant after the game. I have little time to plead my case, since the team is leaving tonight for Boston. If all goes well and we don't kill each other, I'll travel with them.

Jax slides into the booth across from me. He's immediately agitated, his knee bouncing and his fingers dragging through his damp hair. "If this is about Aurora, the answer is no. We're married."

I guess we're jumping headfirst into the bullshit. No longer hiding and knowing he's not about to re-injure his hand with Ethan beside him, I say the first thing that comes to mind. "That's fine. Doesn't mean I won't get down on one knee and propose to her someday."

He tips his head back, a manic edge to his bark of laughter. "Why would you? You can't marry her."

Ethan inches toward Jax, resting his elbows on the table and subtly shielding his bestie, prepared to intervene if necessary.

Undeterred, I lean in. "Because she deserves it. People

have commitment ceremonies without actually getting married. It's symbolic."

"Oh shit." Jackson chuckles and shakes his head. "You're crazier than I am."

"Really? Tell me she hasn't expressed wanting a proposal from you. Did you get down on one knee?" I turn to Ethan, whose expression is sour. "And an actual commitment from you. She wants the gesture, I guarantee it."

They exchange a glance that wipes the smug grin off Jackson's face.

"Are you fucking delusional?" he snarls, no longer snarky now that I've called them both out.

I kick back in the seat and cross my arms over my chest. "Calm down. I have no plans to steal her from you. I'm here to keep her safe—and you."

His lip curls. "Like fuck you are. You can't stay away. You're here to weasel your way in."

"What?" I smirk mockingly and shrug. "Your wife isn't allowed to have friends?"

"Friends, my ass."

My smile grows; I'm enjoying how easy he is to annoy. "Doesn't matter. You need me."

Ethan's jaw clenches so tightly, his temples visibly throb. "This is your pitch? Talking in circles? Being manipulative?"

My body stiffens. If Jax thinks I'm manipulative like his father, he'll never trust me. He needs to know I'm on his side, and a part of him must want what's best for Aurora—even if that includes me.

"I'm not trying to manipulate you. I was with her when neither of you were. First, it was hockey and her modeling, then it was your relapse. I've always been there for her. I was by her side when she was anxious about seeing Ethan again, standing outside his door, taking deep breaths. I listened to her cry herself to sleep night after night in New York. I was the one who held her after she saw the pictures—"

"Enough," Ethan growls. "Stop with the guilt trip."

I inhale deeply, allowing the air to expand my lungs as I recall my reason for being here. "All I'm saying is, she's my priority, and she deserves to be cared for. You struggle without me."

Jax rolls his eyes, unconvinced, and I snap.

"Kyle had someone watching you, watching us all. You have evidence, right? Evidence worth harming you for—or *her*? I'll protect you. She loves you. She'd *never* leave you. Why the fuck are you so worried?"

Ethan skewers me with his intense gaze, his body looming over the table, his tone dropping to a lethal level. "Don't think *I'm* replaceable. You have no idea what I'm capable of. I'll go to great lengths to protect what's mine."

What's mine, as in Jackson too. They're fiercely loyal to one another, far more than so-called friends. If I hadn't let Jax kick my ass, if I'd defended myself and wounded him, Ethan would've slit my throat. I'd be lying next to Kyle.

"Believe me, I know. I'm not trying to be killed. I'm on the job, but I can protect you. I can protect her." My attention shifts to Jackson. "Aurora's safety is still a priority, right? We need to go over what I found at Kyle's, including your iPhone."

13
ETHAN

We step off the elevator and onto our floor.

"This is a bad fucking idea," Jackson hisses.

I follow close behind, trying to keep up with his angry pace. "What do you want to do? You heard what he said about your father, and we can't be with her twenty-four seven."

He throws his arms up. "He wants her. It's going to fuck up what we have."

"It doesn't have to. Aren't you happier when she's taken care of? When she's safe? I know I am, and you play better when she's in the stands smiling."

Do I like Reece? No more than anyone else. Does Aurora? Obviously. Can I ignore him? Probably. I do most of the time. Is he useful? Will he protect them? Absolutely, and that's what matters.

Jax and I can focus on hockey and Aurora without all the worry and complications. Reece can give her all the flowery shit.

"That doesn't mean we should add him to our relationship." He stops at my door. "This," he gestures between us, "is perfect."

I swipe my key card and push open the door. We need to get to Boston. We're already running late, as usual, and still, he doesn't go to his room. He follows me in.

"You and I spend a lot of time together. We haven't always gotten along." I recall the days he was throwing helmets at me and smirk. "It took time." I grab my partially packed bag from the floor and toss it onto the bed. "And I'm not suggesting we add him," I tack on, because I'm not.

I have no idea how this will play out. It's up to Aurora. My priority is having someone with her while we travel, someone who'll make sure she eats and has everything she needs.

She's comfortable with Reece. They were alone for months and never crossed the line. Why would they now? She'd never betray us.

Jax cocks his head and furrows his brows. "You think it's the same? You think if I spend time with him, he'll become you?" He rakes his fingers through his perfectly tousled hair. "He'll only tear us apart."

I grip his shoulder and give the tight muscle a squeeze. "I won't let that happen. Now, go pack." I unzip my duffle and pull out a hoodie. "I promised Aurora I'd stay with you two tonight."

"Does this mean nothing to you?" His voice elevates, taking on an edge of panic. "I'm not sharing a bed with him."

"Calm down." I shrug off my suit jacket and lay it on the bed then kick off my dress shoes. "He doesn't want us, only Aurora."

"Calm down? Seriously? Do you want him?"

My head snaps up, and I blink at Jax. "What?"

He thrusts a hand in my direction. "Will you be sleeping with him? Fucking Aurora with him?"

"No," I stretch out the word. "What in the world is going on?"

"You fuck her with me. Why not with him?"

"I'm not interested in him." In my shocked state, the words slip off my tongue.

"Are you interested in me?"

Everything goes white, and the room tilts. Oh my God, I'm having a stroke. "I'm... What?"

"You watch me fuck Aurora. You're okay being naked together. You use my cum as lube." He lists my sins off, one by one, using his fingers. "You gave me a striptease a few nights ago."

My pulse skips a beat or five, then races. Not a stroke—I'm having a heart attack. No, worse: I'm aroused, my dick twitching in my suit pants. *Why is my dick twitching?* "That's...that's not what I meant."

He steps closer. "What did you mean then? Why wouldn't you do the same with him?"

My mouth goes dry. I'm woozy. Can you have a stroke *and* a heart attack? At the same time?

"It's just sex." Even as I mumble the words, I know they're a lie. I lived that way once; it's not even close. Before, I never thought twice about my sexual partners. Now, I can't *stop* thinking of Aurora and Jax.

His face twists into a grimace, his brows furrowing deeper. "You're okay with anyone?" He swallows hard. "It means nothing to you?"

"No, I'm not saying that." I yank the hoodie over my head, only to realize I'm still in my dress shirt and tie. What the fuck is happening right now? "It's sex. It's fucking great. Do we need to dissect it?"

"So you won't mind if I'm with him, if I fuck her with him? Since it's just sex?"

My brain goes to them in bed touching. Not Reece and Aurora, but Jax and Reece. I wince. I flash back to the drive to the hospital after Kyle hurt Aurora. I was livid, shaking with rage. My chest felt like it'd explode, the same as now.

With a clenched jaw and a threatening stride, I press Jax against the wall. "Is that what you want?"

He doesn't answer. His pupils dilate, his lips part, and dangerous, forbidden thoughts slam into me. *My fingers around his throat, his mouth on mine, our tongues intertwining...*

I'm suspended in the air, unable to breathe. "Don't look at me like that."

His voice goes places it doesn't belong. "How am I looking at you?"

Like you'd worship me.

And fuck, I want that. *I want my captain.*

I saw this coming from *him*, not *me*, and I never expected it to be this intense, this all-consuming.

I ball my fists, fighting the urge to reach out and cross that line. "Don't."

His gaze flickers to my lips. "Why?"

A cold sweat breaks out over my entire body. "You're my player. I'm your coach."

"That's it?" The corner of his mouth curls up. "Yet you sleep with me, live with me, have me pinned against the wall."

I stumble back and gather my wits. This can't happen—I can't be what he needs. It's better to kill his fascination now and save myself the heartache. "I'm not doing this, Jax. It's sex, nothing more. You're being too emotional, too attached." I lay it on thick. "I don't want Reece. Calm the fuck down."

His devilish eyes sharpen with hurt and disgust. He pushes off the wall. "See you at practice, *Coach*," he throws over his shoulder.

The door clicks shut, and I collapse onto the bed. I stare blankly at the endless city lights and sink into self-loathing.

Fiery orange flecks, the color of autumn leaves, circle his pupils. Every word, every detail, replays in my mind, that scorching gaze seared into memory.

I hate myself. I extinguished more than just the desire in his eyes; I killed the light in them too. He feared Reece would destroy us, and I'm the one who tore our relationship down. There's no returning to sharing a bed, a girl, a family, not after what I said.

"See you at practice, Coach."

We're back to the beginning, back to him despising me, and I can't blame him. Wait—why did he say he'd see me at practice? I'll see him tonight. Unless...

I shove my feet into my shoes and haphazardly toss my clothes into my bag. I don't bother hanging my suit. I cram it in with the rest and rush out the door.

He wouldn't take off, not again. He wouldn't do that to Aurora. Still, I have a feeling he isn't with her right now. He's too angry, too wounded.

I drop my luggage at their room and bound down the stairs to the lobby, just in case.

He's not there, and he's not at the valet, the restaurant, the gym, or the pool.

I find him at the rooftop lounge and bar, leaning over the glass railing, staring out at the Manhattan skyline, no drink in his hand, thank fuck. I'd never forgive myself.

It's a beautiful winter evening, not a flake of snow or drop of rain, only a crisp breeze dancing in the air. Still, it's far cooler than Jax prefers.

Up here, there's hardly anyone. Sensing me, he peers over his shoulder. Our gazes meet briefly before he glances away, his eyes wild, wrecked, a punch to my gut.

I swallow hard against the burning in my throat and wrap my arms around him from behind. "I'm sorry."

"Nope. Fuck that." He tenses and makes a weak attempt to escape me. "Stop touching me."

If he wanted, he could fight harder. I'm taller and bulkier, but he wouldn't think twice about throwing an elbow or a headbutt at anyone else, no matter their size. Instead, he allows me to hold him while his heart beats an angry rhythm.

I don't deserve his trust, and words fail me. "I didn't mean it," I manage.

"Yes, you did."

"No..." My argument dies, because, fuck, he's right. "I meant to hurt you, to push you away. It's a knee-jerk reaction, and I'm sorry. I'm an asshole."

He shifts his weight and drops his head back against me. "You are."

I gaze at the Queensboro Bridge for a long while. "I found out my mother died the morning of my last game," I blurt. "We were at home, and the team wanted me to sit out, but I refused. I talked a lot of shit, played tough, but that night, I wasn't focused. My mind was elsewhere. I turned my back on the defender and got leveled. Didn't stand a chance; my head hit the ice, and it was lights out. I lost everything that day, everything I'd worked my entire life for, and I've been..." *Trying to recover that weightlessness, that feeling of security, ever since.* "I've been coaching, you know?"

It was all I had once, but not anymore.

Before I can fully process that thought, the icy wind whips his hair across his face, and he brushes it aside. His blond hair is getting longer, taking on a darker, sandy-brown hue, and his tan is fading. I bet he's eager to get back to the West Coast. I doubt he'll ever be truly happy in New York.

He clears his throat. "Do what you need. Focus on your career. I can take care of Aurora and the baby. I won't bother you."

I won't bother you. Did I not hear the same from our girl? Who's next? My kid? What the fuck is wrong with me? Am I having a midlife crisis?

One thing's for sure. "I don't want to lose you or Aurora. I'm just...broken."

"No, you're not." No hesitation, no wavering in his voice. "You're the greatest man I know."

That might not be saying much, but my eyes water. I hug him a little tighter. "Can we go back to the way we were? Please?"

He doesn't respond, and my stomach flips as my chest tightens. "Jesus, you're giving me a heart attack."

He snorts. "You're not having a heart attack, old man. I won't allow it."

I nuzzle the curve of his neck with my beard, and he shivers, a tremor rippling through him.

"Stop it." He elbows me in the ribs. "Go play with your boy toy."

"He's not my boy toy," I say through gritted teeth, putting him into a headlock. "I'm about to make you my boy toy if you don't shut up." I playfully shove him away.

He spins around and flashes me that crooked grin. "Promise?"

* * *

"Princess." Reece smiles politely and opens the back door of the SUV.

"Viking," she greets with nothing more than a curt nod, not even a glance.

His smile widens, and the corners of his eyes crinkle with amusement. Rather, he understands her better than I do; their nicknames hold some deeper meaning I'm unaware of, or he's ecstatic to hear his name from her mouth.

Whatever Reece is grinning about, it's enough for Jax to flip me the middle finger as he rounds the front of the vehicle.

I arch a brow. "Is that an offer?"

"It wasn't aimed at you." He smirks. "You were just the one staring at me."

Dick.

I take Aurora's hand and help her into the backseat, climbing in after. The valet loads their ridiculous amount of luggage and shopping bags into the trunk, and Reece gets behind the wheel.

It's hard to ignore how much he likes her. Loves her? It's in the way he refuses to pull away until she's settled. The way he sneaks glimpses of her in the mirror, though her head rests on my shoulder. The way he plays her favorite pop music—but not too loud, because she gets overwhelmed easily. The way he carefully drives as if he has the most precious cargo on board—which he does, and I'm confident I made the right decision by letting him in.

I peer over at Jax to gauge his thoughts, only to find him already looking at me. Our gazes meet, but before I can read him, he glances away. He rests his head on Aurora's shoulder and closes his eyes. She runs her fingers up his neck and into his hair, and I kiss her temple. My two favorite things, right here, together.

Nothing is better than this.

The next day, I'm standing behind the player's bench. It's a tied game against my former team, and I'd be lying if I said I wasn't a wreck inside.

Jax doesn't speak to me. No banter. No borderline flirting. He engages with his teammates and maintains his usual high level of intensity, even after missing a much-needed goal, but he pays little attention to me.

His behavior is no different from any other player, but my heart physically aches. I could use his brand of humor today, along with two more goals.

"O'Reilly, fucking score, will ya?" I shout over the roaring crowd and the blaring music.

He could crack about a dozen sexual innuendos, but he doesn't. He huddles with his linemates and plans a flawless play, where he executes a fake and passes to Grant, resulting in a goal. Then, he drafts another with an assist from our goalie, Killian, which nobody expected. It's an impressive performance, one they'll be replaying on *SportsCenter* all season long. If he keeps this up, I won't be able to afford his next contract.

At intermission, we're up by three, and I slap his helmet in celebration. I get no response. Coming down the tunnel, he laughs and jokes with Grant, and I head into the locker room with my temper focused on a new target.

I know who I'll trade if I lack the money to keep my star player.

Jax doesn't need to be distracted by his best friend. In fact, he doesn't need two best friends.

14
REECE

I bump shoulders with Aurora. "What's wrong, princess?"

She's fidgeting in her seat more than usual, crossing and uncrossing her long legs. The team is winning and Jackson is killing it, but as the clock counts down, she grows increasingly anxious.

Perhaps I'm making her uncomfortable. I've been careful not to violate any boundaries, though the mere sight of her triggers vivid memories of a dream I can't erase. Even days later, I swear I could smell her in my bed, feel the phantom weight of her body on mine, hear her soft moans. It drove me fucking mad.

"I didn't know we'd be sitting up here with the other team." She lays her hand on her stomach, something she does when nauseated or anxious. "I had the twins find me one of Ethan's old jerseys. I was planning to surprise him."

Ethan arranged these seats. We're in a suite with a handful of Boston fans, sitting outside the box, overlooking the ice. I've noticed a few people eyeing us, but no one has approached. Besides, she hasn't removed her jacket; only the bottom half of the oversized jersey is visible.

"You're nervous about wearing his New York jersey to a Boston game?"

She has Jackson's bedazzled name and number on the back of her jacket—it's clear who she belongs to. I'm not familiar with hockey etiquette, but I'd think being the wife of the visiting team's captain would be more troubling than sporting the coach's old jersey.

"Well, I couldn't wear it to the New York game. I would've been cheering for the other team, and it was Jax's first game back. I thought maybe it'd cheer Ethan up tonight." She hangs her head. "It was dumb."

I still don't understand. "What are you worried about exactly?"

"Boston is his former team, owned by his ex's family. If someone sees what I'm wearing, he'll be angry. I won't see him for days—if he even allows me to travel with him again." She wraps herself tighter in the jacket. "He doesn't like attracting attention. It was a stupid idea. I don't know what I was thinking."

Is that why Ethan has been staying away from her? Because she attracts too much attention? He's dating a gorgeous, twenty-two-year-old *Sports Illustrated* model who's also his star player's supposed wife. He's bound to be in the spotlight.

"No, it's not stupid. Why would supporting him be stupid? It'll be okay. You're with me, and we're leaving once the game is finished."

"Oh," she mumbles with a hint of disappointment.

The pieces are falling into place. Ethan needs her here to appease his lead scorer, since Jax is a mess without her, when he'd rather she be safe at the hotel. No media. No distractions. He wants complete control.

I take her hand, and our fingers intertwine in their

familiar dance. A jolt of adrenaline floods my veins, my skin prickling, hypersensitive to her touch. I breathe deeply, trying to calm my racing heart, but instead, I inhale her intoxicating scent. God, she smells amazing, and I nearly groan as arousal slams into me.

Focus, idiot.

What were we talking about? I clear my dry throat and stretch my legs to adjust my pants discreetly.

"How's work?" we both ask, then grin.

"No work—for me. Ethan doesn't want me working, but *technically*," her golden-brown eyes light up, "I'm still representing the brand, and they're sending me the spring line. Don't tell him."

So Ethan might've been telling the truth, and she actually traded work for me to be here. I refuse to believe it. "Your secret is safe with me, *but* that means you have to attract the paparazzi, have your picture plastered everywhere. He might not approve."

"True. True." She nods. "It just feels strange not working, not having an income, like I'm forgetting something important."

I know that feeling all too well. Not the lack of work, but the fear of missing some critical detail. "No worries, angel. You have a solid team. We won't let anything happen."

"Thanks." She smiles softly and lays her head on my shoulder. "Are you sure you wanna be my glorified babysitter?" She peers up at me. "*And* my bodyguard? *And* my nutritionist? *And* my driver? *And* my therapist?"

She acts as if being with her is a burden, but it's an honor. I have the privilege of serving her, protecting her—my dream girl. That blows my mind.

"Who else is gonna make you nap when you're cranky?"

Our eyes remain locked. I desperately want to kiss her,

but knowing my luck, it'd be broadcast on the Jumbotron, and her husband will beat me to death with a hockey stick while his bestie stomps my skull in.

The roar of the crowd becomes deafening, and her attention snaps to the game. Jax is on a breakaway, and she gets to her feet. He scores, and she throws her arms in the air, cheering. After bumping heads with Killian at center ice, he searches for her, points his stick, and she blows him a kiss.

She takes her seat, face flushed, and I realize something.

"Jax does that to you." I gesture toward the goalie. "That forehead tap."

She tilts her head, brows furrowing, then she gasps. "Holy crap, he does!" Her cheeks flush deeper, her expression adoring. "Oh my gosh, that's so sweet," she coos.

I roll my eyes, and she playfully knocks her shoulder into mine, giggling. I don't fault her for who she loves, and I don't fault either of them for loving her. After everything we've been through, we all deserve to love whoever the fuck we want.

"There's food. Do you want anything?" I ask at intermission.

She twists in her seat, glancing behind her at the buffet in the center of the suite. "No thanks, but you can go ahead."

"Will you at least have a snack? They have cheese and sparkling water." I wag my brows suggestively.

She smiles at my antics. "I might eat some cheese."

"I know you'll eat cheese. Come on."

The moment she sees a couple standing at the food counter, she abandons me to grab a bottle of water from the fridge. She's not fond of social situations and will avoid people if she can, but knowing she'll share with me, I load up my plate with her favorites.

She's gained a bit of a sweet tooth while pregnant, and when she walks by to return to our seats, I ask, "Should I grab these chocolate-covered strawberries?"

That gets her attention. She leans in, and her eyes widen with a serious case of food lust. "Yes," she mouths with ferocity.

I can't help but chuckle. God, I wish she'd look at me like she does chocolate.

The man across the buffet faces us. "You must be my special guest," he says to Aurora, wearing a well-practiced grin.

He appears to be in his late thirties, with salt-and-pepper hair and a sharp gray suit. Next to him is a blonde woman, about the same age. Until now, their backs had been to us as they chatted and sipped wine. I caught him sneaking glimpses at Aurora, but that's expected.

"Aurora Embers." She gives him a charming smile. "Nothing special, I promise."

The woman's head snaps around, her mouth agape, eyes burning with unmasked hostility, and Aurora practically burrows herself into my side.

Gray Suit extends his hand, seeing only Aurora. "Trent, agent and friend of Coach Blackwood, and I highly doubt that."

Coach Blackwood. Not Ethan, meaning he failed to tell Trent who Aurora is to him. You know, the mother of his child and girlfriend.

Aurora sets down the bottle of water and gracefully takes his hand. "Nice to meet you. Thank you for allowing us to use your suite."

"Not a problem. Coach said you'd be as quiet as a mouse, but he didn't mention how stunning you are."

She presses her lips together and shakes her head in amusement.

"I bet you get that a lot, though." He winks.

The scoff that escapes me is louder than intended and full of annoyance. "She isn't the one, not unless you wanna eat a hockey puck traveling at a hundred miles an hour."

He forces a laugh. "Oh, I know *all* about her husband." He smirks at Aurora. "And you."

Somehow, I doubt that, not with the way he's flirting.

The blonde scrutinizes Aurora's outfit, and her lip curls. "Who are you?" Her Boston accent is as thick as molasses.

Aurora squares her shoulders, no longer charismatic or amused. "I'm a model and Jackson O'Reilly's wife."

Oblivious, Trent snorts. "She's being modest. She was on the cover of *Sports Illustrated* and featured in *Maxim's* Hot 100 this year."

I'm starting to hate this guy.

The woman gives Aurora another once-over, paying close attention to her rounded stomach, and sets down her wine glass. "You're married?" Her brows rise. "This is a joke, right?" Her shrill words hang in the air, the room going silent. "Did he really think putting you in his *agent's* suite would hide you from me?" She enunciates each word with clipped precision, her voice seething with barely contained fury. "Oh, I've been waiting for the day he tried to show off his whore."

My muscles tense, a coiled spring ready to snap. "Excuse me? I don't care who you are—don't threaten her, not even slightly."

Trent puts an arm between us. "Whoa, hold up."

Blondie's furious glare shifts to him. "Did my ex put her in here?"

"Yeah? She's a guest of mine. Is there a problem?"

Aurora embraces me, her eyes wide with panic, her hands gripping my shirt beneath my leather jacket. "¿Nos vamos?" she whispers. "Please?"

She wants to leave. I have no idea how she suspected I understood Spanish. I know what I need to communicate effectively on the job, but I'm not fluent by any means.

Behind her, Ethan's ex continues to rant. "Only that she's carrying my ex's *lovechild*." Her voice rises for all to hear. "Speaking of…how far along are you exactly? Far enough to force him into a divorce? Is it even his?"

Aurora's eyes well up, and she swallows hard. Forgetting all about the food and stellar conversation, I guide her out the door.

From the corner of my eye, I watch Ethan's ex follow us. I dip my head, my hand on the small of Aurora's back. "Don't answer. Don't engage."

We get to the elevator, and the blonde opens her mouth to speak, but I cut her off.

"I'm not only her security detail, I'm also a federal agent. Keep talking, and I'll have you charged with harassment. You touch her, I'll personally escort you out of this building in handcuffs, and it won't be pretty."

She raises her hands in mock surrender. "No harassment." An ugly grin plays on her lips. "I thought Aurora might want to exchange addresses for Christmas cards. We're family, aren't we? Considering her child and I will share a last name."

I should keep my mouth shut, but I can't. "Wow. I see why he divorced you."

"Because he got someone pregnant, obviously."

She has reason to be bitter. Ethan was still married when he met Aurora. I don't need the entire story, but I wish the fucker would've given me a heads-up.

Right or wrong, I don't protect Aurora because it's my job. I protect her because it kills me not to, and I have the mental scars to prove it.

"No, because you're repulsive. You don't even compare. Now take your shit to Ethan."

The elevator slides open, and thankfully, it's empty—the game must be in play. We step inside, and I position myself in front of Aurora, shielding her. She wraps her arms around me, her head resting on my back—another realization: her love language is physical touch, and she needs my comfort.

The doors shut. I turn to her and lift her chin, but her gaze remains downcast, fixed on the floor. She won't look at me, and I can tell by the faint quiver in her lips she's struggling to suppress her tears. I'm struck with the powerful urge to hold her, let her fall apart in my arms, but I know she doesn't want that right now. She's trying to be strong.

It's probably crossing a line, but I kiss her forehead. "Just breathe. We'll be out of here soon."

Her breath shudders, a ragged sigh fighting its way free. "I didn't even get a chocolate-covered strawberry." She attempts to joke through her tears, but in no time, her lip pouts, and her body shakes with sobs. Covering her face with her hands, she cries, "I hate her so much."

I take hold of her wrists and lower my head until her gaze meets mine. "She doesn't matter. These arrogant assholes do not matter. No one matters but you and the baby." I wipe away her tears and smeared makeup with my thumbs. "I'll get you some chocolate-covered strawberries. Now, the doors will open any minute. Chin up, princess, and straighten your crown."

15
ETHAN

"I'm sorry, man!" Trent says for the millionth time since calling. "How was I supposed to know?"

I pinch the bridge of my nose, a dull ache throbbing behind my eyes. "What the fuck did you think I meant by someone special?"

"Ah...Jackson O'Reilly's wife, the swimsuit model. Who else?"

My pregnant girlfriend. Yes, Jackson O'Reilly's wife. Yes, the swimsuit model. Yes, I should've told him, but I didn't have the time or energy for *that* conversation.

Struggling to maintain some semblance of privacy in the back of this motorcoach, I grind my molars, exacerbating the headache. "Why were you with my ex?"

"I rep a few players now that you're no longer their coach." The buzz of a crowd muffles, and he lowers his voice. "Jesus, why didn't you tell me who you were dating? Or screwing? When did you get her pregnant? I need answers! I want to live vicariously through you."

He chuckles, and I want to punch myself in the face. Those questions are precisely what I was hoping to avoid.

"Fuck off, Trent." I end the call before I completely lose my temper.

The last thing I wanted was for my ex-wife to meet Aurora. I can't imagine how vile she was to her. Actually, I can. I endured her abuse for six years.

"Where is she?" Jackson asks, his tone heavy with exasperation.

He's sick of my shit, and I can't say I blame him. We're en route to the hotel, and he likely wouldn't have sat with me if I hadn't sounded heated on the phone. "In the room, napping."

He doesn't even spare me a glance. "You talked to Reece?"

"Yeah, he's with her. He's worried my ex will show up at the hotel."

That captures his attention, and he finally peers over at me. "Will she?"

"Not putting anything past her. She can't contact me since I've blocked her—like Aurora wanted."

I'm sure she has a laundry list of accusations against me. She'd take me back to court if she could. She's vindictive.

"If she comes to the hotel, I won't be nice. I'm warning you now. I don't give a flying fuck about your ex or *saving face*." He shakes his head in frustration. "Stop running and hiding and make a fucking decision."

"Everything will be okay once we get to LA," I tell him, more to convince myself. "Aurora's embarrassed. I'll—"

"No," he cuts me off, his jaw tight. "Do you hear yourself? You're making this harder than it needs to be. Choose. In or out."

My palms grow clammy, slick with sweat. "It's not that simple."

He sits up straight, readying for a fight. "It is that simple. You're just not that committed."

I mirror his defensive stance and lower my voice. "That's not fucking true."

"Yeah? Prove it." He juts his chin. "I guarantee if roles were reversed, every single person would know that baby was mine, that she belonged to me despite being with you. She wouldn't have sat in my agent's suite without an explicit threat of violence if something happened to her, *especially* if I knew I had an ex floating around. I've made mistakes in the past. I'm not about to fuck up the future. Make. A. Fucking. Choice."

Defeated, my body sags, and I rake my fingers through my hair. I'm screwing up, and I'm so damn exhausted from the weight of all this stress and secrecy.

I love Jax. I love Aurora. My chest tightens at the thought of losing what we have. I lift my head and meet his gaze. "I should have told Trent. I should have warned Reece about my ex."

"And everyone else? Us?"

Us? Me and him? I have no fucking clue. "We're family. We'll figure it out."

"We're a mess." He takes a deep breath and releases it slowly. "You're so worried about something happening, you keep Aurora at arm's length, leaving her confused and unprepared for the inevitable. Believe me, I've been there. I didn't tell her about Kyle, and she ended up at one of his parties. It's Murphy's Law or some crap." He gestures with his hand.

"What would you have me do, oh wise one?"

"Live your truth—or *our* truth. You want Reece here? Make him work for it. People will find out. So what?" He raises his chin. "Those who talk shit…"

Grant pops over the seat in front of us. "Get hit," he finishes, flashing his stupid smile. "Who are we hitting? Who hurt my favorite team wife?"

Jax drills him in the shoulder. "Mind your fucking business, G." He directs his crooked grin my way. "See how easy that was?"

I cock my head. "I'm thirty-five, not twenty-five. I'm a coach, not a player. I don't go around hitting people."

"You should start."

"I'm gonna start with you."

"Do it," he taunts with that devilish smirk.

16
JACKSON

"You seriously put her in a suite with your ex? With no fucking heads-up?" the Viking gripes as soon as we enter the hotel suite.

He's reclined on the couch, new combat boots kicked up on the coffee table, arms folded over his chest. He's wearing his usual black tactical pants and a black fitted T-shirt, always in uniform.

The bedroom where Aurora is sleeping is directly opposite him. I bet he sat there, staring at the closed door, his tongue hanging out, panting.

Ethan tosses his suit jacket onto the back of the chair facing Reece then plops down. "No. Why would I do that? My agent had seats available. Obviously, I should have told him who she was."

I plonk my ass beside Reece, putting myself between him and Ethan, and knock his feet off the table. "Is it necessary to dress like that? What could you possibly have in all those pockets? You're wearing cargo pants, for fuck's sake."

"And you're wearing skinny jeans, rich boy. Sorry, my dick needs breathing room." He opens a pocket, the Velcro ripping—fucking *Velcro*—and holds his palm out. "Your girl's lip stuff and ID, because she's forgetful." He tears open another pocket, and metal jangles. "Handcuffs I threatened Ethan's crazy ex with, or in case your girl wants to get kinky." He winks.

Agitation swarms in my chest. "Keep your handcuffs in one of your twenty pockets, and she's my *wife*. Get it through your thick skull."

"I will once I see the marriage certificate." He dismisses me, turning to Ethan. "Trent knew she was Aurora Embers, the model. Knew what magazines she was featured in. Knew she was with Jackson. He laughed when I told him he'd be eating a puck if he didn't stop flirting with her."

I offer him a fist-bump, and he gives me a side-eye before he halfheartedly bumps knuckles.

"I don't know the entire story," he continues, "but your ex is quite unhappy about the pregnancy."

I can't picture Ethan with anyone else. The image makes me sick...and murderous.

Coach rests his head back and scrubs his fingers through his thick, wavy hair. "I fucked up, okay? I'm far from perfect."

"Glad you're finally realizing that." Reece shoots a glare in my direction. "About time someone told the truth."

I'm not about to spend the rest of my life thwarting his attitude. He doesn't even know me. "You want some truth? I don't trust you. Your presence sends me into a dark place—not because you're in love with *my wife*, but because you talk like a cop, dress like a cop, and treat me like shit. After our meeting at the hotel, I could taste the craving to get fucking obliterated, and I almost did. Every single day, I'm fighting a battle you have no fucking clue about." My chest heaves and my heart races. "There's my truth for today."

Reece glances helplessly at Ethan, who stares at me with a pained expression, his eyes glassy.

"Last night?" His Adam's apple bobs. "After we argued?"

I give a half-assed shrug. "Yeah."

"Fuck, Jax." He reaches over the arm of the chair and pulls me into a headlock, his cheek pressed to my hair. "Don't you dare relapse or harm yourself. Tell me. Scream at me. Punch me. We'll brawl if we need to. Understand?"

"Yes, asshole." I chuckle and elbow him in the chest. "Let me go."

"I'm proud of you." He releases me and drops back into his chair.

He might be the only person besides Aurora who has ever told me those four words. How can I not be attached to him? If he doesn't want me to love him, he needs to stop caring for me.

The atmosphere feels awkward, so I do what I do best: keep running my mouth. "While I was up on the roof, I realized, no matter what, we'll work through it." I shift my attention to Reece. "Aurora will get over the videos eventually. You're not holding them over me."

His brows furrow, and he cocks his head. "I'm not. I wouldn't say anything or use them. Fuck, I removed evidence from a federal crime scene for you."

"But that's what you're pissy about, right? The videos?"

"You recorded her without her knowledge. That's fucked up."

Ethan glances between us. "Someone fill me in."

"When Aurora and I started dating, I had cameras installed throughout my downtown penthouse. I kept track of her while I was away, kept videos of us together. I watched her pack and leave me before...I went into the hospital. After we separated, I couldn't stand to be there, and Kyle used the place. I have those videos too. I kept everything."

Reece misinterprets my disgusted expression and rolls his eyes. "Don't worry, I didn't watch the videos of you two together. I'd rather not see your dick."

I arch a brow. "You sure? You seem awfully interested in my dick."

"Positive," he grumbles.

If he wants to bust my balls, he'd better bring it. I can do this all day. "Let me know if you change your mind." I mimic his wink.

Ethan clasps the back of my neck and clears his throat. "That's not gonna happen."

The corner of Reece's lip twitches, begging to smile. "Anyhow, the only other person who knows about the phone is my partner. He's a hacker, and he agrees: there's no way to surrender Kyle's videos without leading investigators to the website, where they can subpoena the rest, even if deleted. They'll want to know why you withheld evidence. You'll be questioned, and Aurora will find out her husband is a stalker."

It's no different from every other controlling, insane thing I've done. "Why do you think I held on to them?" Not that it matters. I didn't watch Kyle's videos—I *can't* watch Kyle's videos.

"You'd watch her while traveling for games?" Ethan asks. "That's actually brilliant. For safety purposes, of course."

"I thought so too. Thanks." I smile.

"Just don't put cameras in the Santa Monica house."

I give him a blank stare.

"Jackson, no."

"There's an entire surveillance system."

He releases an aggravated sigh. "Which, let me guess: you'll have access to?"

"We all will. I'm not hiding anything." I shrug a shoulder, not seeing the problem. "I'm also having a panic room installed."

Reece perks up. "Primary bedroom? Or basement?"

"Nursery. If someone breaks in, Aurora is going for the baby. No reason to run back to the bedroom for safety."

He raises his brows. "Smart."

There's a hard knock on the door, and Ethan slumps in the chair with a dramatic groan. "Fuck my life."

* * *

"I must say, Ethan, this doesn't suit you," a deep voice emanates from beyond the door. Either Ethan's ex is a man, or...that's a man. "I expected better from you."

"Seriously, Beth?" Ethan barks. "Now is not the time."

Beth. Gross. I hate her already.

"Seriously, Ethan," a woman, who can only be Beth, mocks in a snide tone. "She's here with you?"

"That's typically how relationships work, yes."

"Is it not enough for you to flaunt your whore in front of me? You have to go around Boston doing it too?"

Her voice pierces the air, and I jump from my seat. Aurora doesn't need to hear or deal with this shit.

"Bethany, calm down," says the unknown guy. "Let me handle this."

Before he can *handle it*, I whip the door open, Reece behind me.

An older man with white hair glances between us while the ex plasters on a fake smile. They both share the same dull eyes and reek of vanity and old money.

Ethan's face is flushed from his cheeks to the tips of his ears. I casually drape my arm over his shoulders; he shoots me a warning glare but doesn't push me away.

Reece leans against the doorjamb, arms folded over his chest.

The man, whom I'm guessing is Beth's father, settles his attention on me. "I'm sorry, son, but this is a private matter. None of your concern."

Son. What a condescending asswipe.

"Well, *Pops*, that's where you're wrong. Your girl called my wife a whore, and that's very much my concern."

His bushy white brows nearly hit his receding hairline. "What? I thought..." He gestures to Ethan.

"Aurora is my wife and Ethan's girlfriend. We're together," I clarify, motioning between us.

I feel Ethan's stare burning a hole in the side of my face, but he doesn't deny my words.

"We're having a baby, and I'd greatly appreciate you not waking our girl." See? I can be nice. I even add, "Thank you."

Their heads snap back as their jaws hang open comically.

"Ethan, son, this can't happen." Pops shakes his head in disapproval. "We brought you into our family—"

That does it. All niceness leaves my body, and ridiculousness creeps in. "Hold on." I interrupt, raising a hand. "Hold on one damn minute." I shut my eyes, inhaling deeply and exhaling slowly.

"What are you doing?" Ethan mutters, his tone laced with amusement—a tiny bit.

"I'm trying to muster a fuck to give." I open my eyes and click my tongue. "Nope. I've got nothing," I say for all to hear. "Not a single fuck to give. Looks like you'll have to *fuck off* instead." I raise my voice, my patience eviscerated. "You're not his family!"

Ethan pats my chest. "Okay, take the crazy down a notch."

"I could always arrest them." Reece shrugs.

"On what grounds?" the ex cries in pretentious audacity.

"Harassment. I warned you, but you didn't listen. Now, you're stalking our girl." He turns to me and Ethan. "Or we can file a restraining order. I can get a judge on the phone while we're all here."

"What? No! I—" Beth wavers and glances at her father for help.

"That won't be necessary." Mr. Beth lifts his hands in surrender. "All we're asking is that you keep your transgressions out of the public eye and away from us."

"Transgressions?" I clutch my proverbial pearls with feigned astonishment. "All love is beautiful. We don't discriminate here."

Reece nods. "Agreed. That sounds like hate speech. I'll add that to the restraining order."

"What about terrorism?" I ask.

"Fuck me," Ethan curses, face to the heavens. "Please, not another one. I can't take another smart-ass."

I scoff. Reece's humor is dry. He's not nearly as funny as I am.

Mr. Beth closes his eyes and shakes his head, as if he's trying to wake from a fever dream. "This is a lost cause. We're leaving. Let's go, Bethany."

He grabs her by the elbow, and the two march toward the elevator, Bitchy Bethany spitting and sputtering the entire way.

"Have a delightful night!" I call out. "Toodaloo, motherfuckers!"

Ethan shoves me inside and bear hugs me from behind. "For once, I'm actually thankful for your craziness."

I throw him off. "Ha, ha... Hi, babe!" I go from deadpanning to feigning cheerful innocence.

Aurora stands in the middle of the open living area, hands on her hips, in nothing but Ethan's jersey. Her hair is in a loose bun on top of her head, her face pale, her lips bright red in comparison.

"What's going on?" She yawns. "I thought I heard voices. Why are you guys fighting?"

Before anyone can answer, Ethan stops dead. "Holy fucking Christmas, is that my jersey?"

"Wait!" I step between them and block his view of her, just to be an ass. "Babe, are these skinny jeans? Reece said I'm wearing skinny jeans."

17
AURORA

"Are you sure about this?" My gaze traces over the burly bouncer outside the noisy sports bar. "The place is packed."

The post-game crowd is loud enough to be heard from the street. Not my usual scene. I'm more of a stay-at-home-and-read type of girl.

Ethan takes my hand and helps me out of the Uber. He dips his head, a smirk playing on his lips. "I'm feeding you then fucking you in that jersey. We won't stay long."

The bouncer acknowledges us with a nod as we enter. The place is surprisingly spacious. Booths line the brick walls, and TVs hang on every available surface. Pool tables are on one side and a dance floor occupies the other, the room filled with people and pulsating music.

He wraps a protective arm around me, and we head toward a roped-off section in the back, where the crowd and noise diminish. He guides me in front of him, and another bouncer grants us entry. We step into the VIP area, and I stiffen. At the bar, Trent stands among a sizable group of guys.

My date said it wasn't necessary to dress up. I'm in his

gently altered jersey, leggings, a leather jacket, and white Converse, my hair in loose waves. He's in jeans and a black button-up. He conveniently failed to mention we were meeting people.

Trent and Ethan greet each other with that handshake-half-hug-clap-on-the-back thing guys do.

"Aurora, nice to see you again." Trent places a hand over his heart. "Sincerely, I apologize for earlier. That was all my fault. I misunderstood the assignment."

"Is that why we're here?" I place my hands on my hips. "So you can grovel for Ethan?" I tease, and they both chuckle.

I don't blame Ethan for his ex's behavior. It stings that she gets to keep his last name, but I honestly can't blame her either. I'd be pissed too if he got someone else pregnant—although I believe I appreciate him more than she ever did. Still, that doesn't mean I enjoy being on the receiving end of her wrath.

A newcomer clasps Ethan's shoulder. "Holy shit, you've been busy." Tall and built, he must be an athlete. His gaze is fixed on my rounded stomach, but his tone is lighthearted. He's not judging, just stating the obvious.

"Yeah. Yeah," Ethan deadpans. "Scully, this is my girlfriend, Aurora."

Girlfriend. Wow. Has that ever happened in public, if ever?

Scully offers a quick handshake. "We've all been warned to be on our best behavior or risk being banned."

"Trent owns the bar and restaurant upstairs," my *boyfriend* explains. "He wanted to make up for tonight."

With his arm around my waist and his hand splayed over my stomach, he introduces everyone. I try to remember all their names, but it's impossible. Half the team must be here.

The bartender hands him a beer and offers me a mocktail, but I decline. Ethan takes a swig from the glass bottle, his Adam's apple bobbing, and it's so freaking hot.

He grins and cracks up as they delve into the game, hazing one another. They're familiar, reminding me he lived here only a handful of months ago. He was with this team for six years. That's wild to think about. It feels like *we've* been together for years, not months.

I realize, not for the first time, that I have no clue what he's into—outside of hockey and sex. Maybe going out is something he needs to unwind. We don't go anywhere. Jax doesn't drink, which eliminates bars and most other places. Maybe Ethan misses hanging out with the guys.

A pang of insecurity hits me as I watch him. He's ruggedly handsome, even when brooding, but he's a dream when happy. His gray eyes sparkle with mirth, and his smile lights up his entire face. Let's not forget about those dimples that rarely make an appearance.

Feeling my gaze on him, he glances down. His lip twitches in response to my staring and leans in for a kiss, whispering, "I love you."

His fingers grasp my chin, his beard tickles my lips, and he tastes like the citrusy beer he's drinking. It's different and electrifying, and a shiver runs down my spine. *He's* different —possessive as usual, but with a touch of tenderness and intimacy.

"Shit, man. I can't recall ever seeing you kiss someone."

Trent's voice disrupts the moment, and a fiery sensation spreads across my cheeks.

"No joke, Aurora," says a player—Larsen, perhaps. "You need to tell us how Coach nailed a baddie."

Ethan scoffs and takes another swig of his beer. He doesn't seem bothered by the question, but my heart rate speeds up and my stomach plummets.

I swallow my nerves. "Ah...we met at a charity event in LA over the summer." That's vague enough, right?

Trent and Ethan exchange a glance. Given the group's uncomfortable silence, I'm guessing that was the wrong answer.

The air freezes in my lungs. Was he married all summer? When did he announce his resignation from Boston? When did he move to LA? August? Thinking is currently beyond my capabilities.

He hugs me tighter and gives a sly smirk. "I got her pregnant; she's stuck with me."

The guys burst into laughter, and I can't help but join in, a sense of relief washing over me.

Trent shakes his head. "A terrible predicament you got yourself in, man."

Ethan's eyes connect with mine. "Truly awful."

18
REECE

Jackson emerges from the bedroom in only gray sweats, his hair wet from a lengthy shower. This suite, although the size of a small apartment, isn't soundproof. I heard everything from the living room: the hour-long shower, the blow to the wall...

My gaze shifts to his right hand. It's not swollen or bruised, not any more than it was prior, and there's no blood or broken skin. If he didn't hit the wall, what did?

Without a word, he walks into the kitchen, opens a cupboard, grabs a glass, and fills it from the tap. He chugs one, then another, staring straight ahead. He stands on the opposite side of the island, facing me, but he definitely doesn't notice me.

Any other time, he'd call me out for gawking. He'd sneer, *"Like what you see?"*

But right now, he remains quiet, his mind elsewhere, his eyes haunted, face pale. His chest rises and falls with rapid, shallow breaths. He's crashing, with no one else here to deal with him—only me.

He places the glass on the counter with more force than necessary and shakes his head.

I rise from the couch and approach with caution. "What's up with you?"

His gaze connects with mine, but it's vacant. "No," he mumbles. That doesn't make sense, and his speech is hollow.

A knot forms in the pit of my stomach. If he took something, I'll knock his ass out and drag him to rehab.

Panic creeps in, and my voice elevates. "Jackson, what the fuck is wrong? What did you take?"

Annoyance crosses his face, and he curls his lip. "No." He blinks once, twice, his dilated pupils focusing. He shakes his head again. "No, I did not."

Holy shit. "Are you hallucinating?"

"No, I'm... It's a flashback."

Flashbacks, I can understand and deal with. I've been there myself a few times. "Okay, did something happen? Is it me?" I scan the shorts and T-shirt I changed into. "You swear you didn't take anything?"

"No, it's not you, and no, I'm not high." His fingers tremble, and he grips the edge of the counter, his knuckles turning white. "I got a text." He drops his head, and there's an agonizing pause before he glances up, eyes glazed over. "It's..." He trails off, his awareness fading as he envisions whatever has him so shaken. "Aurora." Her name sounds ripped from him, raw and jagged.

I step closer, my heart in my throat. "What about her?"

"They want her. Can you get to her?"

His mind must still be in the dark, caged. If he thought there was a genuine threat to her, he'd be gone. He wouldn't be standing in front of me.

"Where's your phone? Please tell me you didn't break it."

Even if he did, I'm five steps ahead, forming a plan for every likely scenario. I'm zoned in.

He gestures to the bedroom, and I don't delay. I find the phone intact on the bathroom floor. Thank fuck these things are damn near indestructible, and his password is still Aurora's birthday.

The message is already open on the screen, a gritty picture that takes my brain an absurd amount of time to process. It's a rusty jail cell built underneath a set of wooden stairs. Inside, there's a filthy, decaying mattress on a wet cement floor. There's no blanket or pillow, nothing but a bucket in the corner.

I read the accompanying text, and my vision blurs, darkening around the edges:

> 9-2740
> I miss you, but your girl will do. I'm saving the spot just for her.

The ID is anonymous—five numbers generated randomly.

I know this is a scare tactic. I know not to engage. But violence like I've never known has my fingers moving without thought of consequence.

> Touch her, and I'll tear you apart piece by excruciating piece.

And I will. I'll call on every broken shard of me to destroy this motherfucker.

Actions and operations race through my mind. On my phone, I check Aurora's location. She's at a sports bar across from the arena, a few blocks away. I consider alerting Ethan, but interrupting their date is a surefire way to send her into a panic, and she'll have questions.

> I need eyes on Aurora.

CHARLIE

> And I need to stop enabling your obsessive stalking.

> This is legitimate. We received a threat.

CHARLIE

> Location?

While I'm sending her address to Charlie, Jackson's phone buzzes with another text:

9-2740

> How about you keep your mouth shut and save us both the trouble? K, pretty boy?

My dark mood descends into the fiery depths of hell. I storm into the kitchen and slam his phone on the counter. "What did you say to Kyle when you met with him? You tipped him off, didn't you? Did you tell him you had evidence?"

Jax stiffens and balls his fists, his muscles flexing and bulging. He's shirtless, tattoos on display, his pulse visibly pounding beneath his sternum with each ragged inhale he draws.

"Means nothing." He leans over the island, his tortured face inches from mine. "I grew up in it. All the memories." He taps his temple. "*I'm* the evidence."

His words, rough and raspy, give me chills. The message, the picture—it's unfathomable. No one should go through the shit he's had to endure.

Still, I have to keep him talking. "Who sent the text?"

"Can you protect her?"

"Yes." *With my life.* "Who?"

His shoulders slump with a shuddered sigh. "Kyle's former partner."

"How are you so sure?"

He swallows hard. "I just know."

Unfortunately, I need more than that. I open the text and slide the phone in front of him. "That sound like him? Would he call you pretty boy?"

His demeanor flips, and his eyes become cold. He fists my shirt and drags my upper body across the counter. "Are you fucking stupid, Cop? What do you think?"

My skin crawls. This is his abuser. It all adds up, and I realize then that Ethan was right. I had Jackson wrong. He wasn't merely entangled in this. He was a victim. His abuse wasn't only psychological, which is why Ethan is fiercely protective of him. Aurora too.

I raise my hands in surrender. "Easy, Jax. I want him dead as badly as you do."

"Doubt it." He shoves me away. "Stop being an insensitive prick."

Thirty minutes ago, I would've said he was acting like a child, but now, I get it.

His oppositional behavior isn't all about protecting Kyle or himself, nor is it about protecting Aurora, though that's there. It's a trauma response. Engaging in this case is reopening wounds that never fully healed—*will* never heal.

"Just give me a name. I'll find him."

19
ETHAN

"Wow," Aurora breathes, her wide eyes reflecting the fairy lights hanging from the ceiling. "Are we alone?"

Above the bar is not exactly a restaurant. It's an exclusive event venue used for small gatherings. We held our season opener and closer parties here most years.

Tonight, it's prepared for a party of two, with a private chef and a romantic ambiance, all arranged by Team Trent. I'm no good at flowery shit. I thought make-up sex in my office was passionate. Clearly, I have a lot to learn.

Her dreamy expression has me grinning, and my cheeks are aching from all this smiling and laughing.

I take her hand and guide her toward a table adorned with flickering candles. "Just us and the chef."

We sit in front of the stone fireplace, lit with a roaring fire.

She narrows her eyes, her gaze suspicious. "What's going on?"

"What?" My tone is far too enthusiastic to pull off nonchalance, especially when a smirk follows.

"You're being nice. It's weird." Laughter bursts from my chest, and she joins in. Then, her brows furrow, and she frowns. "You're happier here."

"What?" This time, the word comes out with confusion.

"It's okay. Your friends are here. You lived here. You're happier here," she repeats with more conviction.

If she believes I'm happier anywhere other than with her, she couldn't be more mistaken. I shake my head. "No. I've low-key dreaded coming here all season. Everything I tried to prevent ended up happening. I got a lovely visit from my ex, and so did you."

Our dinner is intimate—again, thank you, Trent. We're seated on a worn leather loveseat, and I lift her legs onto my lap. "By the way, Reece told me what she said, and she didn't take my last name. She's a fucking liar."

My ex kept her well-known surname, and I didn't give a shit.

Aurora rests against the plush backrest. "I won't lie, that makes me pretty happy. Your ex is quite awful." She flattens her lips and widens her eyes dramatically. "I can totally see why you'd want to avoid her, but downstairs, with your players, that might be the happiest I've seen you."

My response is immediate. "I'm happy because I'm with you. I'm happy because I knew you'd like this night. I'm happy you didn't leave me after dealing with my bitch of an ex and my shitty mood. You're here in my jersey, gazing at me with the same adoring eyes you've had since the beginning. No other person will look at me the way you do." My throat swells with emotion. "It's been a hell of a week. It's over, and I get to take you *home*. Finally."

Her, staring at me with love in her eyes—like she is now, like she was while I was simply drinking a beer and laughing with friends—that right there is everything to me. Nothing compares, and I'll protect that adoring gaze, that feeling, with my life.

She gives me an affectionate smile. "I'm ready to go home. We have a doctor's appointment and Thanksgiving next week."

"Holy shit." I forgot all about Thanksgiving and, fuck, Christmas.

I'll have to buy gifts. I've never really had a family Christmas. My ex went on vacation with her parents every year. Sometimes, I joined, and other times, I worked. She bought all the presents, including her own, and that was fine by me. I was a terrible husband, but I hope to be a better boyfriend.

"Yup, and I was thinking, if it's okay with everyone, we can take my grandma dinner?"

Big brown eyes plead with me, as if I'd ever say no.

I squeeze her thigh. "Of course we can—or we can invite her to the house."

Her face lights up, her lips parting. "Can we? I've never asked the nursing home because we had nowhere to go." She places a hand on her chest. "That would be so wonderful." She fans herself. "Okay. Okay. I need to calm down, or I'll cry my eyes out when they tell me no."

I chuckle at her ramblings. "They won't say no. We'll figure it out."

Oh, it's happening. I'll bribe a nurse if I have to. I might go as far as kidnapping to see Aurora this excited again.

We chat about this and that for the rest of dinner, just enjoying each other's company. She rolls her eyes when I force her to eat a few pieces of filet mignon with her vegetable pasta and two slices of bread.

She's eating better, at least when she remembers, and hasn't fainted—well, as far as I know—but her picky eating habits still concern me.

I lift the glass bottle in front of her. "Do these sparkling waters make you feel full? Maybe we need to switch to regular water."

With a theatrical gasp, she whips her head toward me. "Ethan Aiden Blackwood. You've already taken my coffee away. What's next? Cupcakes?"

I can't stop grinning. I fucking love her. "I regret telling you my middle name."

Peering down, she places her hand on her stomach. "Don't worry, baby. I won't let Daddy take away our cupcakes."

My entire body flushes with heat. For a moment, I lose the ability to breathe and fear I'm having a stroke. Nope, just feelings.

Daddy. I'm going to be a daddy, and I'm not horrified. Not one bit. Not even a little. Jesus, what's happening to me? Next we'll be in the bath, searching Pinterest for baby names.

The chef places a plate in the center of the table, interrupting my existential crisis. "I heard someone likes red velvet cupcakes." This is no cupcake. It takes up the entire platter. "A red velvet molten lava cake topped with homemade vanilla ice cream and strawberries." He dips his head. "Enjoy."

Along the outside of the white plate, written in chocolate syrup, are the words: *Be Mine?* I take my thumb and smear the top of the question mark.

"What are you doing?" She giggles.

Then, I clear the B and e. "There. That's better."

It's left saying: *Mine.*

She cocks her head and smiles. "I don't get a choice?"

"No." I offer her my thumb for her to suck the chocolate off. She does, and my cock jerks. "I meant it when I said you were stuck with me."

20
JACKSON

"You don't have to sleep on the couch." Aurora's brows pinch, and her eyes search mine. She lowers her voice. "What is it?"

When they came back from dinner, she made a beeline for my lap. One glance and she knew. Then she glared at Reece, probably thinking he did something, or it was her date with Ethan that was bothering me. Neither could be further from the truth.

I want her and Coach to work through their issues. I want him to be a part of us, and if anything happens to me, I trust him to care for her most. My feelings toward Reece are conflicted, but as long as he protects her, I can tolerate him.

The problem is, I won't get a wink of sleep in the bedroom. I'll be preoccupied, listening for noises and attempting to fend off the nightmares, the flashbacks, the demons tormenting me.

Even sober, I'm fucked up. My worst nightmares were after the bottle-throwing incident—not that I regret almost killing the piece-of-shit predator, but the guilt of hurting Aurora was unbearable.

I took her to Laguna Beach to convince her not to leave me. I promised her everything, including sobriety.

Then, the guilt festered, the withdrawals kicked in, and I had horrifying nightmares. Not only the usual twisted flashbacks, but new, demented terror…

I stepped into the kitchen of my childhood home. My ears rang with the eerie echo of my heartbeat. The air was harsh, cold in my lungs. The marble tile was gleaming, and my boots smacked as I walked. I remember thinking I had to be quiet, or I'd alert someone. That someone could've only been Kyle, a dark, lingering presence in the back of my mind.

At my feet, I found my mother's crumpled and broken body. I sank to the floor and pulled her into my arms. The icy touch of her skin passed through my fingertips, spreading through me like death personified, aching in my bones.

The lines between reality and illusion blurred, and when I shifted my gaze, the face that stared back at me wasn't my mother's. No, it was Aurora's—her eyes lifeless, expression frozen in agony.

It felt as if my heart was ripped from my chest with a chainsaw. I woke up from clinging to her dead body in a cold sweat, gasping for air. The guttural screams from my nightmare were strangled in my throat, suffocating me.

I scrambled out of bed, went to the minibar, and downed every drop of alcohol. My promise to quit drinking lasted less than forty-eight hours.

Still, she stayed. She never confronted me, but she knew. I hated myself, but she continued to love me. The more she did, the greater the self-loathing and guilt consumed me, the worse I treated her.

I already fear the nightmares, and I can't put her

through that again. They can enjoy the bedroom while I lie awake on the couch.

Instead, she sits on my lap and tells me about tomorrow. Her touch brings me peace and chases away that numb, icy sensation. My thoughts slow when she's talking to me, drowning out the chaos in my mind.

"One day at a time." She runs her fingers through my hair. "In the morning, we're packing up in New York and heading home." She gives me a big, bright smile. "Next week, we have a baby appointment and Thanksgiving. I need you to make everything. Unless you want me to try…"

She knows damn well I don't want her to cook.

"No. I got it. It'll be our first Thanksgiving in our first house. It has to be epic."

"It will be," she says with certainty. "Ethan said we can have Gram over for dinner, so we'll have an extra."

My brows shoot up. "Seriously?"

"Yup." She grins, excited. "You can invite Grant and Kill. You have a home game on Wednesday. I'll get everything ready if you give me a list."

"I got it."

"I'll help."

I inhale her warm, sweet scent, and my tense muscles relax. "Okay."

She trails kisses along my jawline, as if we're the only two in the room. "I won't sleep without you."

I remain quiet, tracing the delicate curve of her neck, unable to admit I won't be sleeping either. "You have Ethan, baby."

"Fine. I'll sleep on the couch with you. I'm pretty sure there's something in our vows about sleeping together. In sickness and in health. In beds and on couches."

I can't help but chuckle and shake my head in amusement. "You are not sleeping on the couch. Go to bed, babe. We have a busy day tomorrow."

Her face falls. "Tell me you'll be here in the morning." Her eyes shine with unshed tears. "Say it, Jax."

There's a small part of me that wants to give up. It's a fraction, a sliver, of what it used to be, a tiny voice that tells me living—at least living sober—is harder than the alternative.

It might be true, but nothing—not the whispered promise of peace in death or in getting high—is worth risking Aurora and the baby. "I'm not going anywhere."

Ethan clasps the back of her neck. "Go get ready for bed. I need to talk to Jax."

21
ETHAN

"Hey," Reece says to Jax, nodding toward the bedroom. "Go. I got it."

There's turmoil in Jackson's eyes and weariness on Reece's face. Something happened.

They're both being vague, which in itself is odd, but for them to be getting along, even the tiniest bit? Shit must have hit the fan.

Our life is chaotic. Jax could be upset about many things—Kyle, the case, Reece's crush on Aurora...

Or he's still pissed at me and refuses to share a bed.

With a frustrated groan, Aurora goes to the bedroom, shutting the door behind her. We have at least fifteen minutes before she finishes her skincare routine, thirty if she braids her hair.

I cross my arms over my chest. "What's going on with you?"

He lowers his head and drags his fingers through his disheveled hair. "I'm exhausted. It's your date night. Go have fun. I don't mind sleeping here."

Who is this person? Jax doesn't sleep without Aurora

and is always first in line for *fun*. He's also not afraid of confrontation. If he wanted to sleep apart because I was an ass, he'd be insisting *I* slept elsewhere.

This isn't the Jackson I know. He's a whirlwind of emotions, but he's never this distant or flat. He's a fighter to the core, but tonight, he seems to have lost the battle.

The water comes on in the bathroom. Aurora is on step one of her twenty-step nightly routine. We have time before she returns, but she *will* return. She won't abandon Jax.

I sit on the coffee table across from him and rest my elbows on my knees. "If this is about our argument or the bullshit I said, just get in the fucking bed. I didn't mean it, and you know she won't sleep without you."

His knee bounces. "It's not. Please drop it and go be with her. She's wearing your jersey."

Arms folded over his chest, Reece leans against the doorframe. "I'll take watch. I'm used to it. Go to bed, Jax."

Take watch? Warning bells ring in my head. I glance between them. "Someone tell me what's going on."

Jackson shoots him a lethal glare. "What happened to *keeping it between us*?"

"*Us*." Reece circles his hand to include the three of us. "He needs to know. You can't hide this."

Slumping back into the couch cushion, Jax shakes his head in frustration. "Whatever."

I understand why Aurora is worried he might leave—or worse. His jaw is clenched and his chest heaves. He's about to either bail or detonate.

Tonight is not my night to be a surly bastard. I clasp his shoulder. "Look at me."

The weight of his anguish is palpable when his gaze meets mine.

"I'm sorry. I didn't mean to push you away, to where you

feel you can't trust me. Whatever it is, we'll work through it. Just tell me."

"That's not it." His eyes glisten, and he swallows hard. "I don't want Aurora to know."

I shift my hand to his nape. "Okay."

"When something happens, you withdraw. She doesn't need that. *We* don't need that."

I nod in agreement. "I won't." Then, for whatever reason, my impulsive fingers move from his neck to run through his messy hair.

He swats me away, scowling, and I smile.

"Sorry, it's bugging me. I've never seen your hair like this."

Unlike his usual impeccable style, it's blah and lifeless.

His scowl deepens. "It air-dried. I'm not naturally perfect."

I grin, even though, appearance-wise, he is quite perfect. "Wow, that must have killed your ego to admit out loud."

He shoves my shoulder. "Can you not be an asshole, for once?"

"I dunno." I shrug. "Do we need to hug this out, or you gonna tell me what's wrong?"

All humor washes away, and he sighs. "I got a threatening text."

Tightness grips my chest. "From who?"

He drops his gaze and clears his throat. "One of Kyle's old partners."

"Show me." He makes no move for his phone. "Jax..." I warn in a low tone.

Reece steps closer, his hands up in a placating gesture. "Before you freak out, my entire team is working on it. She's safe."

"This is about Aurora?" I ask through gritted teeth. "Show me the fucking text."

Jax unlocks his phone and gives it over, the message already open on the screen.

The floor shifts beneath me. With every word I read, my pounding heart becomes louder until it's the only sound I hear. My lungs struggle to fill with air, each forceful breath slow and shuddering. A chill spreads across my skin like thousands of tiny electric shocks.

I lock eyes with him. Shame and torment reflect in his gaze, and my blinding anger subsides—slightly.

"You were planning to keep this from me?"

"Parts of it, yeah."

"What the fuck? Why?"

He gives me a blank stare.

Am I missing something obvious? I reread the text. "This sounds like Kyle."

"It's not." His temples bulge and release. "He didn't call me pretty boy."

"Kyle is most definitely dead," Reece adds. "I saw his bloated body myself."

This piece of shit is why Jax tensed when I called him pretty. I figured as much, but it still hurts to think about. I struggle to accept what's right in front of me. "You're worried this person will come here. Is that why you won't sleep?"

He cracks his knuckles. "Among other things."

"Like what? Tell me, Jax!" My voice rises in frustration.

"Nightmares, okay?" He juts his chin, his nostrils flaring. "Now, can you leave me the fuck alone and go to bed?"

I hold his furious gaze. He's hostile, defensive. If I don't back off, he'll bolt.

With the three of us and whatever Reece arranged,

nobody is touching Aurora. I'll send the text to Rocco and focus on it tomorrow. For now, Jackson is my priority.

"No. I love you, Jax. A threat against one of us is a threat against us all." I return my fingers to his soft hair. "If you're staying up, I'm staying up. If you have a nightmare, I'll be there."

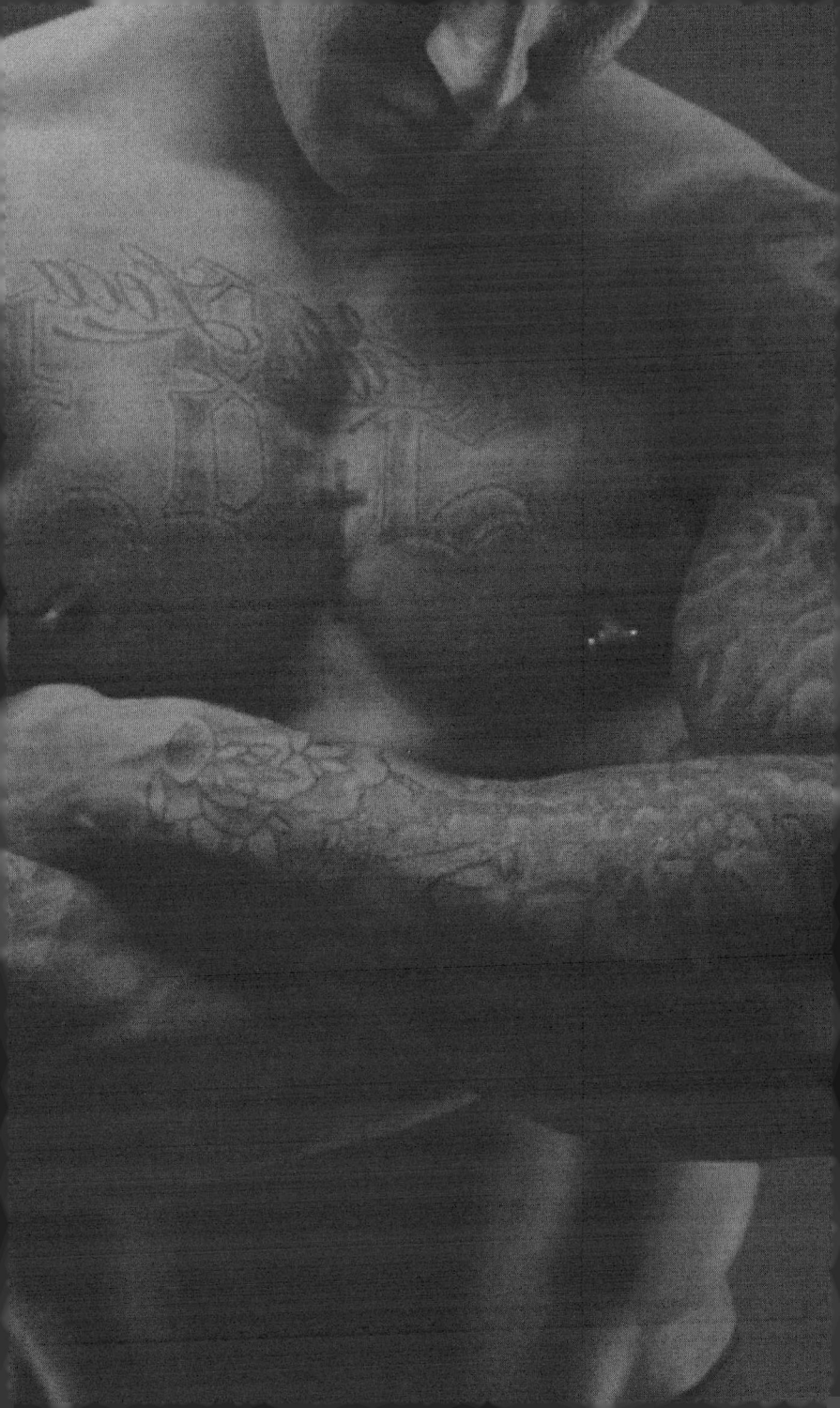

22
REECE

Ethan and Jax grab their mattress, tip it upright, and knock the pillows and bedding onto the floor.

I lean against the wall of the bedroom, watching. I'm only here for moral support.

Well, not really. I'm waiting for these two idiots to attempt to get the king-size mattress through the doorway. They're both smiling; I guess that's all that matters.

Aurora peeks her head out of the bathroom and instantly grins. "What are you doing?"

"We're having a slumber party," Jax calls out.

They reach the door and exchange baffled glances, and she bursts into giggles.

I shake my head, but a smirk escapes me. "Bend the mattress, morons."

What did I do with my years of tactical training? Helped two professional hockey players maneuver their bed into the living room so they could cuddle while one was having nightmares.

I haven't seen anything this ridiculous since boot camp.

It's sweet, though. I just wonder if Aurora knows they love each other, maybe as much as they love her.

Dumb and Dumber grunt, groan, and laugh as they push the curled mattress through the doorway. The top is wedged in the corner and scraping along the doorframe, but they don't seem concerned. Who cares if the hotel charges you for a new mattress when you're a millionaire? Billionaire, between the two of them?

Anything for Jackson.

The words cross my mind, but they're not as bitter as before. He's struggling, and they'll do whatever it takes to get him through it. I can respect that.

Aurora joins me in watching the mattress fiasco. Long, dark waves cascade down over her shoulders. Her bare face reveals a dusting of freckles across her nose and cheekbones. She's in shorts and one of their T-shirts, per usual, her little belly popping out.

She peers up at me, as beautiful as ever. "Are you staying for the sleepover?"

"Do you want me to?" My voice is lower and raspier than intended, but having her next to me does something to my insides.

"Only if you bring candy or popcorn."

Those pouty lips curve into a flirtatious smile—intentional or not, I don't know.

My chin dips and my eyes narrow. "You don't even like candy."

She gasps, feigning horror. "Not true. I like chocolate-covered peanuts."

"Goobers," Jax yells from the living room, always listening. "I'll get candy. Grab the pillows."

We gather the bedding while Ethan and Jax stock up on candy and drinks from the lobby gift shop.

Aurora tosses the pillows down and faces me, her mask dropped and eyes full of suspicion. "What's going on?"

She's smarter than they think, no longer a naive girl. It's entirely possible she caught bits of conversation, especially Ethan's booming voice. Unfortunately, I promised them I wouldn't tell her anything about Kyle or the threat.

I reach out and tuck a strand of hair behind her ear, tracing the length. "Jax is struggling with the case, that's all. He'll get through it. He has you and Ethan."

She steps closer, and my heart rate kicks up a notch. There's only a sliver of space between us. Then, she encircles my waist, and the air catches in my lungs. It feels like forever since she randomly hugged me. Her body is pressed to mine, reminiscent of the dream I had, and I have to beg my dick to behave in these gym shorts.

I hesitantly wrap my arms around her. "What are you doing, princess?"

Her eyes sparkle with mischief. "I'm hugging you. I used to hug you all the time. You don't like hugging me anymore?"

"You know very well I like hugging you. Too much. What are you doing?"

The temptress grins. "I wanted to say thank you for defending me earlier."

She's lying and not even trying to hide it. It's written all over her devilish face.

"I'll always defend you. Now, your husband will be back soon, and I don't feel like losing my balls tonight. Tell me why you're tormenting me."

A silent laugh rumbles through her. "I'm just happy you're here."

I tangle my fingers in her hair and give a little tug. "You're a damn liar."

She bites down on her bottom lip in an attempt to hide her smile, and my body ignites like gasoline thrown on a bonfire.

"Aurora…" I warn.

Her eyes soften, and the tension between us intensifies.

"I'm not lying. I want you to stay."

My throat goes dry, and I force myself to swallow. "Why?"

Does she want me to stay as security? More? I'm staying anyhow, at least until the threat is resolved. Does she think because something happened, I'll be returning to LA, like when Kyle died? Is she worried I'm leaving?

My thoughts are a mess.

"You're good here." She shrugs. "You seem good with Jax."

Jax. Not the answer I wanted.

My palms are sweaty, her head cradled in my hands. She feels too close, and I slide my fingers free from her hair and step out of her embrace.

Things were rough while I was gone. Ethan and Jackson were fighting. Aurora and Ethan were fighting. Aurora was alone, and she hates being alone. Tonight, despite everything, we're all getting along. Does she think *they're* better with me here, or does *she* want me here?

She's touching me, giving me looks that go beyond friendship, and my mind instinctively bristles at the sheer impossibility of her genuinely wanting me.

There's no way. It's unfathomable, and my confidence shakes.

My face heats, and I ball my hands into fists at my sides. "I'm not here to manage *Jax*. Don't use your body against me. I'm not your plaything. I'm a person with *feelings* you're messing with."

* * *

What the fuck is wrong with me?

I'm still bitter.

That's the only explanation.

I told her I wanted her, told her I'd take whatever she was willing to give, even friendship, to be a part of her life. She asked me if I was sure repeatedly, and I said yes—every damn time.

Then, she tells me she wants me to stay, and I snap at her?

Jesus fucking Christ, I have issues.

I know Aurora. She's affectionate, speaks better with her body than words, and hates to feel rejected. She'll never give me another chance, never put herself out there again.

From the kitchen table, I watch her in my periphery as I work on my laptop. She clings to Ethan on the couch, her head on his shoulder, her arms around him. Her gaze is glued to the TV, but her eyes are emotionless. She still wears the forlorn expression I left her with.

I'm a total fucking dick.

Maybe she was excited to tell me she wanted me to stay, excited to have me here, excited about the sleepover, excited everyone was getting along. Maybe she wasn't playing me but being playful, and I ruined it by being jealous of Jackson.

Who isn't jealous of Jackson?

I bury myself in work, researching Kyle's former partner and reassigning my team. Movement catches my eye, and I glance up. She approaches with her head down, making a beeline for the fridge, and I take my chance.

Recklessly, I reach for her, my fingers close around her waist, and pull her to me. She stumbles between my legs, her hands finding purchase on my shoulders, her eyes wide and searching with an intensity that takes my breath away.

"Lo siento." Expressing the apology in Spanish isn't necessary, since I'm not at all being cautious, but it sounds romantic.

She swallows. "Está bien. No te preocupes." Of course she would say it's okay.

I have no idea what the last phrase means, but it's provocative rolling off her tongue.

Jackson and Ethan must think so too. Both of them are staring at us with their mouths hanging open. That, or I'm about to be killed.

I know the word 'stay' only as a command used during arrests. I haven't a clue how to say 'I'll stay,' but I try anyway. "No te muevas."

She furrows her brow and tilts her head in confusion.

It's cute, and I smirk. "What did I say?"

She grins. "Don't move."

So close—just not in this instance.

"Manos arriba...?" *Hands up*? I joke.

She flashes a gentle smile and obeys—and, holy shit, new kink unlocked.

"Um, how about hands *off*?" Jax interrupts, glaring daggers my way.

She steps back, and my arms drop to my lap, feeling empty.

He scoots to the edge of the couch. "So we're using secret languages now?"

She walks away, going to the fridge for a bottle of water.

I meet his annoyance head-on. "It's called Spanish."

"No fuck," he says at the same time Ethan asks Aurora, "You speak Spanish?"

She takes her seat beside him. "Rarely, but I grew up speaking both languages."

He directs his scowl my way. "And you know Spanish?"

"A little. For the job."

"Well, isn't that convenient?" Jackson grumbles before dumping an entire box of Snow Caps in his big mouth.

"Actually, it is. When she wanted to leave the game, she was able to tell me without worrying about others overhearing."

"Wow, it's incredible how you have a secret language with everyone except me." From the death glare Ethan is giving her, he does *not* think it's incredible—at all. "You communicate with Jax through your eyes and understand each other's thoughts. Now, you speak Spanish with him." He nods in my direction.

"That's because with us, she's quieter," Jackson says, quick to calm his bestie. "But with you, she speaks her mind. You both get heated and yell. Nothing is secret."

"Clearly, something is secret." Ethan cants his head at Aurora. "Got something you wanna tell me?"

Jax grabs the bowl of popcorn from the coffee table and pops a piece into his mouth. "Yeah, share with the rest of the class."

I'm glad his snarky attitude has recovered. It's better than worrying if he'll take off. But fuck, he's aggravating, and he knows it.

She presses her lips together and shakes her head.

Ethan arches a brow. "Easy way or the hard way?"

I push from my seat and place my hands on the table. He's too rough. I understand he pressures her to open up, and Jackson must trust him. Otherwise, he wouldn't be sitting back and stuffing his face, but I'd never tolerate anyone threatening her, even Ethan.

Her shoulders slump. "I'm not hiding anything."

His expression remains rigid, his steely gaze locked on hers. "Do we need to discuss this alone?"

I stand to my full height.

"Fine." She rolls her eyes. "I gave him a hug." She gestures my way. "You didn't say no hugs. I told him I wanted him to stay, and he got angry. That's it."

Jax makes a show of the popcorn. "Ooooh, this is getting good."

I'm about to dump it over his head.

"Angry, how?" Ethan asks.

Walking into the living area, I lean against the counter and cross my arms over my chest. I guess we're doing this.

"He said I was playing with his feelings." She glances at me. "Which wasn't my intention. I'm sorry."

Jackson scoffs. "He wanted you to play with him in other ways."

"Can you shut the fuck up?" I snap. "You make no sense."

"Dude, she isn't gonna fall all over you. She's not like that. Whatever girls you've been fucking with, she's not them."

Aurora's gaze drops to her fingers in her lap.

Ethan chimes in. "I don't think that's it. I think she was being playful, and he's not playing. This is too serious for him."

"Same thing." Jackson shrugs.

Except it's not the same. He knows talking shit about other women will drive her away from me. He tried the same with Ethan.

I let out a slow, frustrated breath and roll my neck. "It doesn't matter. I'm staying. I'm sorry for getting angry, princess. It won't happen again."

They might discuss everything with each other, but that's not me. I'll figure this out with Aurora when the time is right. I'm afraid my feelings for her will ruin our friendship—if they haven't already.

It was unfair of me to expect more from her, to be resentful when she didn't explicitly say *she* wanted me to stay.

23
REECE

It's getting late, after midnight. Aurora is the first to abandon the couch and curl up on the mattress piled with pillows and blankets. She's not asleep, but her eyelids are drooping. I'm sure she's exhausted but holding out for the guys. I know she isn't staying awake to watch the show because—surprise, surprise—it's a five-hour documentary on hockey.

The only light is from the glow of the TV and my computer screen. My eyes are sore, screaming at me to take a break. You wouldn't expect it, but an absurd amount of documentation is required in law enforcement. If it's not documented, it didn't happen, and I'm not provided the resources necessary to do my job.

"Hey, Viking. Shut it down and stop avoiding us."

I'll never admit when Jackson is right. Still, I save my progress, close the laptop, and flop into the armchair. "Don't hate me for this, but I don't watch hockey. I have more important shit to do."

Jax gives me the side-eye. "Blasphemy. You watch my games. Don't lie."

"Because I'm forced to."

"Liar," he says under his breath.

Aurora glances at me, probably gauging the truth of my words. I shoot her a wink to let her know I'm joking. If she believes I'm obligated to go to his games and don't enjoy it, she'll find a reason for me to stay home. Honestly, I don't mind. I'm not there for the game.

Ethan shifts to face me. "Did you play sports?"

Since his fit of jealousy, he's been quiet, his eyes fixed on Aurora's every move.

"I grew up in the South. Anybody who's anybody plays football."

I followed the script and did what was expected of me my entire life, including playing football from age five. Football is life, and I went along with it, since that's what good ol' Southern boys do—just like my father, his father, and every father before him, I'm sure. The same goes for joining the military.

Thinking back on my childhood is like watching a movie starring someone else. It doesn't seem real. The last time I went home, it felt as though I woke in a complete stranger's house. I didn't belong, but they continued to treat me as family.

"What position did you play?"

I blink a few times to get my head straight. "Linebacker throughout high school. I didn't play after that. I went to boot camp."

He makes a thoughtful sound in the back of his throat. "Were you any good?"

Jax throws his hands in the air, his nose scrunched in annoyance. "Oh my fucking God! Stop," he blurts.

Ethan's expression hardens. "What the fuck is your problem?"

Our girl sits up, legs crossed and arms outstretched behind her, to watch the drama unfold.

"Really?" Jackson deadpans, eyes squinted. "I know exactly what you're doing."

Aurora and I exchange puzzled glances. Ethan can't be interested in me playing for him. I'm almost thirty, have never played hockey, can't even balance on skates, and my list of injuries from the military is a mile long.

Technically, I'm disabled, per the Department of Veterans Affairs. Definitely not playing hockey.

Ethan leans in, narrowing the gap between them on the couch. "Oh, yeah? What am I doing, Jax?"

"You're recruiting his kids before they even leave his balls."

What? I have no idea what he's suggesting, but I'm cracking up, laughter bursting from my chest. His thought process is truly remarkable.

They stare at each other, having some wordless conversation before Ethan says, "Every team needs an offense and a defense."

Jackson stiffens. "*You* played defense, dickhead."

A smirk plays on Ethan's lips, and his eyes shine with amusement. "Then there's the goalie, who holds the key to the team's success."

Without warning, Jax lunges at his bestie, snarling, "You're getting on my last fucking nerve."

If it wasn't for the grin on Ethan's face while Jackson tackles him to the floor, narrowly missing the coffee table, I'd step in.

They land with a loud thud, vibrating the room, and it wouldn't surprise me if security came knocking at the door.

"Jackson Vaughn!" Aurora chides.

She gets to her knees, her hands out as if she might try to separate them, but Ethan's booming laugh cuts her short.

I swear, I'm watching the beginning of soft porn. They're wrestling. If they start kissing, should I leave?

Both are equally matched, Ethan with size and Jax with speed and rampant energy, but ultimately, I think Ethan could unleash some severe damage if he wanted.

Laughter fills the air as they tussle, pushing at each other's shoulders and chests. Ethan grasps Jackson's jaw, pressing his head back, and Jax retaliates with a forearm to Ethan's throat.

Ethan winces and releases Jackson's face to push the arm from his neck.

Jackson's smile vanishes, and he jumps aside. "Oh shit, I forgot about your neck. Sorry. Fuck. Are you okay?"

"What's wrong?" Aurora scrambles toward them. "Are you hurt?"

"No," Ethan croaks. "I'm fine." He rolls his shoulders. "It's more of a precaution than anything."

She glances between them, her expression filled with worry. "What happened?"

Jackson's brows furrow. "Did you never Google our boyfriend?"

Ethan shoves him, taking him by surprise. Jackson nearly falls flat on his face, and I can't help but snicker.

"Ah...yeah," Aurora drags out. "Once, and I regretted it. The first thing I saw was pictures of him and his, you know, *wife*."

Jax presses his lips together and nods. "Okay, valid reason not to Google your married baby daddy, who got you pregnant in the back of a limo while you were on the rebound."

So that's the story. Interesting.

Her face flushes. "Jackson, seriously? Just tell me what happened."

It's Ethan who answers. "I took a nasty hit, bounced my head off the ice, and broke my neck."

Her mouth falls open with a gasp. "I didn't know that. I thought you stopped playing because…"

"Because…" he prompts with raised brows.

"You know, 'cause you're, like…old…er," she says, her voice so fucking innocent, it sends Jackson collapsing to the floor in a fit of laughter.

Just another day with these three.

24
JACKSON

It's pouring rain—icy, slushy fucking rain. Hail pelts the windows, creating a chaotic rhythm that fills the loft.

I enjoy the sound. It's peaceful, it could lull me to sleep—especially since I didn't sleep much last night, even with our slumber party. What I don't enjoy is being nailed by frozen golf balls while I load our shit into the vehicle.

Dear Mother Nature, is this necessary? There's absolutely no purpose for this weather. None.

Ethan grew up here, and look at him. He's gloomy. I'd be a miserable bastard too if I didn't see the sun until I was thirty-five.

My eyes catch on the mismatched, decades-old furniture, and I smile. Despite the bitter cold, I'll miss this place. I'll miss the mornings I sat here eating donuts and listening to the twins razz each other over stupid shit, like who was better at *Call of Duty* or whose body count was higher. Foolish arguments, since I'm fairly certain they only play together, and I don't mean just video games.

Aurora was right: this loft is a dream. It's isolated but not lonely, and Ethan's family has everything to do with that.

"Wife," I shout over my shoulder. "Don't let them throw out the furniture."

Between now and when we play here next, which is in March—and with Aurora's due date, who knows if we'll be traveling—the loft is being remodeled, completely gutted.

"Okay, *husband*," she yells from the kitchen, where she's making coffee with the Viking.

I grab our bags from the bedroom closet and toss them on the bed. Then, exhausted by the mere thought of packing Aurora's clothes and saying goodbye, I plop my ass onto the mattress and drop my face into my hands.

Tears burn behind my eyelids. Fuck, I don't want to leave. I don't want to return to LA. I don't want to deal with the paparazzi or the LAPD. I'll be forced to confront Kyle's death and make arrangements regarding his estate.

I'd rather hide out in dreary New York.

I'd rather have nights with the three of us in this bed.

Someone snatches my baseball cap and ruffles my hair, breaking me from spiraling thoughts.

I glance up, and there he is, standing between my legs. I don't know what else to say but, "Give me my hat, asshole."

Ethan flips it around and puts it on, his thick, wavy hair escaping.

It looks good on him. "You never wear a hat."

He takes it off and chucks it onto the bed. "Gives me a headache."

"That's 'cause you need a real haircut."

"A *real* haircut? You mean a hundred-dollar haircut."

"Yes, a twenty-dollar street barber is not taming that mop on your head."

He smiles, and those gray eyes gleam. "Your wife likes it."

"Joke's getting old, just like you."

He laughs on his way to the closet, returning with an armful of Aurora's clothes and laying them over the foot of the bed. "What's wrong with you? You don't wanna leave?"

"No." It comes out a little petulant, I won't lie.

He flashes me a doubtful glance. "You wanna stay in this loft? With the cubicle walls and slanted floors? Are the donuts that good?"

"Yes, and I like this bed." I hold his gaze.

He shakes his head. "Both of you, so fucking clingy."

I don't miss the tiny twitch at the corner of his mouth. He loves us and he knows it.

He comes between my legs again and slides his fingers through my hair. It's new, and I don't hate it—far from it. My heart skips a beat, and I have to force myself to breathe and not lean into his caress.

For once, I feel awkward. What to do with my hands? I know what I *want* to do with them, but if I touch him, he'll probably avoid me for days. "Don't act like you don't like it." My words come out breathless, and I'm sure I'm giving him that *look* he called me out on.

Unsurprisingly, his cheeks flush, his arm drops to his side, and he averts his gaze.

I deflate, my shoulders drooping. "Why are you afraid of things being good?" We could be so fucking good together— more than just sex, no matter what he says.

"Ask yourself that." He walks away to get another load of clothes or to avoid me.

"What's that supposed to mean?"

He juts his chin toward the kitchen.

I curl my lip. "Reece?"

He shrugs. "It's easier with him here. I have a lot less to worry about."

"Except he's in love with her. Do you not worry about that?"

Leaning in, he lowers his tone. "Don't you want someone who loves her to care for her? I like knowing we can focus on our jobs without worrying about her and our family. With him here, I know he won't let anything happen to her—or *you.* If you haven't noticed, you two take a lot of energy. Imagine adding a baby."

"I don't have to play."

He crosses his arms over his chest. "I want you to play. I want to coach you. You're talented, and it's good for you. I'll never force you or hold our relationship over your head, but we can make this work."

A thought comes to mind, and I can't hide my grin. I see why Aurora acts like a brat to get his attention. "I'll play, just maybe not score. I'm not feeling very motivated."

"You'll score."

I cock a brow. "Will I?"

He hits me with that death glare. "I can be very creative with punishments, Jax. Don't test me."

My stomach does somersaults. Why is my stomach doing somersaults? Fuck, do I *want* him to punish me, to be rough with me? Damn, I think I do. "Oh, yeah?" That's it. Two words. That's all I manage.

"Yeah," he answers with certainty. "Did you know there's a birth control that lasts up to five years? Another kid while I'm coaching might not be a good idea. I'm sure Aurora will understand."

All playfulness, or desire, or whatever I was feeling, dies. "You wouldn't dare."

"If I have to worry about you two and can't focus on my job *and* my star player isn't performing…I won't have the energy for sex or a second baby."

"You manipulative bastard. I hate you. You better take some fucking vitamins and Viagra."

He chuckles and heads back to the closet.

"I'm serious! I'm only twenty-five, old man."

He throws another pile of clothes onto the bed. "We can all get what we want."

"He has a career. You don't even know where this'll lead."

"I do. I once joked about bringing a fourth into this love triangle, and she named *him*. Have you ever seen her comfortable enough to hug someone else? He's confused, thinks she's just affectionate. She's not. I've watched her around Grant. She gives him a stiff, half-assed hug." He takes a deep breath and releases it slowly. "She won't cheat on us, but she asked for him specifically as her bodyguard."

A derisive scoff escapes me. "He wants more than that."

"She's pregnant. Maybe if she wasn't..."

More reason to have another one. "I can fix that."

I pack and mull over his words. When we finish, I grab a bag and hoist it over my shoulder. "You're saying with Reece around, you'll be less stressed? You'd be open to seeing where this leads and having a bigger family?"

"Theoretically, yes." He zips up a duffel. "You ready, brat, or you gonna pout some more?"

I shake my head. "The shit I do for you."

He weaves his fingers through my hair. "Don't act like you don't like it."

25
AURORA

"Babe."

"Babe."

"Aurora," says a raspy, pained voice.

Jax.

"Hmm?" I mumble, still trapped in the fog of sleep.

Ethan lifts a shoulder under me. "What's wrong?"

"Migraine." Jax takes a few labored breaths, his face buried in the pillows. "I need meds."

That wakes me fully, and I scramble off the bed. "Where?"

"Closet. Black bag."

It's dark, we're at our new place in Santa Monica, and I don't know this room. We've barely settled in. We were all tired and miserable between packing the SUV in the snow, saying goodbye, the six-hour flight, and the time change. Then, after we landed, Jax and Reece disagreed over who was driving.

Jax hired someone, and Reece wasn't comfortable with an unvetted person knowing our location. Jax argued anyone could find our address, that the house was gated, and the Viking was being paranoid. Reece scoffed and said that was ironic.

In truth, my husband is stressed. The closer we got to LA, the more his knee bounced and he tugged at his hair. This migraine is likely a result of tension and lack of sleep.

I extend my hands in front of me and locate the wall. I move forward, feeling my way until I come upon the entrance to the walk-in closet.

"Babe, I have to turn on the light."

He makes a smothered noise.

I hit the switch, and the room fills with light. I blink to allow my eyes to adjust and spot his leather bag on the far side of the closet. I riffle through the backpack and find four bottles of pills. None have labels that specify headaches, migraines, or anything besides the name and strength.

When I return, Ethan is sitting against the headboard, massaging the base of Jackson's skull, and I'm jealous. I feel a headache coming on in the future.

"Which med?" I ask, gently.

Jax holds a pillow over his face with his forearm, even though the light from the closet hardly reaches the bed. "I need two. They don't say?"

I reread them to be sure. "No."

"Fuck," he curses.

Ethan grabs his phone. "I'll text Doc."

"Reece will know. He's a medic." I'm already out the door.

Soft baseboard lights illuminate the hallway. Opposite the primary bedroom is the nursery, followed by a guest room Ethan wants to use as his office.

Reece's apartment is across the house. It's adorable, with a double-sided fireplace and a reading nook. I could live happily on his side alone. It has a separate entrance, a patio, and access to the pool and beach.

I knock on his door. It doesn't take long for him to answer, and suddenly, I'm staring at a hard, inked body without a stitch of unmarked skin, and holy shit... "You have piercings?"

My face heats. Did I say that out loud?

He chuckles, a deep, husky sound full of sleep. "Angel, you're lucky I'm wearing pants."

My gaze falls on gray sweatpants then immediately darts up. Nope. Not going there.

Another throaty chuckle. "What are you doing here, princess?"

What am I doing? Oh, right. Meds. Headache.

I break from bulging tattooed muscles and nipple piercings. My God, that should be illegal. "Umm...what are these for?" I fumble the bottles between us and nearly drop a few.

Dark-blue eyes twinkle with amusement. "Give me those." He holds each bottle up individually, reading the labels with a deepening scowl. "These Jackson's? What's going on?"

"He has a migraine."

"I'll need to talk to him." He shuts the door behind him. "Lead the way."

We enter the room, and Ethan is playing with Jackson's hair while on his phone.

"Hey, man." Reece kneels beside the bed. "You got a headache? Anything else?"

Jackson shifts from where his face is tucked into Ethan's side. He winces and throws his forearm over his eyes. "Nausea. There are two meds, one blue, one white."

Reece examines the bottles again. "You sure? Is it bad? I'm no doctor, but—"

"What's in them?" Jax cuts him off.

He clears his throat. "The blue one is a psychoactive sedative that can be habit-forming. The small white one for nausea is fine, but it'll make you sleepy—though, I'm positive you need sleep. You have another for psychosis and an anti-anxiety med for nightmares."

"Fuck that." He rolls away.

"Babe..." I start. Unsure what to say, I glance at Ethan.

He brushes Jackson's hair off his forehead. "You promise it's nothing else? Will you tell me?"

Jax peeks his eyes open. "Yes."

"Okay." That stormy gaze focuses on Reece. "Any suggestions?"

He sets the bottles on the nightstand. "I have an over-the-counter trick, non-habit forming. We can start there."

Jax fists the pillow, breathing heavily. "Anything but the psych meds."

Twelve hours later, it's four p.m., and we're all still in pajamas, snuggling in the media room. It's Ethan and Jackson's day off, and nobody wants to break our cocoon, not even Reece.

"I love this place," I say to no one in particular, my head on Ethan's lap. I may have whined my way into getting a neck massage as well.

He peers down at me and smiles wide. "Me too."

Jackson shifts his palm on my stomach. "Me three."

The baby kicks more forcefully than ever, and we both gasp, our faces lighting up with excitement.

Ethan pushes Jax's hand aside to feel the baby move. "I guess he agrees."

"Y'all make me wanna vomit," Reece grumbles from a plush leather recliner. "I regret helping you. Go back to bed and suffer."

We all burst into laughter.

26
AURORA

"Wow, you've become the help. Jesus, look at this place. You've been bought."

"I asked you here to check over the security, not run your mouth."

"If Jackson kept videos of them fucking from his last property, I'm sure he's well-versed in setting up security."

"That was internal. I want every inch of the exterior covered."

"Once this is sorted, are you returning to the hotel?"

"I'm undercover. Why would I leave?"

"Because there's an entire investigation beyond this mansion. You're dragging your feet and being played by pussy, man. Sorry."

"You saw the text Jackson received in Boston. She's being threatened by the people we're working to take down. My job is here."

"And that's all?"

"That's all."

Frozen in the hallway, I replay the conversation in my head. I was going to greet Charlie when I overheard voices coming from the security room. Now, my entire world is blown apart.

I feel foolish.

Boston. Why Ethan's voice was raised, why Jax was upset, the only reason Reece is here. I'm being threatened, and they didn't tell me.

That, I can understand. Ethan told me to forget about the case. I can deal with them wanting to protect me, but Jackson has videos of us together? From where? The downtown condo? Laguna? Both? Reece and Charlie know. Does Ethan know too? Of course he does; he knows everything.

I'm alone.

Reece is here for his job. *That's all.* I guess his partner doesn't like me much, and here I was, excited to see him again. He thinks I'm playing Reece, which sheds light on Reece's anger when I hugged him and asked him to stay.

I'm so stupid.

In a daze, I stumble through the house and out the door. I stand on the back patio, eyes fixed on the ocean, unsure of what to do next. I'm living a lie. I need to think—away from here.

"Princess."

Startled, I whip around.

Reece's brows pinch. "What's wrong?"

I place my palm over my wildly beating heart and tight chest. "I'm leaving."

His scowl deepens. "Why?"

"I want to leave."

He steps closer. "Okay. I'll take you wherever you wish to go."

I step back. "No. I don't want to be near you." My voice cracks and my throat burns. Tears blur my vision, and I angrily wipe them away with my knuckles.

He advances again, and I retreat.

His jaw clenches, his temples bulging. "What did I do, angel?"

I catch movement behind him, and we both turn to see Charlie approaching.

He waves. "Hey, Aurora."

I have nothing to say. My chest hurts too much to speak more than a few words, and honestly, I don't feel like talking to him at the moment.

They exchange a glance. Reece lifts his chin toward the house and gestures for his partner to leave us. When he faces me, his eyes betray his guilt. "What can I do?"

The confirmation is even more gut-wrenching. "Go away."

He blows out a breath. "I can't do that."

"Charlie seems to think you can. Just leave."

He shakes his head. "I'm not leaving you."

Tears stream down my face. "Fix the security and go home."

"You're my home," he says with such conviction, I almost believe him.

"You said yourself I was playing you."

Frustrated, he interlaces his fingers behind his neck and flexes his biceps. "Fuck, Aurora. I was caught off guard, and I didn't mean what you overheard."

"And everything else? The videos? The threat?"

"We're just trying to protect you. It's being taken care of."

I sniffle, drawing a shuddering breath. "The videos everyone has seen but me?"

"No one has watched them but your husband." He slips his phone from his pocket. "It's not my story to tell. I'll call him, and he can explain."

"He's at practice, and I'm leaving."

Reece presses the phone to his ear. "I can't let you do that, angel."

I glance at the beach behind me. I'm more familiar with this area than he is. I can run, lose him, get an Uber. Women run while pregnant.

He lowers the phone from his mouth. "I'll catch you. It's been a while since I've chased a suspect, but I'll do it. You're not leaving my sight, Aurora. Don't even try it. I'll carry you back kicking and screaming if I have to."

I scoff and walk away, following the edge of the pool. I step onto the grass, and the blades prick my feet, a sharp reminder I'm not wearing freaking shoes.

I'll be fine on the beach, and I can book an oceanfront room or find an Airbnb using my phone, bypassing the front desk or check-in. Call me stubborn or petty, but I have no intention of playing their games or complying with their rules.

Just as my toes sink into the cool, soft sand, muscular arms wrap around me, and a hard body presses against my back.

"I'm gonna be honest with you, princess. The likelihood of you leaving is slim to none. Your husband has videos of you from years ago because he's a full-blown stalker. Ethan will do anything to keep you and Jax safe. He met with his father the day before Kyle was killed, and I bet if I called him right now, he'd have zero remorse and redden your ass for threatening to take off."

I swallow hard, my throat thick. "Sounds like more reason to leave."

He ignores me and continues. "Even when I was away, I watched you in New York. I'd track your phone's location and have Charlie hack into the surveillance cameras to see you. One of us *will* find you."

"You're all crazy." Every breath I suck in feels strained, my lungs constricted, unable to fully expand. A suffocating fog descends upon me, making it difficult to articulate my thoughts.

I don't even know what I'm angriest about. Reece lying to me when I thought I could trust him most?

I'm tired of it all. The lies. The pretending.

The tightness in my chest intensifies, throbbing with every beat of my heart, and I clutch his forearms.

He bends down and effortlessly lifts me into a bridal hold. "I understand you're mad. I understand what I said hurt you, and I'm sorry, but you'll have to be mad in one of the ten bedrooms."

Pissed off and humiliated, I kick my legs and attempt to free myself from his grip.

The asshole chuckles, his body vibrating with laughter. "You're so fucking adorable, especially when you're furious, Tinker Bell. Is that where you got your middle name?"

I push against his chest. "Shut up."

He adjusts me in his hold and snatches both of my wrists in one massive hand. "Your husband is going to flip when he sees this." His face breaks into a wolfish grin. "If you want revenge, now is your chance. What do you say?"

"Revenge? Clearly, he enjoys watching."

His feet come to a halt on the path beside the pool. "Huh. That makes sense." He flashes that smirk again. "Must be why he doesn't like me. He has a thing for brunettes."

"You're being a real dick today."

"And you're being a stubborn, pain in my ass."

"Then leave!"

"Nah, I think I'll stay and watch Ethan handle you.

Sounds exciting. Maybe I'll let him borrow a pair of my handcuffs."

"He prefers a belt." We cross the threshold, and I attempt to break free with wiggles, kicks, and elbows, but it's useless. "You're going to need those handcuffs to keep me inside this house."

"Oh yeah?" That goddamn stupid fucking grin. "Don't tempt me with a good time. What bed would you like me to handcuff you to? My room has a fireplace and books. I'll even leave one arm free so you can read."

He heads toward his apartment, and I dig my elbow into his sternum.

"Keep fighting me, baby. You're only earning me bonus points with your harem."

I slump in his arms. "God, I hate you."

He kisses my nose. "You can hate me in my bed. I like you feisty."

27
REECE

I drop the angry hellcat onto my bed, fully expecting her to jump up and claw my eyes out. For such a small person, Aurora is fierce when she's mad.

Instead, she crawls toward the pillows and climbs under my covers. I was only going to handcuff her if absolutely necessary, but I didn't expect her to obey.

Maybe she's tired. She could use a nap.

One thing's for sure, though—this will really fuck with my fantasies.

She crisscrosses her legs, gets comfortable, and raises her chin. "I read a true crime documentary where an undercover agent spent nineteen years with a woman. They got married and had a kid. All the while, he was investigating her father, and it was all part of his job. The marriage wasn't even legal."

Unsure where this is going, I fold my arms over my chest. I support the mission, but I draw the line at forced intimate relationships, and I'd never have a child with someone I didn't intend to be with.

Why is she researching this stuff? I open my mouth to ask, but she continues.

"And you think *I'm* some diabolical mastermind taking advantage of *you*?" Her voice escalates, ready to tear me apart. "For what? I'm going to stroke your ego and play with your feelings so you'll bring me fucking pastries?" she shouts then sucks in a breath, amping up for my next scolding. "You're fucking delusional."

Okay, she's mad, mad. Angrier than I've ever seen her.

"Did you forget I had no idea who you were? I let you into my life. I trusted you—*depended* on you. You lied to me as *part of your job*," she air quotes. "And I forgave you."

She takes another gasping inhale, and I step toward her, ready to intervene.

"You're in our house, included in our family. How dare you allow someone to say I'm nothing but pussy playing you? You're not even getting any!"

Her voice cracks and her lip quivers, and without thinking, I'm in bed with her, boots and all.

"What are you doing?" she hisses and pushes at my chest.

I grab her wrists with one hand, holding them above her head, and yank the blanket over us with the other, trapping us in our own world. Per Jax, there are no cameras in the bedrooms, save for the nursery, but you never know with him.

She trembles, fighting back tears, her breath coming in ragged gasps.

I brush my knuckles along her cheekbone. "You're okay. Just breathe. You're panicking, angel, but nothing has changed. Jax and Ethan are only trying to protect you. Your husband is the same unhinged, reckless person he has always been. He had no intention of anyone seeing the videos, and if I hadn't found his phone at Kyle's, nobody would've known." I release her wrists and sweep her hair from her damp face. "I'm not going anywhere. You're safe. You can trust me."

She glares daggers at me, and I lie on my back, giving her space. I never considered how my actions affected her. At one point, I was the one she depended on, the one constant in her life, and I ripped that away when she discovered I was an agent. In Bryant Park, she asked about the future indirectly. Her hesitation is understandable. She'd never compromise her loyalty to Jax and Ethan.

For whatever reason, maybe because she thought I was leaving again, she got up the courage to ask me to stay, and I shot her down.

Then, Charlie.

She rolls onto her side and rests her head on my shoulder, her arm around me. "What are we doing?"

"I don't know." I'm just as confused as she is.

"I'm sorry I kicked you."

"I'm sorry for what you overheard. I'm still living a double life, and sometimes, it's easier to be dismissive. I didn't mean it, you know that." I lean down and nuzzle her because I can't help myself. Her skin is incredibly soft, and her seductive scent messes with my head. "Are you worried I'll leave you? It's only us. Be honest with me."

A shaky breath escapes her. "I am honest with you. I told you I wanted you to stay."

Fuck, I wish she'd give me a straight answer. Or one I can understand, at least. "Why do you want me to stay?"

She peers up at me, eyes red and her lips swollen. My heart slams into my rib cage. Our faces are only inches apart. I could easily weave my fingers through her hair and kiss her, as I've imagined many, *many* times.

"What's the point of asking if you'll only get angry with my answer?"

Our gazes lock, and I sense the significance of this moment. A heavy silence hangs between us, the unspoken truth threatening to crush me either way. It's time to face reality and confront whatever this is—no more playing. No more pretending. No more fantasizing. No more beating around the bush.

When I stay silent, she releases a disappointed sigh, and her shoulders sag. "You want me to tell you what to do. You want me to say things I can't, make promises I can't. I'm giving you everything you said was enough, but it's not, is it?"

Her lips tremble. A tear slides down the bridge of her nose, and I brush it away with my thumb, my fingers lingering on her cheek.

Is this enough for me? I'm not so sure anymore. I find myself wanting more and more, and that's where the frustration lies.

I swallow hard, my voice rough when I say, "I guess not."

"So, yeah. I'm afraid you'll leave because eventually, you will. I want you here for selfish reasons. A part of me wishes you'd stop doing this—coming into my life and pretending to be what I need, pretending this is enough for you, pretending you're staying." She searches my eyes. "I won't blame you if you leave. You should. You deserve better. You deserve someone who'll love you without boundaries."

I'm not pretending. I've told her this before, but none of that matters. What matters is how she feels, and her words have my stomach taking a dive.

I glide my fingers into her hair and cup the back of her head. "Say that again."

Her brows furrow. "You deserve better."

"Keep going."

"You deserve someone who'll love you without boundaries."

"Do you love me? *With* boundaries?"

Her lips part as her eyes well up, tears clinging to her long lashes. "That's not fair of me to answer." Her voice is barely above a whisper.

I nod. My throat goes dry, and I swallow again. "I'm not pretending. I'm here because it physically hurts me to stay away. I leave because of my job, which may continue to happen, as much as I don't want it to." I kiss her forehead then her nose, tasting the salt of her tears. "I'll always find my way back to you."

She lays her head on my chest and closes her eyes. "Ethan wants you here. Jax wouldn't let you live here if he didn't."

The implication of more, regardless of her intentions, goes straight to my heart…and other places.

Needing to clear my head before I do something stupid, I pull the blanket down. The room is darker now, full of shadows, as if the universe wills us to have this moment alone.

"Do you think this is weird?" She yawns and covers her mouth.

"Which part?" I chuckle. "Our life is quite unusual."

"Us lying together. The four of us living together. Me being pregnant. You not allowing me to leave, carrying me into the house. Aren't you worried Charlie will say something?"

She places her small hand on my stomach, and I interlace our fingers.

"At home, we can do whatever we want. I'll talk to Charlie. You've been pregnant the entire time I've been with you.

I cared for you in New York, carried you to bed, and you were pregnant. Nothing has changed."

She makes a sleepy sound of agreement.

"You wanna nap in your room or stay here?"

"Here."

I hold her close, replaying her words in my head until she drifts off. Then, I carefully break free of her to find my partner.

28
ETHAN

Jax gazes up at me from the bench, his damp hair falling onto his face. He's shirtless, with the lower half of his gear still on.

His best friend sits beside him. I interrupted their conversation about riding. Grant was offering to go to Kyle's with Jackson to get his Ducati. It's not a good idea. Jax doesn't need to be on a motorcycle or at Kyle's right now, and I make a mental note to discuss it with him later.

Jax lifts his chin. "Hey, what's up?"

"PR wants you." I nod toward the door. "You up for media?"

They wanted an interview in the locker room, with him breathless from a hard practice, sweaty and half-naked, but I held them off. I'm not about to let them bombard him.

PR hasn't granted reporters access to him since he relapsed—well, besides the tunnel incident, which was outside our management. After his suspension, they did a photo shoot but wouldn't allow any Q&A.

His first home game, following the night he relapsed, is tomorrow. We've won every game since his return, and we're on our way to clinching the playoffs. He's playing better than ever, and the team hasn't been this good since his rookie year.

Everyone is itching for a piece of Jackson O'Reilly.

But he's been in a weird mood. Up and down. Unpredictable. He barely sleeps. He's edgy; I feel it.

He rakes his fingers through his wet hair. "Will it get them to leave me alone? My phone hasn't stopped buzzing."

"I make no promises. Might as well get it over with."

He snatches a towel from his cubby, wipes his face, and changes quickly.

We exit the locker room, and the PR team swarms in. A girl I don't recognize smiles at Jax and reaches to fix his hair.

He knocks her wrist away. "Don't touch me."

Her face flushes bright red, and silence descends among the group. No one seems to know how to handle him.

I clasp his shoulder. "What's wrong with his hair?" I glance between him and the girl.

She shakes her head, her eyes glassy, and everyone averts their gaze.

I shrug and tousle Jax's hair. "Be nice."

"Do they play with your hair before you go out there?"

"My hair isn't wet and in my face."

"Still, they know better than to touch me."

I take a deep breath and let it out slowly. This is going to be a disaster.

Jax steps up to the mic, and the cameras flash. I stand to the side with my arms crossed over my chest. I rarely hang around when players are interviewed, but my presence may ease his agitation.

Patty, head of PR, signals a reporter to begin.

Some sports journalist gets to his feet. "Hi, Jackson.

Congratulations to you and your fiancée on your engagement."

"Wife." Jax clears his throat. "We're married."

"Wow!" More cameras flash. "Congrats."

He offers a sharp nod. "Thanks."

"You were double-teamed against Boston. During your last breakaway, what made you think you could waltz through the defense like that?"

Jax glances my way. "Is this a trick question?"

Laughter rings through the room. They want a cocky, provocative sound bite from him, ideally a jab at the opposing team.

Instead, he says, "There were three or four defensemen, if you count the goalie. It's my job to get past the defense, and it's the defense's job to try to stop me. If I balked every time I was guarded, Coach wouldn't be very pleased with me." His lips curve into a crooked smile full of secrets.

"You seem to have a close relationship with Coach Blackwood," says the next reporter.

Jax doesn't even attempt to hide his devilish grin. "You could say that."

More laughter. The tips of my ears burn, and I clench my jaw. I'm about to have a heart attack. Someone needs to shut this down—immediately.

I glare at Patty, and she shrugs.

There's a list of subjects reporters are instructed to avoid, such as Jackson's relapse. They're not invited back if they don't, so they're obliged to meet our demands. Why am I not on that list?

Because you're his coach, and he's a player. How would they restrict questions involving that relationship?

I'm on the verge of calling this whole thing off when Jax

says, "Coach would go to bat for any of his players. That's the man he is. You don't get any better than him."

My gaze connects with his. He gives me that longing look again, and I lose my breath. My world tilts. Panic must be written all over my face, because his expression sours. During the rest of the interview, he remains short and dismissive.

On the way home, it's quiet in the car, and I can tell he's annoyed with me. He stares out the passenger-side window, his knee jumping. I release the gearshift and grab his leg to stop him from fidgeting. "We're fine. Just be careful of what you say. I don't need to be fired."

"Whatever," he grumbles. "Like that'll ever happen."

"I'm serious. Not all of us have unlimited money. This is an opportunity of a lifetime for me."

A cocky smirk plays on his lips. "What? Being with me?"

My God, I nearly roll my eyes. "Coaching you. We're heading to the playoffs."

"You'll always be my coach. You'll be the only coach I ever have. If they fire you, I walk. It's that simple. We'll be sitting at home doing whatever the fuck we want with the unlimited money *we* have."

Well, shit. What do I say to that?

A notification dings his phone, and I remove my hand from his thigh as he pulls it free of his pocket. He scrutinizes something on the screen while I make my way down the Pacific Coast Highway. The ocean view is unlike anything I've seen in New York. I can understand why they love it here.

"Motherfucker," he mutters.

"What is it?" I lean out the window and punch in the code for the gate, getting it wrong the first time. What was the date the baby was conceived? June? Only Jax would set this code. On the third try, the light turns green.

The garage is full of boxes delivered from Jackson's downtown and Laguna penthouses that neither he nor Aurora wants to go through, and I park in the driveway. The car doesn't even come to a complete stop before he jumps out and storms into the house.

I'm hot on his heels. "What the hell is going on?"

He passes the entrance, strides through the kitchen, and hangs a right to Reece's side of the house. Fuck, this can't be good.

"Motherfucker erased the security feed." He doesn't bother with the handle. He lifts his leg and delivers a powerful kick to the bedroom door.

The impact echoes through the hall, the splintering wood filling the air with a sharp *crack*. My brain must be tripping, because the only thought that comes to mind is *shit, we'll need to get that fixed.*

My sight is instantly drawn to Reece's bed, where Aurora jolts awake.

She was asleep in his bed. I have no time to process what this means because Jax is rushing at her, eyes blazing with murder.

He towers over her, his fists clenched into tight balls. "Where the fuck is he?" Fury reverberates in his growled words.

She clutches the blanket to her chest and scrambles away from him. "We didn't... I...I was having a panic attack and fell asleep here."

He thrusts his phone in her face, and she flinches.

"Then why the fuck did he erase the security feed? Hmm? Tell me that, Aurora!"

The harshness of his raised voice brings tears to her

eyes, and once he's in reach, I grab the back of his shirt and yank him to me. He's in a rage, and he'll never forgive himself if he hurts her—and neither will I.

Her pleading gaze connects with mine. "Nothing happened," she sobs.

Reece comes barreling through the door, Charlie behind him, and Jax struggles against me.

"Calm down." I get an arm around his throat. "They didn't do anything."

"What the fuck is wrong with you?" Reece glances from Jackson to Aurora. "Ven aquí," he tells her, which must be Spanish.

She rushes out of bed, fully clothed in the same leggings and T-shirt she was in when we left today. I highly doubt they slept together. She hides behind him, using him as a shield, and clutches his shirt.

He interlaces their fingers, drawing her arms around him. "You're lucky she's still here."

I freeze. "What did you say?"

Jax fights against me, struggling to shake me off. "He's trying to take her," he chokes out.

I loosen my grasp on him, ready to intervene with Reece if necessary. "You won't make it out of this house."

Charlie steps beside Reece, his hand at the small of his back. He's in uniform—black tactical pants, a black shirt with HSI on the sleeve, black combat boots. He's a smaller guy, but it's clear he's prepared.

Reece throws his hands up. "I'm not trying to take her. I brought her back. *She* wanted to leave."

"Why?" Jax and I say in unison, both of us aghast.

He scoffs. "You watched the footage."

Jax tenses in my hold. "You deleted the footage."

"What? No, I didn't," Reece says, taken aback, before his

head whips to Charlie. "You're a real fuck-up today, you know that?"

Sorry, Charlie mouths with a grimace.

"Can you fix it?" Reece asks.

His partner presses his lips together and shrugs.

Reece releases a heavy sigh. "Aurora overheard Charlie talking shit and decided she was leaving." He gestures toward the beach. "I picked her up and brought her back with her literally fighting me. I might have bruises. I nearly caught a knee to the chin for *your* videos." He fixes Jax with a pointed stare. "I brought her to my bed to watch her. She started panicking, and I stayed with her until she fell asleep."

Jax's heart hammers against my chest. "My videos? You told her about the videos."

"I..." Charlie falters. "I may have mentioned them...and said some things I was wrong about. I *adjusted* the security feed to make it up to Aurora."

"For fuck's sake." Jax pushes away from me. "Were you two police academy dropouts? The feed stops at her standing outside his door and restarts when Reece leaves to go to the security room. That's not at all suspicious."

Reece pinches the bridge of his nose. "Charlie, get out."

I sink onto the patio lounger, close my eyes, and breathe in the salty night air. Days like these put me in the mood for a stiff whiskey. "I'm getting too old for this shit," I groan.

Charlie left with a mumbled apology. Reece was too agitated to let Jax talk to Aurora alone, so I convinced my hothead captain to take a break outside.

Nearly every room in the beach house flows into the

outdoors. Some rooms, such as the bedroom suites and the living area, feature retractable glass doors that open to the backyard oasis. Jax and I are in a private corner of the terrace. Palm trees and lush greenery surround us, creating the illusion of privacy without compromising the ocean view.

Despite the breathtaking scenery and refreshing breeze, he persists in pacing.

I've become desensitized to him. It's not right, but I've grown accustomed to his temper. We're both rough around the edges. I can deal with his outbursts. Aurora, on the other hand...

With a sigh, I pick my head up. "What do you need, Jax? You can't come charging in here, screaming and breaking shit. It can't happen. Not with a baby. I won't allow it."

He pauses mid-stride. "She was going to leave."

"But she didn't. Reece was here. That's his job, remember? I'll talk to her. Right now, I'm talking to you."

He plops his ass on the foot of the lounger. "He doesn't have a job here, not while he's still an agent."

"Give him one or don't." I shrug. "Not if you'll flip out every time he touches her."

"I thought they were fucking behind our backs. I thought he screwed with the security to hide what they were doing. Why else would he?" He gestures, palms up. "Unless he wanted her for himself? You would've done the same. She was in his room, in his bed."

Would I have been furious if I'd caught them fucking? Probably. Would I have screamed at Aurora? No. Punished her? Yeah. Gone after Reece? Maybe.

The only thing that'd make me irate is him taking her from us, and Reece knows that. I doubt he'd cross the line and have sex with her, but despite everything Reece has done for Jax, he still doesn't trust him.

"They're not fucking. Jesus, come here." I reach out, grab his T-shirt, and pull him to me.

He obliges, his back pressed against my chest. "Haven't you hugged me enough for one day?" As cocky as ever.

"Just shut up for once and listen." I wrap my arms around his shoulders. "You don't need to yell and break shit to be heard, okay? That's in the past. I hear you. If you have a problem, tell me, and I'll fix it."

We stare at the inky-black sky, the rhythmic crashing of waves filling the silence between us.

Eventually, his taut muscles give way, and he relaxes completely, sinking into me. "Okay," he exhales.

"You did an amazing job with this house." I rest my head on his. "It's perfect. I can't imagine what I owe you."

Every detail of this place is meticulous, from the gourmet kitchen to the luxury spa bathroom with a steam shower—which took me fifteen minutes to figure out how to turn on—to the eighteen-foot custom velvet couch in Tiffany blue that Aurora adores.

And you can't tell me he didn't plan Reece's apartment. He could've put him in the pool house but didn't.

"Whatever," he says under his breath. "I'm not worried about money; you shouldn't be either."

"Still—" I start.

He cuts me off, changing the subject. "Your office is downstairs, not next to the nursery, so you'll have peace and quiet."

See? Calculated.

I go along with it. "What's yours?"

"The gym, the ocean, the giant bed." There's a smile in his voice.

"So let's work this out, okay?" I have a sudden urge to play with his hair, but I resist. "You're beating your head against a wall with Reece. Someone has to be with her. He cares about her. He didn't let her leave. He stayed with her while she was panicking and talked her down. She's obviously attached to him. I know sex has a much deeper meaning for you; if that's your concern, they're not having sex."

His knee bounces, and I give in to the temptation and weave my fingers through the back of his hair.

"He's not...*us*." His voice softens. "I'm connected to you."

I swallow hard. "I love you, Jax. There'll be times when we're together, and she'll be here, for whatever reason. He can be with her."

"I want the three of us."

"He changes nothing. You have us."

"No. You don't want a commitment. If I joke around with you in front of others, you take days away from me. I can't imagine what you'd do if I touched you outside of here."

"That's not true. I'm committed to both of you. I'd never be with anyone—"

"It's not a commitment if you have to hide it. A commitment shows the world you're taken."

I scoff. "Nobody wants to be with me, and I don't wanna be with anyone else. Besides, you don't have anything. Aurora has your ring. What do you have?"

"I have several tattoos. One on my ring finger." He flashes the tattoo in question. "You want me to get a tat of your name?"

"No—"

"No, because you're afraid someone will see it." He tries to sit up. "Right?"

I tighten my arms around him, not ready to let him go. "We *can't*. There's no way to escape it. I'm your *coach*."

"Who cares? No one. They can't say you're biased toward me or show me favoritism—you've sat my ass out more than anyone, and you'd do it again. You give more to the team than anybody else. They won't fire you."

Aurora and Jax love to push my limits, and I cave every damn time, especially to him. "You want matching tattoos?"

He whips around to meet my gaze. "Are you serious?"

"Will it help you chill the fuck out?"

He gives me that shit-eating grin and leans back into me. "A little bit."

"What else?"

"The tat must be on your finger."

"Inner, like yours. I still need to look semi-professional."

"Fine," he grumbles. "We share a room on the road."

"That's pushing it."

"I'm supposed to be your roommate."

"Then don't flirt with me in front of the team."

He doesn't even attempt to deny it. "People know we're together."

"No," I say stubbornly. "People *think* we're both with Aurora."

"See, there you go again."

"You can't flirt with me, brat. It's unprofessional."

"Fine, I won't flirt with you." He's threatening me, some hidden agenda in his tone.

I smirk. "Are you better now?"

"No. I need a good fuck," he says with all seriousness.

I scoff and shake my head. "Well, have fun with that. You scared the shit out of Aurora." I rake my fingers through my own hair. "What about Reece?"

He bolts upright. "Ew! I am not fucking Reece!"

"What is wrong with you?" I can't help but laugh at the pure horror on his face. "Not to fuck, you moron. What will help you trust him? Besides the fact that he's protecting you."

His answer is immediate. "Quit his job."

"That's a stretch and quite controlling."

"Whatever you wanna call it. You're the same way, so don't start."

He got me there. I did force Aurora to quit her job. "I doubt Reece will go for that."

I'm not sure he *can*. I'm positive there are rules or stipulations against quitting the government to live permanently with the person you were supposed to be investigating.

"You want someone in our family who comes and goes? And what about Charlie? Did Reece give him the gate code? You know how many agents Kyle had in his pocket? Now I'll need to reinstall the entire security system."

His speech is coming a mile a minute, but before I can dive further into his paranoid musings, the sound of light footsteps draws our attention.

"Hey." Aurora's voice is soft and uncertain.

Jax reaches his hands out. "Come here, babe."

He slides over, creating space for her to fit comfortably between us. Without hesitation, she complies, and they settle in beside me.

I breathe a sigh of relief. My world is complete when they're in my arms.

29
AURORA

"I'm sorry." His tone is pleading but playful—classic Jackson.

I bet if I spun around, he'd give me those puppy-dog eyes I typically fall for.

Unlike him, I'm not in a joking mood. Call me crazy, but I don't enjoy being screamed at. Plus... "Reece is leaving. He doesn't want to cause problems between us."

I'm struggling to pinpoint the source of my irritability. Is it the lies and secrets? Jackson's furious accusation that Reece and I are sleeping together? It's not the worst I've had to deal with from him, not by far. Maybe it's the disappointment of Reece leaving?

I like the Viking. They keep me in the dark. I don't know everything, but I know Reece is good for us. He allows them to focus on hockey, and we're not so overwhelmed.

"Shit." Ethan sits up. "Now?"

"No. After the baby's appointment tomorrow, since I don't have a ride." My words come out more bitter than intended. I'm trying to be understanding, but my frustration keeps resurfacing. "He said he'll stay in his apartment to prevent another fight."

The guys have a morning practice and an evening game. I'll meet them at the doctor's office in LA. I could get up at the crack of dawn and go with them, but I value my sleep, which, lately, I've been getting little of. I'm no longer vomiting as much, but we've been traveling, and I'm exhausted.

"I can always leave you the car," Ethan offers.

Jackson and I stare at him. The lack of vehicles is not the problem.

"What?" he asks. "You're doing that twin thing, scowling at me identically."

"I can't drive. I don't have a license."

Ethan's brows nearly hit his hairline. "Seriously? I spent six figures on a vehicle, and you don't have a driver's license?"

"I've never needed one." I'm far too fearful to drive. Can you even imagine? I'd be a nervous wreck driving a luxury SUV. "I thought you bought it for you."

"I'd rather she wasn't behind the wheel," my husband adds.

"Of course you would." Ethan gives Jax a hard stare. "What do you wanna do then?"

The gentle glow of the outdoor lights casts a shadow over Jackson's green eyes as they meet mine. "Is that why you're upset? 'Cause the Viking is leaving?"

I hesitate, and Ethan interlaces our fingers, his thumb running over my knuckles.

"Not if it's going to hurt you or if he's a source of trauma for you."

Jax is not fixable—no one truly is. He is, however,

worthy of love and healing, and unfortunately, having Reece in our home prevents that.

A little voice inside my head questions my innocence. I was in his bed, after all. I said things I had no right to and crossed lines I shouldn't have. I knew Jax's temper, knew he'd be livid, but I wasn't attempting to hide anything.

He cocks his head. "That's not what I asked."

"I'm disappointed." Despite the lump in my throat, I force myself to say the words. "I want him to stay. I think he's good for us. He just spent twenty minutes telling me it's your past that doesn't trust him and explaining why he needs to leave." A tear slips out, and I brush it away.

He caresses my stomach and nods in contemplation. "So..." he drags out the word. "You're not mad at me?" That boyish smile curves his lips. "Except for running Reece out of here?"

I tilt my head, gaze at the sky, and gather my thoughts. The night is dark but not overcast, allowing the stars to take center stage. For a moment, I lose myself in the glittery void.

Earlier, I wanted to escape all three of them, but now, I realize we're all messed up, confused, and doing our best to make this work. I want everyone to be happy, preferably together. "I can deal with everything else, but not you screaming at me, intimidating me."

Ethan grabs Jackson by the nape and gives him a tug. "It won't happen again, will it?"

His answer is immediate. "Nope."

"Who's going to talk to Reece?" Ethan asks Jax. "You or me? She needs to eat."

Some silent conversation takes place between them, and Jax smirks. "When are we getting tattoos?"

Ethan shakes his head. "You're such a child. Set it up."

"Fine," Jax relents. "You deal with Reece—he likes you better. I'll cook dinner."

I stand, tuck my hands into my hoodie and head into the house.

We enter the living room, and Jax wraps an arm around my neck. "I love you. I love you. I love you," he chants. "We'll work it out with Reece."

"I love you." I encircle his waist. "Do what's best for you."

"You're what's best for me. If you trust him, I'll try to do the same."

We reach the kitchen, and he plops me onto the onyx island.

Ethan strides down the hall. Jax hands me a bubbly water then rummages through the stocked fridge.

I open the glass bottle and take a swig. "You two are getting tattoos?"

"Hopefully." He sets packages of fruit on the counter. "We'll see."

"Of like...crossing hockey sticks? Or..." I bite my lips to suppress my mischievous grin.

He throws a grape at me. "That's vulgar."

I giggle, and it echoes through the mostly empty space. "Not as vulgar as you stealing my boyfriend. Don't think I haven't noticed."

He pops a grape in his mouth, all smug. "You have another one. Get over it."

"Ha-ha, funny," I deadpan. "I have a question, though. Where were the cameras?"

"Downtown penthouse, in the smoke detectors."

Fucking Jackson.

30
REECE

The patio door slides open and shut, heavy footsteps approaching, undoubtedly Ethan's.

"If you're here to apologize for him, save your breath." I raise the bottle to my lips and take a long swig.

He winces and drops into the Adirondack chair beside me. "You can't drink here."

I figured as much, but my talk with Aurora left me restless, and I grabbed a beer to ease the discomfort.

She chose Jackson and always will. When I asked if she still wanted to leave, she refused. She'll never leave him, and he doesn't trust me. It's him or me—I won't allow her to remain caught in our crossfire.

"I didn't expect anyone to come out here."

"Jax might, though, so please don't." He runs his fingers through his chaotic hair. "Throw out whatever you have or finish it."

"Charlie brought over a six-pack, sorry. It's been a while, and he was hoping to hang out. I'll take it with me when I go."

He releases an audible breath. "That's what I wanted to

talk about. Have you thought about what you're doing after this case?"

"Every day. Why?"

He stretches his legs out in front of him. "Can you resign?"

"Possibility. Why?"

Tired eyes meet mine. "I'll match your pay."

Miffed, I shake my head. "You two think everything is about money—everything can be solved by throwing money at it. You couldn't pay me enough to put up with him."

He clenches his jaw, and the muscle furrows. "You grew up normal, didn't you? Then, in the military, some shit happened. Now, your rose-colored glasses are shattered, along with your good-guy persona. You look at Jax and all his mistakes and can't fathom how we could love him. Maybe you think the same of yourself, and him receiving what you deem him unworthy of really pisses you off, doesn't it?"

The scorching heat of humiliation ignites my face, and my body breaks into a cold sweat. I ball my fists. "He treats her like shit and always has. He doesn't deserve her."

"Neither do I." He shrugs his tense shoulders. "Neither do you. But she needs us."

Something in the way he says 'us' has me dropping my guard, finishing my beer with a long pull, and sinking back in the chair. "He doesn't trust me. I'm only making things worse for her."

"Jax is deeply perceptive. He can pick up on intentions almost instantly, and he's highly attuned to our surroundings. He'll continue to distrust you if he detects animosity or deceit."

Fair enough. Between us, the roar of the ocean, the

rustling palms in the breeze, and Aurora's melodic laughter fill the silence.

A smile tugs at my lips—I love that sound.

"I don't need your money." My military pay is sufficient, and my living expenses are minimal. "Unless you're expecting me to contribute to this extravagant mortgage."

The last line is sarcasm, but he responds anyway. "This house is paid for by Jackson. I'm expecting you to contribute in other ways."

My heart rate quickens, and my brows pinch in annoyance, mostly with myself for feeling an ounce of hope. "Like what?"

"Security. Stay here. Do what you're doing. Just do not involve anyone else."

"Not involve anyone else?" I scoff. "I removed his phone from a federal crime scene to protect him, and he still doesn't trust me."

"You know what I mean. No one at the house. I told you to keep that shit away from him." He gestures with his hand. "Now, he wants to reinstall the security and change the codes. He's…"

"Paranoid," I finish for him.

He side-eyes me. "He has reason to be."

"I get that, but he has no reason to scream at her. I don't give a fuck what he does to me, but I'm not sitting here while he terrifies her."

"Me neither," he snaps. "He won't do it again."

"Doubtful." I need another drink—a water, anything. My idle hands feel awkward, and I go to twist the diamond in my ear, only to remember it's not there. Technically, I'm not at work. I could replace them.

"You think I'd let something happen to her?"

"I think your love for Jax blinds you to what he's capable of."

"I know what he's capable of. Him and I aren't much different. He lacks self-control. He needs guidance, not retribution."

Is he serious?

"I'll guide him right through a fucking wall if he ever screams at her again."

His expression hardens. "You won't touch him. You'll go to your superiors, explain you've fallen in love with your client or whatever, and quit."

Serious and delusional.

"And what will that get me? Arrested and imprisoned on multiple counts of tampering with evidence and obstruction of justice?"

"Jax's trust. Aurora's trust. The chance to be with her. Isn't that what you want?"

An absurd grin spreads across my face, and, dammit, I can't stop it. "Is that what you're offering?"

He narrows his eyes. "That's not up to me."

"So it's up to her *husband,* then?"

"No, it's up to Aurora. Jax knows I'm trying to convince you to stay. He knows she wants you here. About the only thing she's upset about in this clusterfuck of a day is you leaving."

Foolish male pride swells in my chest. "I'll consider it. But Charlie would never betray me. He deleted the footage to protect me and Aurora. He thought you'd be against me hauling her back and lying down with her. He didn't mean to set off your bestie."

"He messed with the security, and now, Jax thinks it's unsafe. He'll most likely have the whole thing ripped out and reinstalled."

I shake my head in disbelief. "If you really wanna help him, have Rocco send someone—anyone familiar to him. He trusts you and them by default. It'll ease his mind."

He slips his phone from his pocket. "Fuck, that's brilliant."

"The most stable I've ever seen him was in New York. It's not me or Charlie. It's LA fucking with his head. It's sad to say, but the best thing Kyle did was send him to boarding school."

Focused on his phone, he says, "We're both committed to this team for two more years." A smirk plays on his lips. "And you know he hates the snow."

Then, it hits me—the reason behind Jax's paranoia and why I am unable to resign.

I blow out a heavy breath. "I can't quit right now, and you don't want me to."

Ethan peers over at me, his brows pinched in question.

"Kyle's former partner, Hugo, still works for the LAPD."

He sets his phone down, his eyes darkening. "Fuck."

"It gets worse. He made police chief a week before Kyle's death. He's one of the highest paid in the country—nearly twice as much—petitioned and approved by the board of police commissioners."

"Meaning Kyle."

I nod. "We're investigating him and the LAPD, but…"

"It's a long and corrupt process," he answers.

"Hugo likely knows about me. Kyle, or someone using Kyle's phone, sent pictures of us in New York to an untraceable number. Given the threatening text toward Aurora, Hugo's afraid Jax will talk. I have a hunch Kyle kept the LAPD away from Jax—"

"Yeah, because if he were arrested, Kyle would lose his paycheck."

I lean in and lower my voice. "Here's my worry: Jax tipped off and blackmailed Kyle to prevent us from using Aurora as bait. Kyle warned his partner, who wanted Jax silenced. Kyle refused because he wouldn't get a dime of Jax's inheritance if Jax wasn't alive, especially with the baby's paternity in question."

Ethan's eyes widen, and his tone deepens. "So they got Kyle out of the way once he was no longer needed."

"Exactly, and I can only protect Jax and Aurora by being employed with an agency that outranks the LAPD."

31
AURORA

Ethan steps between my knees and takes my face in his hands. Stormy-gray eyes bore into mine. "You and I are gonna have a talk."

I slide my fingers under his shirt and wrap my legs around his waist. "I missed you today."

"Don't suck up to me." His voice drops low and stern. "I need you to be safe, Aurora."

That deep scowl between his brows tells me he's serious and stressed out, which only makes me double down on the love and humor to cheer him up.

I hook my ankles at the small of his back and press our bodies together. "Jax, did you measure these counters? They're the perfect height."

My husband, working at the stove behind us, snorts.

Ethan shakes his head, not even a hint of a smile. "Who's in charge here?"

"You are, and I love you." I trace the firm, defined lines of his abdominal muscles, the heat of his skin radiating under my touch. "We'd fall apart without you. Truly."

He weaves his fingers into my hair and tugs my head

back. "How about I add to your punishment every time you attempt to mollify me, brat?"

"I quite enjoy every punishment you give, so sure." I know the punishment is coming either way. Might as well make it fun, right?

He cocks a threatening brow. "Really? Do you enjoy it when I sleep elsewhere?"

Nope, that's not fun. That's the opposite of fun.

A sharp pain pierces my chest, and sadness kills my playful mood. He'll do it too. He won't just sleep in the guest room. He'll stay at his downtown penthouse or somewhere equally depressing.

"See? That right there—that's how I feel when I think about losing you." His grip on my hair loosens. "What did I tell you about leaving or threatening to leave?"

"Not to." I grasp his jeans at the waistband. "How come Jax gets hugs when he goes off, but I get punished?"

Another snort from my husband.

Ethan's big hands cup the back of my head, and his thumb caresses my jawline. "Let me handle Jax. You focus on being my good girl. Got it?"

Well, when he says that... How can I not give in? "I was hurt and mad. It was a lot to take in."

"And what are you supposed to do instead of running?"

"Talk to you, but you were at practice."

"So? Did I not step off the ice to call you in New York? And when you've had panic attacks, did I not stay on the phone with you, no matter where I was?"

I release a frustrated sigh. "You lied to me."

"I told you to forget about the case, that we'd deal with it. You knew there were things we weren't telling you, and for good reason."

"I know that *now*. Reece explained everything, but it was still a shock to find out all at once."

Plus, I was angry at Reece and Charlie, but that's a separate issue.

"And what did Reece say?"

"He told me to go have a fit in one of the ten bedrooms until you got home." I gesture with my free hand. "And that if I tried to leave again, he'd handcuff me to his bed."

Ethan smirks. "I'm starting to like him."

The sound of a wooden spoon slamming against the counter rings through the air, and I bite my lips to hold back a snicker.

Ethan glances over his shoulder, and the tendon in his neck pops. I want to run my tongue along it. He's dressed down today, in faded jeans and a pullover, his beard growing in. He's rather delicious.

"What's your problem?" he asks, clueless he's become his star player's newest obsession.

"Whatever," Jax mutters, rolling a meatball with more force than necessary.

I'm surprised it's not a pancake—a beefcake?

My chest vibrates with a stifled chuckle at both my own joke and Jax's reaction, bringing Ethan's attention back to me.

"You two are a pain right in my fucking ass."

I pucker my bottom lip. "But we love you."

He meets my pout with a smug grin. "We'll see how much you love me when you're getting up at five a.m. to go with me to practice."

"No." Horrified, I draw out the word. "Anything but that. Can't we bang it out instead?"

"That's a fantastic idea," Jackson agrees.

Ethan ignores us. "I warned you I'd handcuff you to me. I told you—"

"I've been good," I interrupt. "I haven't given you attitude lately. I've been taking care of myself. I haven't even thought about work, and I wasn't planning to go far—I didn't even have shoes on, nor did I have any money."

"That's not helping your case," his deep voice rumbles.

"I'm exhausted. I'll stay with Reece the entire time. You'll have nothing to worry about."

"He didn't say he'd stay, baby girl."

Pushing Ethan aside, I hop off the counter and make a beeline for Reece's room. "He will. I'll go ask him." More like beg him—just not with my body. Apparently, he doesn't appreciate that, and now, he's about to find out how awkward I am.

"We're still banging it out!" Jax yells after me.

32
REECE

"Um, I'm selfish. I am. I know that."

She's adorable. Cheeks flushed, Aurora stands in front of me, her hands clasped at her chest, as she no doubt tries to convince me to stay without saying the words.

I bite the inside of my cheek to stop from smirking.

Her gaze strays to the bookshelf behind me, anywhere but my face. "But sometimes, it's like that, you know? When a person..." She fiddles with her fingers, and her expression becomes curious. "Who brought these books?"

"I haven't a clue. I'm assuming whoever your husband paid to furnish the house." I relax into the plush reading chair and stretch out my legs. "You were saying?" I bring her focus back to the painful conversation at hand.

This is not unpleasant for me at all. I'm enjoying this awkward attempt at getting her way immensely. I love it when she's tongue-tied. Any minute now, she'll give up talking and resort to nonverbal communication.

"They say when you..." Her attention drifts to the ceiling, as if she's praying to God for help. "...when you love something you should set it free, and if it loves you, it'll return." She gestures with her hand. "But what if the bird doesn't know you love them, and they find someone else to love them, you know?" Her face reddens further, and her breath quickens.

My chest vibrates with a silent chuckle. I should save her from this nervous fit she's having, but I'm too entertained.

This might be better than her persuading, flirtatious hugs.

No, definitely not, but I suspect her rambling is because of my *one* mistaken rejection.

Her hair is up in a ponytail, her pulse visible, fluttering at the base of her throat. "So, sometimes, you have to be selfish or lose what you have." She nods repeatedly to convince herself that was a good argument.

I muffle my grin with my fist. "I see. So what you're saying is…?"

She shifts on her bare feet, toenails painted teal-blue, the color of their hockey team. "After my doctor's appointment, are you leaving?"

Ah, there it is.

"I haven't decided yet." I put on a severe scowl. "Why?"

She swallows. "We could hang out." Noticing my tough façade, she babbles again. "I don't know what you like, but we could do something before the game. Get pizza, or…" She flattens her lips. "Axe throwing?"

My forehead furrows in surprise. "You think I like axe throwing?"

Her gaze wanders over me slowly. "Shooting?"

This time, my amused grin is unavoidable. "Are you gonna throw an axe or shoot a gun, princess?"

"I'll watch you," she offers with a weak tone.

"You dislike loud noises. You'd hate a shooting range."

"I'll wear headphones and cheer you on."

"With pom-poms?" I joke.

Her eyes narrow. "If you want me to, Viking, I'll wear a full cheerleading uniform. It'll look weird since I'm pregnant, but whatever."

I reach out and grab her hand, pulling her to me. She raises her knee onto my thigh, as if about to sit on my lap, but stops.

"Tell me, angel, what did Ethan say?"

"That I have to get up at five a.m. and attend practice with him," she grumbles.

"And let me guess: you'd like me to save you from your punishment?"

She ignores my question, her fingers playing with mine. "Oh! We could visit the Ripped Bodice bookstore in West Hollywood."

"You want me to take you to the bookstore?"

"No... Well, yes, but only if you want to. We could do something else if you prefer."

"Pizza and smutty books sound perfect."

"You don't have to. We can do anything you want."

"*Anything* I want?" I tug her hand until she falls into my lap.

Her ass lands on my thighs, her hands on my chest, and that white-hot sensation races through my veins. My cock thickens; obviously, I didn't think this through.

A soft gasp slips from her lips, and her pupils dilate.

"You're terrible at this," I say, a little too breathless.

She releases a shaky sigh. "I've been trying to tell you that."

"I must admit, it was cute—pretty painful to watch but cute."

She rests her head on my shoulder. "Yeah, well, I'm woozy. You need to take care of me."

I laugh so hard, tears prickle the corners of my eyes. "You should've tried that first."

She punches me in the side. "I hate you."

My arms come around her. "No, you don't. From all that babbling, I think you might like me."

"I'll kill you if you tell anyone."

This dizzying, weightless feeling in my rib cage is irrational. "Your secret is safe with me."

Silence hangs between us. I could sit here for days without moving or speaking, just holding her.

Except for one swelling problem.

Her fingers glide into my hair, nails scratching my scalp, not at all fucking helping. Soon enough, I'll have to imagine corpses to stop from dry-humping her.

She wiggles on my lap and smiles against my throat.

"Aurora." I tug her ponytail. "No teasing."

She snickers. "You deserve some torture for making me sweat through that speech."

"Is there even a shooting range in LA?"

"I have no idea," she breathes. "I was having a seizure."

God, I love her.

33
JACKSON

I set a giant bowl of spaghetti and meatballs onto the center of the table, along with warm Asiago bread. "If they don't come out here in five seconds to eat this dinner I made—"

"Don't even fucking start." Ethan chuckles, his attention on his phone. "Leave 'em alone."

I slump into the dining chair next to him, one of those tall, ladder-back styles that match the weathered farmhouse table. I didn't think the rustic aesthetic would pair well with the black countertops, but the bronze accents and wooden beams pull it all together perfectly. Plus, it was on Aurora's Pinterest, so...

"And why would I do that? How are you so calm? Oh, that's right: you've been pitching him since New York."

"Yup, because I need him. *We* need him. If I can deal with you, you can deal with him."

I stand, pushing back the chair, my hands flat on the table. I'm restless, torn in a hundred different directions.

Ethan drops his phone and grabs my shirt for the hundredth time today. "I'm joking. Relax."

He's tactile—always has been, especially with Aurora,

and that seems to be passing on to me. Not that I'm complaining; it helps ease my agitation.

"I need eyes on her. I'm installing cameras in his room."

"Do you trust me?" He ignores my last sentiment, so he must agree.

Cameras in Reece's room would've prevented today's disaster—or not. Maybe I would've strangled him. Perhaps it's better I don't know what they're doing.

Straightening, I lean against Ethan's chair. "Of course I do."

"Then trust me on this, okay? Imagine what we can achieve with the three of us. Imagine having someone else to protect our family, someone who'll always be with her and the baby."

"Did he say he'd quit his job?"

A knowing glint appears in Ethan's eyes. "Not yet. He's in a position to protect you."

Irrational fear erupts in my stomach like a swarm of angry bees. "Fuck that. You know who else was in a position to protect me?"

That piercing gaze narrows. "Do I need to worry about you, more than normal? Do you need to see someone? I'd never let anyone hurt you or Aurora. I mean it, Jax. I'll do whatever it takes, and if that means having Reece here, then so be it."

I sit, drop my head into my hands, and rub my eyes. "How can you be so positive about everything?"

His hand clasps the back of my neck and massages the tight muscles. "You're gonna give yourself a headache. I planned to spend my life alone, and although that sounds appealing," his voice carries a smile, probably picturing peaceful days and quiet nights, "I can't imagine returning to the silence. I have Aurora and you, and we'll have a baby soon. We have this house and a family in New York. We possess the power to do anything we choose. You taught me that." His fingers move into my hair. "Tell me what you need to get through this. We have our entire future ahead of us."

What do I need? Ultimately, our family's safety. I want to say I can manage myself, but the more I'm around Ethan, the more I realize I've been spiraling since my rookie year, and I was out of control as a teenager before then.

He and Aurora are my only refuge. Without them, I'd go out in a blaze of glory, killing all these motherfuckers who haunt me.

He continues to caress me, his soothing touch battling the war waging within. "You wanna return to New York?"

Before I'm able to answer him, footsteps echo in the hall. When I lift my head, all I see is Reece's smile. My gaze connects with Ethan's. "Can I please murder him?"

"No. We need him to protect Aurora and the baby—and the next baby you want so badly."

"Manipulative much?" I mumble as they take their seats across from us.

"Dinner smells amazing." Aurora sets the napkin on her lap. "What are you two whispering about?"

Reece follows suit, that smug smile never leaving his ugly mug.

Nope, I can't do this. "How fucking awkward this is."

Ethan grips my knee under the table, easing some of the sharp emotions in my chest.

"Let it go," he growls.

Aurora places a piece of bread on her plate. The Viking butters the slice for her, and I roll my eyes.

Someone kill me now.

Ethan's hand shifts higher, and my body becomes distracted, buzzing for a whole new reason.

"Babe," I say, as gently as I can muster. "We are not picking up any more strays. Understand me?"

"Technically, *babe*," she mocks. "If you wanna go there, you and I were kinda sorta broken up."

Reece folds his arms over his chest with an expression that reads, *I told you so.*

I let out a sound somewhere between a scream and a screech. "You already have one rebound!" I point to Ethan, who smirks.

"And *he*," she drags out the word for emphasis, "wasn't there either. He said he wasn't capable of a relationship."

"You don't get a rebound from your rebound. It doesn't work like that!" I shout.

She leans over the table. "Didn't you just promise to stop yelling?"

"Would you rather I yell or kill someone? Because I swear to God, Aurora, I will murder anyone else and bathe you in their blood." Damn, that feels good to get off my chest. "And if you," I point at Reece, "ruin this, I'll kill you too."

He rolls his shoulders. "I'd love to see you try."

I glare at him and snatch Aurora's plate before he can serve her. Childish? Yes. Do I care? No. "Don't forget you sleep under my roof."

Ethan tightens his grip on my upper thigh. "Are you done? Can we eat now? I'm fucking starving."

"Me too," Aurora agrees. "Spaghetti is my favorite."

I scoop pasta onto her dish. "No, it's not." It is, but I want to argue. I want her attention. "You don't even like meat." That's partially true.

Reece scoffs. "I don't think you know her as well as you think you do. Clearly, that's not accurate."

I pause mid-stab of a meatball, disassociating, because I know I'm not finding him funny.

When my soul returns to my body, I pass him the meatball on my fork the same as I pass a puck—a flick of my wrist, eighty miles per hour, without looking, and dead-on.

Except he moves his head at the last second, and meat and sauce explode all over the smoke-gray wall.

Aurora's mouth falls open with a gasp. "Jackson Vaughn O'Reilly!"

Ethan doubles over, his face practically in my lap, his body shaking with laughter. It better be me he finds funny.

Aurora arches a threatening brow. "If you don't stop, I'm not sleeping in your bed tonight."

"Yeah, okay, *wife*." I serve spaghetti as if nothing had happened. "We'll see how well that goes over. If I'm in this house, you're sleeping with me and Ethan, and no one else."

"Thank fuck you're gone half the year." Reece grips his knife so tightly, his knuckles are bone-white.

I bet he's itching to stab me.

"Thank fuck she's going with me," I snap back.

"Thank *fuck* this conversation is over," Ethan rumbles in his coach voice.

Jesus, why does that give me goosebumps?

34
ETHAN

The kitchen falls silent, save for the clatter of dishes and the running water at the sink. It's clear we just moved in. The house has that new-place echo.

Jax is clearing the table, Reece is loading the dishwasher, and I'm working on my phone, returning emails and texts. Aurora is in the bedroom, doing her nightly routine of God knows what.

It's oddly...domestic.

"I remember the first time I played." Jax breaks the stillness. "I got into a fight in the cafeteria, and the coach recruited me. I knew how to skate. I played a bunch of sports growing up, but nothing stuck. I was terrible on a team."

Reece sets a glass in the dishwasher and mumbles, "Shocker."

"I liked surfing." Jax flashes him a scathing glare. "It gave me a chance to get out of my head. There wasn't much to do at boarding school besides hiking, skiing, or freezing my balls off. So I said, fuck it. I'll try hockey." With surprising gentleness, he stacks dirty plates on top of each other. "The first practice, I got my ass kicked." He chuckles. "I mean, these guys were gonna show me why their country was the best, you know?"

He brings the plates to the sink, and Reece shoots me a worried glance over his shoulder. Jax is talking more than usual—about his childhood. Maybe he's filling the silence, or maybe he's having a breakdown. Nobody knows yet.

"We were on the same fucking team." He crouches and grabs a spray bottle and paper towels from under the sink. "I didn't understand it. In my head, I was thinking, I'm gonna slaughter one of these motherfuckers and get into so much trouble. And yeah, I got crosschecked and snapped. Mitts and helmets came off, and we exchanged blows until Coach called it, but that was it. They hit me. I hit back. By the end of the week, I was sore as fuck, bruised, bloody, and damn happy. Happier than I remember. It was strange, like waking to a dream."

I watch him, trying to gauge his mood, but his back is to me, his focus on cleaning the counter. He's reminiscing about a time when he escaped LA, escaped Kyle, and found life worth living, and I wonder if he's processing the idea of leaving.

He places a bowl in the sink, washes his hands, and organizes spices in the cabinet. "Eventually, I learned if I was fast, I could avoid getting knocked around, and people liked me since I could play. I fit in. I never did at any of the preppy private schools Kyle sent me to. There, I was only somebody 'cause I had money and designer drugs."

"Another shocker," Reece says under his breath.

I might punch him if he doesn't shut the fuck up and let Jax trauma dump or whatever is happening here.

"*Anyhow*," Jax draws out. "That's where it starts. They use rich kids to push drugs and get others hooked. High school, college, raves—it doesn't matter at first, as long as people can afford it."

Reece pauses, both of us seeming to sense the direction this is headed. This is Jackson's weird way of opening up.

"They set up lavish parties within their inner circle and sell a shit ton of overpriced drugs to trust fund kids, all while cherry-picking their victims."

I sit back, my work forgotten. Reece dries his hands and leans against the counter.

Jax positions and repositions a brass pot on the ridiculous twelve-burner gas stove, ensuring it's directly under the pot filler. "Kids wanna belong, feel special, you know? So they'd invite the *chosen ones* to their exclusive parties with celebrities, athletes, politicians, and sex workers. Some are predators. Some are prey. That's what Kyle would tell me when I refused to fall in line—I was a predator, or I was prey." His shoulders rise and fall with shallow breaths. "I chose to be a fuck-up. The kid who always got kicked out of school. The stoned guy at the party. The addict."

My eyes sting. Kyle is lucky he's dead. I might dig up his body and feed it through a woodchipper for my own peace of mind.

"I'm sorry, man." Reece clears his throat. "Give me some names and places, something to go on. I'll do the rest."

Jax mirrors Reece's posture and rakes his fingers through his hair. "I'll name who I recognize in the videos—pictures of faces; I'm not watching them. I'll list those in the LAPD and any headmasters, teachers, and others I can remember. I'll give you the locations I've been to, though my memory is spotty."

"The text you received," Reece prompts. "The jail cell. Do you know where it is?"

Adam's apple bobbing, Jax swallows repeatedly. His eyes

become glazed, and Reece glances at me in alarm, but I'm already out of my chair.

"Hey, it's okay. Take your time." I draw him into my chest, clasping his nape. "I'm so fucking proud of you. You did good."

His arms come around me, and he buries his face in my neck. "I don't wanna be like this. I just want it to end."

I get choked up, and hot tears burn my eyelids. I weave my fingers into his hair and dip my head. "I love you. You've been strong for too long. Tell me who, and I'll fix it. I swear to you."

Right now, I'd do anything, hurt anyone, to take his pain away.

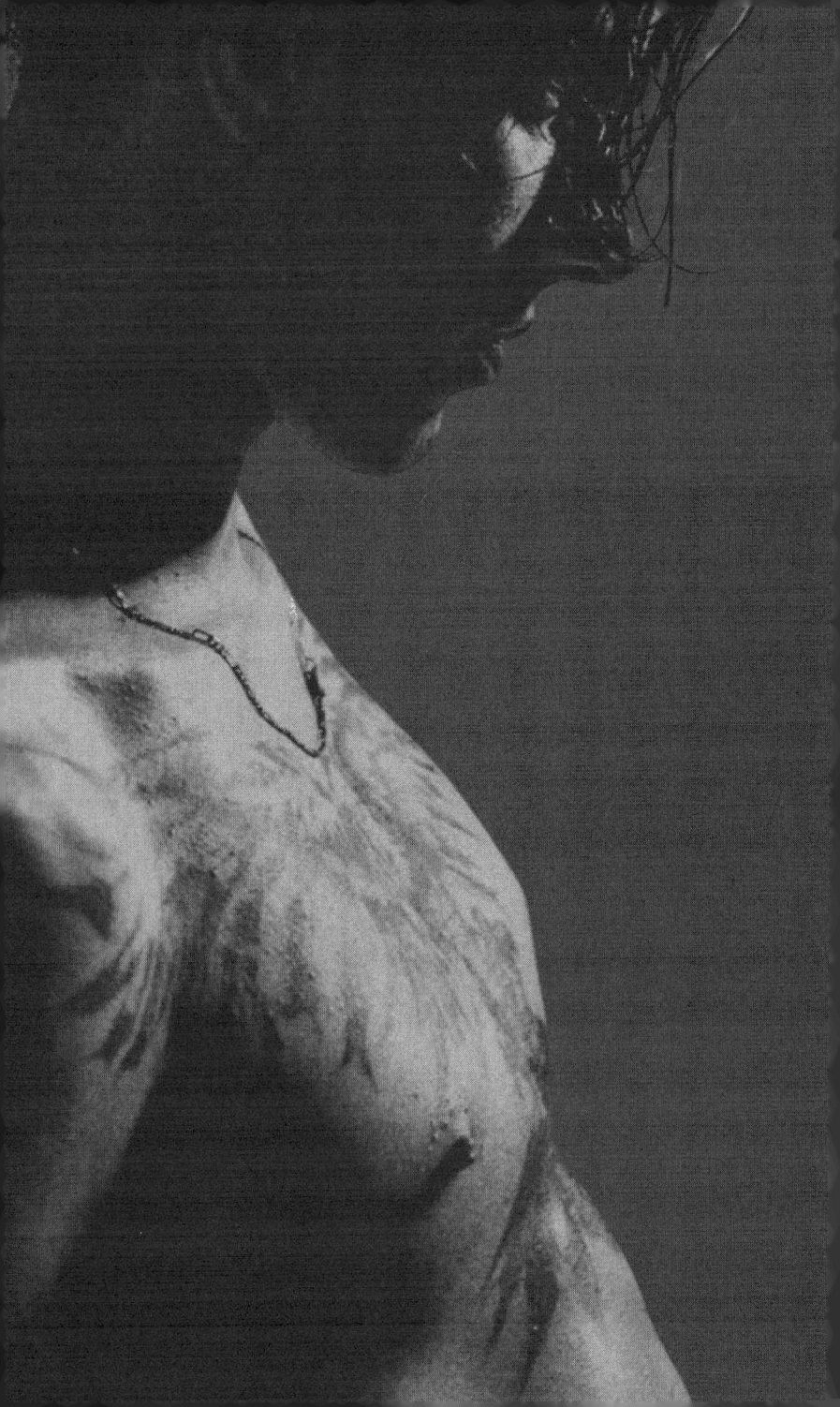

35
JACKSON

Aurora gazes into the bathroom mirror, a black satin robe draped over her, and brushes out her long hair. I activate the steam to warm the room before approaching.

I place my palms on the counter, boxing her in, and kiss the curve of her neck. "You're angry with me. I feel it. I felt it at dinner."

She sets down the brush, twists in my arms, and takes my face in her hands. "I'm worried about you. You're not okay." She runs her thumbs over the dark circles under my eyes. "Something was wrong in Boston, and you wouldn't tell me. Something is still wrong." She offers a soft, playful smile, though it doesn't reach her eyes. "We're supposed to be best friends."

I press my forehead to hers. "I'm struggling."

Her arms encircle my neck. "Because of Reece?"

I can't tell her; I never want her to know the extent of my demons. She'll look at me differently. Maybe that's one reason I dislike the Viking. He knows everything.

"Two things mean the world to me. You and Ethan. I see how Reece fits, but I can't imagine anyone outside of Ethan."

"You're a bit obsessed. You know that, right?" She threads her fingers through my hair. "He's not replacing Ethan."

I ignore her comment, already well aware of my growing infatuation. "I fear losing you. My head is… I'm fucked up and paranoid. A thousand thoughts are coming at me at once. I'm afraid Reece will convince you to leave me, and I don't trust the people he works with."

"You are not fucked up, and you are not losing me. I shouldn't have been in his bed—"

"But you like him."

Her troubled eyes, red-rimmed and glistening with unshed tears, search mine. "Is that so bad?" she whispers. "You love Ethan and hockey. I'm giving up everything for the family you want, and I'm okay with that. But he—"

"I can quit. I *will* quit. We've talked about this."

"Will you?" calls a deep, irritated voice from the doorway. "Because I'm gonna continue coaching."

My body stiffens, and I stand upright. I can't deny it. His words hurt.

I see us as one. If he leaves the team, I leave. If he wanted to relocate to Bumfuck, Alaska, I'd go. I might whine about it, but I'd never refuse. It tears me apart that he doesn't feel the same, and a dull ache splinters in my chest.

He pushes off the doorframe. "Let me explain this again, and then it's over. We move on." He puts a hand on Aurora's shoulder. "Aurora is mine." He clasps the back of my neck. "*You* are mine, and because I love you, I want you to succeed. I want you to play and win. I want you to be happy like you were in Canada or your rookie year."

His stormy gaze bores into mine, his thumb caresses my skin, and the tight fist gripping my sternum loosens. The relief is tangible. My shoulders relax and the panic dissipates.

"And since I'll be by your side, I need someone with my other favorite person." He kisses Aurora's temple. "I need her safe and cared for, and Reece can do that. I trust him to protect you both. You'll grow to trust him."

I highly fucking doubt that. He has the power to separate us, to take me from them, to turn them against me. I have no connection with him. I've tried. Even tonight, he was an ass. He's arrogant. I don't know what Aurora sees in him.

"He's not sleeping in our bed." I sound childish and possessive, but I'm only interested in two people. Both are in this room.

Ethan smirks. "He doesn't want us. He wants Aurora. He tolerates us because that's what's best for her, and you'll do the same." He reaches for the hem of his shirt. "Now, can we shower? It's fucking hot in here."

My expression goes blank, and my stomach swims for an entirely different reason. "Wait. Are you showering with us?"

That smirk stretches into a salacious grin. The fucker knows precisely how to manipulate me. "Will that improve your mood?"

"That depends. What are we doing?" If he's just going to hide behind our girl and wash her hair, then…

Shit, I'd still love it.

Wickedness dances in his eyes before he yanks his shirt over his head and tosses it at me. "I'll let you pick."

"Hello!" Aurora throws her arms up. "I'm right here. Don't I get a say?"

"Of course you do." I free the ties of her robe and palm her perfect tits. "You get to decide whose cock you suck first."

36
AURORA

Jackson sucks my nipple into his mouth and pushes the robe off my shoulders. My confidence shakes. Feeling attractive at almost six months pregnant is difficult, but these two quickly restore my self-esteem.

Ethan strips and drags me into the shower. Jax follows, flipping on the dual showerheads and rainfall above. Steam swirls in the air, creating a hazy, dream-like atmosphere, and the fact that we're naked together doesn't seem so unnatural.

I tip my head back and let the water run over my body. Impatient as ever, Ethan seizes my throat and draws me in for a heated kiss. Our tongues intertwine, and he caresses my stomach.

"Fuck, I love this," he rumbles between kisses. "I still can't believe you're having my baby."

Jackson grasps my hips from behind and presses his erection against my ass. I reach between us and wrap my hand around his hard length. He releases a deep groan and bites my shoulder.

I trace my fingers down Ethan's toned abs and do the

same with my other hand, stroking them both. Hands explore my body, and honestly, I couldn't tell you whose are whose. Both are calloused and scratchy.

Ethan's kiss becomes urgent, his teeth grazing my bottom lip before he fists my hair and demands, "Get on your knees."

Twisting to the side, I lower to the stone floor between them. Ethan guides me toward Jax, and I suck him into my mouth while palming the other.

They stare down at me, eyes half-lidded and full of lust. Their hair is dripping wet, and water runs down their impressive bodies. It's hot as hell.

You know what else is hot? Ethan's hand on Jax's waist, his thumb tracing the indentation of that V-cut muscle. That's fucking hot.

I look up and hold Jackson's gaze. I glide my tongue along the length of his shaft, then wrap my lips around the head of his cock, flicking the sensitive underside.

"Fuck." He clasps my nape and thrusts his hips.

Ethan cups the back of my head, urging me to take Jax deeper, and I gag.

Still, he doesn't let up.

My throat works furiously against the intrusion, and I focus on breathing through my nose. My eyes well up, but I blink away the tears to watch my husband's face contort with ecstasy.

His palm hits the shower wall, his fingers dig into my skin, and his cock jerks in my mouth. My pussy aches for attention in response to his pleasure, and I moan around him.

My hair is tugged, and Jax pops free from my lips.

Intense gray eyes lock on mine, Ethan's bicep bulging

with the force of his grip. He runs his thumb over my bottom lip. "You like that, don't you? Being our dirty girl?"

I stroke his cock with a pleading stare. "Yes."

Jackson's erection is rock-solid in my other hand. He's loving every second of this.

Without breaking eye contact, I run my tongue up Ethan's length, following the path of a prominent vein. I reach the tip and lick along the slit to savor the taste of his salty pre-cum.

Those stormy eyes darken, and his jaw ticks. "Open."

I obey, and he holds my head steady and fucks my mouth. He bumps the back of my throat, and I gag and swallow.

He pulls me away with a growly hum. "You're too good at that."

We continue this way, with me taking turns blowing them until we're all frantic with need and Ethan is yanking me to my feet.

His lips crash into mine, and his fingers tease my clit. I whimper and push back into Jax.

He takes the hint and notches at my entrance. "Fuck." He thrusts deep. "I've missed this pussy."

I moan into Ethan's kiss, my hands tangling in his thick hair.

"Come on Jackson's cock, baby girl." He circles my clit faster. "Get him nice and slick so we can both fuck you."

The smell of coconut oil fills the steamy air, and Jax's fingers find my ass. Understanding the assignment, he pounds into me while stretching my tight hole.

My head drops onto his shoulder. I dig my nails into Ethan's neck, and my legs shake. Someone pinches my nipples, and I can't take it anymore. It's an onslaught of pleasure.

I cry out and shatter in their arms.

Jax slams into me. "Fuck. Fuck. You're gripping me so fucking tight."

"Don't make him come yet." My mind is still a cloud of euphoria when I'm suddenly lifted into Ethan's arms, Jackson's cock replaced by his. "I want him to fill your ass while I unload in your pussy."

"Jesus fuck." Jax eases into me. "Goddamn."

I suck in a sharp breath and tense around them, clutching Ethan's broad shoulders.

His hold on my thighs turns bruising, and he groans, "Relax, baby. Let us in."

Jackson slides past that tight ring of muscle, filling me in one, firm stroke, and a lusty, high-pitched moan escapes me.

Arousal swoops low in my belly. *So full.*

Ethan adjusts me in his arms, his hips rolling as they find their rhythm. "Good fucking girl," he praises. "You take us so fucking well."

His dirty words and gravelly tone shoot straight to my clit, and my orgasm builds rapidly once again.

They fall in sync, rutting into me, and a melody of erotic sounds bounces off the tiles. Moans. Grunts. Whimpers. Wet skin on skin. It's intoxicating, and that submissive haze takes over.

I become pliant and surrender to their desires. It's the most incredible feeling—heady and gratifying.

Jax grabs my chin and forces my mouth to his. He devours me, the kiss rough and desperate. "There's nothing better than fucking you." His warm breath shudders over my lips. "Except for fucking you while you're full of Ethan's cock."

His voice is raspy, his thrusts punishing. He's close.

My body flushes with heat. "Fuck me, Jax. Fill my ass with cum."

With a guttural groan, he sinks his teeth into my bottom lip. His fingers tremble against my skin. He jerks inside me, and the burn of his hot cum sends me over the edge.

"Oh... Fuck, I'm gonna come." My words are barely above a whisper.

Ethan buries his cock to the hilt. "That's my girl... Fuck... Give me that tight pussy."

He hits deep, and I gush around him, screaming in ecstasy.

His head falls back, his neck arched and his lips parted. He hisses through his teeth, and his cock throbs inside me. His pleasure suspends mine, and I lick and bite that strained tendon, moaning the entire time.

No one moves. We're frozen in post-climax bliss.

The three of us pant, trying to catch our breaths, our hearts beating wildly together. My tongue dances with Ethan's, passionate and languid.

Jax trails kisses along the curve of my neck, his fingers in my hair. "That might be the best fuck we've ever had."

"Mmm." Ethan makes a sound of agreement. "I'm gonna sleep like the dead."

Later that night, we're lying in bed. My body is deliciously sore, my head on Ethan's shoulder, and Jackson is curled around me, his arm over my waist and his hand on my belly.

"We need to think of a baby name," Ethan says in the dark.

"How about Elijah?" Jax offers. "It has all our initials. We can call him Eli or EJ. It's perfect."

A chuckle vibrates within Ethan's chest. "You never cease to amaze me, but I like it."

"Me too," I add. "Elijah, it is."

37
JACKSON

"Listen up!" Coach shouts through the locker room. "Tonight, we're hosting Huskies to the Rescue, a special event that showcases a local rescue center. Each of you will get your picture taken with an available dog, promoting adoption and raising awareness. This event was a massive success last year, so put on your brightest smiles and have fun. Oh, and one more thing: we still need a player to foster a puppy."

A hush falls over the room, and every player averts their gaze—everyone except Grant and me.

Ethan lets out a heavy sigh. "Grant fostered last season. Any other volunteers? We have a genuine husky who needs to be adopted. I'm confident they're cute and not at all a ploy orchestrated by the PR team."

The group ripples with snickers and scoffs at his sarcastic remarks while management looks on with forced smiles.

The PR director shakes her head disapprovingly at Ethan, but I don't miss the pleased gleam in her eyes. "The puppy is a he, and his name is Celly."

I caught her staring at Coach during my interview. Okay, maybe not *staring*, but definitely appreciating.

She appears to be around the same age as him, an executive type with yellow-blonde hair, much like his ex. I steal a glance at her hand—no wedding ring.

Annoyance twists in my gut. I swear, if she hits on him, I'm lighting her car on fire in the parking lot.

"I'm positive Patty," he motions toward the woman who can't keep her eyes off him, "will make sure Celly is taken care of while we're on the road."

PR Patty playfully purses her lips, and I get one of my genius ideas.

I raise my hand. "I'll do it."

Ethan's head whips around, his eyes widening in a silent warning, as if to say, *"Don't you fucking dare."*

I smirk. It's his own damn fault for keeping our relationship hidden from management and PR Patty. "We just moved into a new house with a yard. Aurora will be thrilled to have a puppy."

He grimaces, his dark brows furrowing. He opens his mouth to refute but flounders.

Grant, who knows we live together, chuckles beside me and says, "Huskies are rambunctious. They require a lot of attention. Otherwise, they destroy everything."

"Sounds familiar," Coach grumbles, his eyes fixed on me.

I offer a half-assed shrug. "It'll give the baby something to play with."

His body jolts, his aggravated expression turning to one of horror. He extends his hands out, and his voice rises in intensity. "Absolutely not." Catching himself, he takes it down a notch. "It's not safe."

I'd never leave our baby alone, dog or not. EJ is going to be spoiled.

Still, I continue the charade. "We have plenty of help at home. In fact, we just added a new member to the family. It'll be fine."

His cheeks flush, and his ears turn pink. He glares at me, but at least he's no longer flirting with PR Patty.

Oh, and I guess we now have a puppy.

The door swings open, and in comes Celly, cradled in the arms of a young woman sporting a Huskies jersey. He's adorable, wearing his very own tailored jersey and a matching pair of pale-blue eyes. Aurora will be totally enamored with him. I can practically hear her squealing.

"I want her—him." Grant's clipped words are rushed, his expression stern.

"You already have one. You adopted last year's foster," I argue.

PR Patty gestures toward us, and the media team and the girl with the puppy head our way.

My best friend widens his eyes and flashes *the look*. "I want him," he says through gritted teeth.

I frown in confusion until the dog handler approaches, and G is suddenly tongue-tied.

"You're mine—I mean, he's mine," he stammers, his face turning an almost purple shade. "You're here for me."

It's ironic Grant loves dogs, considering how he acts like a puppy himself. He's always happy, often goofy, and fiercely loyal.

He and Killian were the only players who weren't intimidated by Kyle. They stuck with me even after knowing he was a piece of shit. They stayed by my side despite my depression, isolation, and drug use.

The only dispute we've ever had was about how I treated

Aurora. Kill just started speaking to me again at the beginning of this season—after I got sober. Given his past with an abusive stepfather, I can understand why he didn't want to be around me. I can't say I blame him—I was an asshole.

Grant has been my ride or die since our rookie year. We'd often go out and party together, so I know for a fact he does well with women. The way he's currently struck stupid is not his usual style. He's charming and hilarious.

For this reason, I don't argue when he claims the husky. I only wanted Celly to distract Coach from PR Patty anyhow.

* * *

We wait at a stoplight to exit the arena, and Ethan rakes his fingers through his hair. "Thank fuck you didn't take that puppy."

"Not a fan of dogs?" I ask.

"No, I'm not a fan of Patty. I don't need her or the media team at our house."

I scoff. "Afraid your sidepiece will find out you live with us?"

A smile plays on his lips despite his white-knuckle grip on the wheel. "Don't fucking start. That might be a joke to you, but you know who it won't be a joke to? My pregnant girlfriend."

"I'm not joking!" My voice elevates. "Patty doesn't know you have a pregnant girlfriend. Patty wants you to bend her over your desk. Patty is one step away from me burning her car in the parking lot."

He roars with laughter, his head tilted back. "And what if I did bend her over my desk?"

A part of my brain knows he's taunting me, but the impulsive, jealous, and slightly insane side is much, *much* louder. "Then I'd make sure she was in it when I lit the match."

Amusement shines in his gaze, and his wide grin reveals a dimple. "There's something seriously wrong with you."

"You think I'm kidding? I just watched her climb into a black Toyota Sienna. You need me to rattle off the license plate number?"

He dabs tears from the corners of his eyes with his shirtsleeve. "I want nothing to do with Patty, and if you mention this to Aurora and get her going too, I'll never sleep with you again."

"Please." I fold my arms over my chest and relax into the seat. "You love my cock, and you know it."

He chokes out a laugh. "Stop." He shoves my head playfully. "I have to drive. Sit there and don't talk."

38
REECE

"Embers," the nurse calls out, her gaze already on the four of us, along with everyone else in the waiting room.

Jackson flashes a brilliant smile and takes Aurora's hand. He gets about two feet away before he turns to me, eyes narrowed. "Are you coming or what?"

My brows furrow. "Ah... What?"

He comes closer and lowers his voice. "How can you care for her without knowing what she needs?"

I peer beyond the nurse and into the hallway leading to the patient rooms. I'm not fond of hospitals or medical clinics. That antiseptic smell and those glaring, stark white walls evoke some of my worst memories.

Whenever Aurora attended appointments or went to the emergency department, she had the other two, and I found reasons to stay behind. Today was different. I had no choice but to accompany her.

"You don't have to." Her gentle words are sincere, but disappointment lingers in her gaze.

Not wanting her to think I'm disinterested in this aspect

of her life—because that's far from the truth—I set aside my issues and rise from my seat.

I cradle her head and kiss her temple. "It's not about you, angel. I promise."

On our way, I'm not bombarded with the scent of bleach. The air smells faintly of roses, and I breathe a sigh of relief.

This isn't your average doctor's office, which helps. Earthy tones adorn the walls, and large, expansive windows fill the space with sunlight. The design reminds me of the fancy spas Aurora frequents, and for once, I'm thankful for their privilege.

The nurse takes Aurora's vitals while we all eagerly observe. "Girl," she chuckles. "You have quite the fan club." She removes the blood pressure cuff. "I can see how you got pregnant. Jeez."

A nervous giggle escapes Aurora, a blush blooming on her cheeks.

Of course, Jackson has to chime in with a snide remark. "I was here first."

A shit-eating grin spreads across Ethan's face. "Still not your kid."

With her brows raised, the nurse shifts her attention to me and awaits my response. Her expression is free of judgment, and the tension in my shoulders melts.

Coming from a strict conservative upbringing, I never imagined the visit unfolding this way. I expected piercing glares, sneers, whispers, or a cold reception at best—none of which I ever want Aurora to endure. That hasn't been our experience, leading me to accept the plausibility of this foursome.

I shake my head, a subtle smirk curving my lips. "I'm just the bodyguard."

Despite my lighthearted tone and the nurse's amusement, Aurora scowls. "That's not true."

I intertwine our fingers, and shoot her a wink.

The doctor enters and doesn't bat an eye at our band of misfits. "Are we adding another to the birth plan?"

Naturally, it's Ethan who answers. "He'll be with her most often, so yes, just in case anything happens and we're unavailable. Also, is it possible to schedule the delivery?"

He may come across as strictly business and indifferent, but this is how he copes. This is how he shows his devotion—by prioritizing what matters to him, by ensuring Aurora and Jackson are safe and well-cared for.

"It depends on the baby's development and Aurora's health," replies the doctor. "If her blood pressure continues to run high, we might be forced to deliver early. What's your schedule?"

"We're home from February second to the twenty-seventh. March is crazy. We have ten away games."

Jax rakes his fingers through his hair. "When can she and the baby travel?"

He and Ethan share a glance. Good luck to Ethan while on the road. His bestie is going to be an absolute nightmare.

"That also depends. She'll need recovery time based on the difficulty of the delivery. I wouldn't recommend taking a newborn on a commercial flight or to an arena. It's best to avoid crowds or anyone but immediate family for several weeks while the baby builds immunity."

Ethan places a hand on Jackson's shoulder and massages the curve of his neck. "It's an eastern tour. We'll fly privately and stay in New York. We have Reece for that reason."

Jackson's skeptical gaze meets mine, contrasted by Aurora's pleading stare. For a fleeting moment, a surge of irritation wells in my chest. They're using me, manipulating me.

As fast as it comes, it goes, and I realize where that defensiveness stems from—the military. Not being valued, being taken advantage of, being thrust into dangerous situations, witnessing the loss of friends, all for the benefit of billionaire politicians who'll never set foot on a battlefield.

What a ludicrous connection, I chide myself. This is not the same. They rely on me. Aurora depends on me, and if Aurora needs me, I'll unquestionably be there.

* * *

"Coffee?" Aurora asks once we're parked on the street near the bookstore.

I allowed her to sit up front with me for the first time, a decision I quickly regretted. During the short drive, my mind was plagued with thoughts of being in an accident, the airbags deploying, and her getting injured. I glanced at her repeatedly to ensure the seat belt was under her rounded belly properly, not trusting my eyes the last several times.

Because I was focused on her, I almost didn't catch the car ahead abruptly coming to a stop. I slammed on the brakes, and my arm shot out like a steel bar to protect her, reminding me of my mother when I was a boy.

I take a deep breath to ease the knot in my stomach. "Decaf. Your blood pressure is still high."

Before exiting the vehicle, I sweep my gaze over our surroundings, then make my way around the SUV to open her door. It's the day before Thanksgiving, and a fair number of people are strolling the streets of West Hollywood.

She takes my hand, and that familiar jolt of electricity surges through me. I help her down onto the pavement, and with me blocking anyone's view, she discreetly adjusts her oversized, cable-knit sweater dress.

An expanse of toned thigh is visible between the hem and her knee-high suede boots. Ethan raised a brow at her outfit choice when leaving the doctor's office, mumbling about having twins next. I can't blame him there, but she can wear whatever she wants with me. Let some asshole try to touch her.

She tousles her wavy hair, ensuring she's picture-perfect. "I want a mocha latte. Do they make a decaf latte?"

I intertwine our fingers. "I thought you were hungry?"

We walk hand in hand, like any ordinary couple, except I'm her security, dressed in all black—uniform tactical pants, T-shirt, and my worn baseball cap—and she's a hot model.

She nudges her shoulder against my bicep. "I am. I want a pastry."

I lift my brows. "Did you forget about our pizza date?"

"No… I'm just craving a coffee and a muffin." She gives me a pout, knowing full well she'll get her way.

One of these days, I'll refuse her whims—one day.

Instead, I dip my head and say, "You keep pouting, princess, and I'm going to bite that bottom lip."

She freezes, her wide eyes fixed on me, their innocent façade barely concealing a spark of something else.

"Come on." I chuckle and tug her hand. "Let's get you fed before you get cranky."

As we approach the coffee shop, a pedestrian recognizes her and creeps closer, phone poised. Then, a few others take notice, at least one photographer based on the camera.

When we arrive, they block the sidewalk and entrance, snapping pictures. It's only a half dozen people, but a few are yelling, and to Aurora, the noise is jarring.

I put my arm out before her and bark, "Step back!"

An employee swings the door open, and the small crowd stumbles over one another to move aside. We hurry in, and he points to a quiet spot in the corner, far from the windows.

On the way to our seat, I don't miss how he gawks at Aurora's firm, bouncing ass. Don't get me wrong, I'm staring too, but I'm allowed—I think.

Ethan is agreeable, and his word is law in this family—until Jackson throws a fit and suggests I'm taking her for myself. Then, Ethan's heritage reveals itself.

I'm not an idiot. I know she's not leaving either of them, and I'm convinced they'd tear the world apart to find her if she did.

She slides into the booth, and I follow. I give a dismissive nod to the host, my stony gaze locked on his until he turns and walks away.

With an amused smile, she shifts to face me. "What are you doing?"

"He was leering at you."

"No," she says with a giggle. "Why are you sitting with me? You never sit with me."

I push the table toward the other side to have some damn legroom. "I need to have a clear view of the entrance. Do you want to switch? Besides, isn't this a date?"

She cocks her head. "Is it? I'm out of practice. Actually, I've never taken anyone on a date. You're my first. Be gentle." Those tempting lips spread into a devilish grin.

Fuck. How can she arouse me with just her teasing smile?

My voice deepens, and my cock hardens. "I don't think you like gentle, princess."

"How would you know what I like?"

"I know everything about you."

Her gaze falls on my mouth, and a wicked gleam enters her eyes. "That's not true."

My body gravitates toward hers until we're only inches apart. "And what don't I know?"

She edges in closer, the warmth of her breath ghosting over my skin when she whispers, "How I feel."

The air is heavy with unspoken desire. Her seductive scent is intoxicating, and my pulse races, slamming against my rib cage.

I entwine my fingers in her thick hair and breathe her into my lungs. "But I do. I've felt your laughter and tears, your affection and anger, your kindness and pain." I brush my lips over hers. "The rest is an added bonus."

39
AURORA

Reece grazes my lips, avoiding a full kiss. "You're making me soft, you know that?"

Butterflies swoop low in my belly then plummet to an angry death when he withdraws. "Are you gonna kiss me or not, Viking?"

I don't want to initiate something he may not be interested in or uncomfortable with, but I also don't want to be stuck in this uncertain state where we're tiptoeing around each other.

The corner of his mouth curls up in a smug smirk. "I'm working, princess."

I sulk, and as he promised, he takes my bottom lip between his teeth, his bite igniting a shiver down my spine and an inferno in my panties.

He releases me, and I trace my tongue over the indentations he left behind.

I squirm in my seat. "You're evil."

He pacifies me with a quick peck. "You're a distraction I can't afford."

"This is a date," I say, a little too whiny. "Remember?"

I blame my needy behavior on that damn backward hat and those ocean eyes.

I'm also seeing things I hadn't noticed before, since I wouldn't allow myself to look at him for too long. He has a scar on his chin and another under his lip. The tattoo at the base of his throat is a geometric lotus flower surrounded by intricate mandala designs. He has his ears pierced. His hair is growing in darker, with contrasting shades of yellow-blond and rich brown, unlike Jax's sandy blond.

"If I start kissing you, I won't stop." He brushes his thumb over my bottom lip. "Tell your husband to hire more security. Female, preferably."

I snort. "Fine, I'll be good. But our next date is in the pool, half-naked, with my legs wrapped around your waist."

That's unlikely to happen anytime soon, but a girl can dream, right? He did say we could do whatever we wanted at home.

"Fuck." He adjusts his pants. "Now who's evil?"

We break apart at the sound of a quiet "Hello."

While he orders our second breakfast, I place my hand on his upper thigh and draw circles over the firm muscle. Still conversing with the waitress, he shoots me a side-eye and intertwines our fingers, preventing me from taunting him further.

Giving up for now, I rest my head on his shoulder and observe the crowd passing by the window. A lovely patio is in the front, adorned with teal bistro tables and flowerpots filled with pink and white snapdragons. A woman drinks a coffee while reading a book I recognize. A couple walk by, their arms loaded with shopping bags.

It reminds me to ask my husband for a babymoon over the holiday, and while we wait, I daydream of a vacation. I imagine a picturesque white Christmas, one where we'd all be confined to a secluded cabin, a roaring fireplace, and snow falling outside the window. Then, I laugh to myself, knowing Jax would absolutely hate it.

My excitement grows when the waitress delivers my latte with heart-shaped foam. Add the sugar-topped blueberry muffin, and I'm ecstatic.

I beam with appreciation. "Thank you."

She returns my smile, sets down the bill, and walks away. Behind her, a fixed stare holds mine and refuses to break contact. My happiness withers and my pulse races. Where do I know that bald head and weathered face from?

Kyle's party—I'm sure of it. He helped pull Jax off the guy who was hitting on me. He was friendly with Emily. I believe he was a client of hers, though I never saw him after that night.

The memory sours my stomach and spoils my appetite.

I take a sip of my latte, easing the lump in my throat, lick the foam from my lip, and force a grin in Reece's direction. I wrap my arms around his neck. "Do you want to share?" I trail kisses along his defined jawline.

"Aurora," he growls low.

Too bad I have to save that panty-melter for later. "A man is staring at us," I whisper. "He's sitting at the counter."

"I saw—I'm keeping watch."

"I know him from Kyle's party. He dated Emily."

His body stiffens, and I recall Charlie's words about me being threatened. The gravity of the situation sinks in, and a wave of dizziness comes over me. This is more than one of Kyle's associates recognizing me.

Reece removes his dog tags from his shirt, letting them fall to his chest, and adjusts the chain. He cups the back of my head. "You're safe, angel. He can't do shit with me here." The sharp edge to his tone offers little reassurance.

I meet his intense gaze. "What does he want?"

His nostrils flare, and he clenches his jaw to the point where the muscle bulges. "To intimidate you. Pretend you don't see him." His hands cradle my face, and he presses a kiss to my lips. "Eat. I'm going to send a few texts. Everything is okay."

Then why does he have a murderous glint in his eyes?

I eat but taste nothing. Anxiety cramps become intolerable, and I clutch my stomach. Reece slides his phone into his pocket, and with his hand gripping mine, we head to the counter to settle the bill.

The man stands and approaches. Reece's arm comes around my waist, and his massive body moves to shield me.

"Special Agent Crombie." Baldy nods in acknowledgment. "Mrs. O'Reilly," he pauses, his gaze lingering on my body. "Tell your husband I said hello."

40
REECE

"Who told you not to tell me anything?" Aurora's face is pale, her voice wobbly. She's putting the pieces together and is on the verge of a meltdown. "It was Ethan, wasn't it?"

She's not an idiot. She knows Hugo's parting words were a threat. He wants Jax to know he's following his wife and got close enough to talk to her. Couple that with Jax's erratic behavior, and I'm surprised she hasn't had a panic attack, fearing he's in danger.

I give her a pointed glance. "Who else is in charge of this family?"

"Fucking bullshit," she mutters.

We're on our way to the game in Jackson's armored SUV, my partner and another agent following close behind. Not that I'm concerned. It's more of a show of force.

Without support from the LAPD, Hugo is powerless. He would've never made police chief if not for Kyle's corruption, and going after a federal agent would be career suicide.

Hugo is nervous and desperate, driving him to pursue Aurora. We've found nothing that suggests his authority stretches beyond LA. He may have a few politicians in his back pocket, but none who'll impede Homeland Security.

In situations like these, walking the line sucks ass, but now is not the time to go rogue. I need my team behind me to protect Aurora—and Jax—and eliminate men like Hugo.

Besides, I've got Ethan for the shady shit.

I take her hand and kiss her knuckles. Again, I should've seated her in the back, but I worried the isolation would upset her further.

"Angel, it's okay—"

She cuts me off with a scathing glare. "No! It's not okay!" She yanks her hand from mine. "Do you know how stupid I feel? I'm living in a dream world, being spoiled, thinking we're safe to go on dates while you're placating me, distracting me like a child."

Her voice breaks, and I pull into the first parking spot I find. I throw the vehicle into park and unbuckle my seat belt. Charlie drives by, likely to circle the block until I'm ready.

I cup her face and draw her angry gaze to mine. "You've been worked up lately. We're reducing your sugar intake."

She attempts to twist away. "Don't. Just take me home."

I caress her jawline with my thumb. "We're not going home. It's safer to attend the game. While we're there, Charlie will watch the house."

Her hands grip my wrists, her breathing slows, and she leans into my touch. "Jax won't like that."

"He'll get over it. Your security is more important than his paranoia."

"It's not paranoia if it's real. You should've told me it was this serious." Tears well in her eyes, catching the rays of the setting sun and turning her irises a golden amber. "I feel awful. This is a repeat of Kyle, and you're all dealing with it while I'm making plans to sip lattes, buy books, and go on vacations. I could've stayed home. You don't have to babysit me."

I kiss her forehead, then her nose. "Wherever you are, I'll be. If it's home or the bookstore, LA or New York, it doesn't matter. I've been with you since day one. I've chased down your husband's private jet and tracked your boyfriend's team to a hotel in Long Island—to find *you*." I press my lips to hers, but only for a moment. Otherwise, we might never leave. "It's okay to be happy, even when things are falling apart. We *want* you blissfully unaware."

Her lip quivers, and her eyes search mine. "This guy is using me to threaten Jax, right?"

I nod. Her tears spill over, and I brush them away.

"What does he want?"

"For Jax to remain silent."

"Is he?"

"No."

"Then we stay home."

"Okay."

We stare at each other, music playing low in the background.

"Special Agent Crombie, huh?"

I can't resist kissing her again, loving the sound of my name coming from her lips.

"It's short for Abercrombie, but don't tell your husband. He'll never let it go."

Her fingers loosen from my wrists and intertwine with mine. She rests against the seat and furrows her brows. "This relationship will hurt you far more than me."

"Someone once told me a story about an agent who married a Mafia don's daughter. I'll be fine."

She rolls her eyes. "I'm not a daughter of the Mafia."

"Nope, just a girlfriend."

With a slight smile, she shakes her head. "That's not true."

"Okay," I draw out, my tone heavy with sarcasm. "Have you heard Ethan threaten me? It's as if the Devil himself is growling from the depths of Hell." I feign a shudder. "Fucking frightening."

Finally, she laughs. "Believe me, he's given me worse."

I arch a brow. "There's a worse offense than messing with Jax?"

"Yeah." A mischievous grin spreads across her lips. "Messing around with you."

41
ETHAN

Outside Jackson's luxury suite, fans fill the arena, taking their seats, while hype music blares from the speakers.

"You don't need to baby me." Aurora stands between my open legs, her hands on her hips and her jaw set. She's poised for an argument, but I'm too damn happy to see her. It's not often I get time alone with her.

She changed into a jersey dress and matching blue Converse, her hair in a high ponytail and her lips painted an alluring matte red. She'd be more convincing if she didn't look precisely like something I wanted to baby and spoil—then give a hand necklace to while I fucked her six ways to Sunday.

My dick perks up at the fantasy. I may have a sex hangover from the fuck-fest we had in the shower. Is that a thing? Because I'm incapable of being in a shitty mood.

An indecent smile spreads across my lips. I wrap my arms around her and guide her onto my lap. "Are you being stubborn today? Did you forget our deal?" I place my hand on her rounded stomach. "I absolutely will baby you. That's my job." I kiss her forehead.

She runs her fingers up the back of my neck and into my hair. "Then don't either of you gripe about me being spoiled and blame it on Jackson."

Hugging her closer, I breathe in her sweet scent. "Oh yeah? Has Reece been spoiling you?"

He texted me on the way and asked if I'd meet him in Jackson's suite—without Jackson. He gave me a quick synopsis of what had happened with Hugo then left to talk with his partner while I stayed with Aurora.

To be honest, I expected this. Maybe not today, and I half expected it'd be Jax getting arrested without Kyle alive to protect him, but I've been preparing for the inevitable.

I had only hoped Hugo wasn't stupid enough to go after Aurora directly. He did, and she's unharmed and still her sassy self. I'm grateful.

Don't get me wrong, I'm still fucking pissed and have every intention of dealing with the bastard.

"Reece agreed to take me to the bookstore when it was risky and only complained I was distracting him. He's rather spoiling or placating me."

I cock a brow. "*Were* you distracting him?"

A flicker of uncertainty crosses her face as her eyes search mine. "He wouldn't let me."

This is why we have Reece—this is why he's with her. He'd sacrifice himself, his pleasure, and any chance of a relationship to keep her safe and happy. I saw it when he let Jax beat the shit out of him, knowing if he fought back, Aurora would despise him. Recently, when he said he was leaving, it was to prevent Jax from being triggered because it was better for *her*. And tonight, he called in reinforcements despite the likelihood of questions.

At my silence, her frown deepens, and her head dips.

With two fingers under her chin, I raise her gaze to mine. "What's wrong?"

"I'm waiting for you to choke me for being too friendly with Reece."

"I thought I was clear on this. We need Reece as a family. I gave you permission. Why would I be mad?"

She hesitates. "What if he leaves?"

"Is he taking you with him? 'Cause then I'd be mad." I hold her stare. "Is there something you're not telling me?"

She shakes her head. "No, of course not."

"Without you, he won't leave, and I guarantee he told you as much, or you wouldn't be *distracting* him."

Her fingers play with my hair anxiously. "And Jax?"

"I'll handle him." I grab her cheeks and plant a kiss on her lips, adding a playful bite. "No one is mad at you or placating you."

She releases a soft sigh. "What's going to happen?"

"Don't worry about it, remember?" I move my hand to her throat and caress the delicate curve of her neck. "I'll take care of it. Your job is to care for yourself and my baby."

She melts into my touch, her eyes heavy-lidded. "Reece thinks we need additional security."

"*Reece* needs to stop telling you things. I'm already on it. Are you afraid...of Hugo?"

Her pulse races against my palm. "Jax is afraid. This is why he's been moody and not sleeping, right? If he's afraid, it must be bad."

Jax lives in fear, and I don't know how he does it. Some of his fears are unresolved from childhood. He sees them as monsters, but they're just men. They can fall like the rest of us.

"I promise I won't let anything happen to you or Jax."

She lays her head on my shoulder, getting comfortable on my chest.

"There's a lot I don't understand," she says through a yawn. "I'm certain Hugo was a client of Emily's. I saw them together at Kyle's party. She talked about him. If everything is true, why would she date him? She hated Jax because of Kyle. She must've known."

My sweet, sweet girl.

"Baby." I brush my fingers over her cheek. "Did you ever wonder if Emily disliked Jax because he showed her no interest?"

Maybe a part of Emily didn't want Aurora involved with Kyle, but I doubt it. All I've seen from her is jealousy.

"I don't know," she mumbles, the softness in her voice suggesting sadness more than confusion. That, and she's exhausted.

"What do you need, love?"

"Pizza. I promised Reece pizza, and then I had a panic attack. I ruined it."

"No, you didn't. You did well. I'm proud of you. I'll get Reece a pizza."

She faces me, brows raised. "You're in an oddly cheerful mood, Blackwood."

My head tips back in laughter. "You're healthy. My baby is healthy. Our family is safe, and I fucked the most amazing woman last night."

She smiles. "Oh, really? That good, huh?"

"Fucking fantastic." I brush her hair aside to kiss her throat.

The door opens, and I brace myself for an irate Jax, who's supposed to be with Doc. Instead, it's Reece.

His gaze immediately finds Aurora, sweeping over her as he flips his hat backward. I wonder if he does that for her.

"What's the plan?" I check my watch. "I only have a few minutes."

He drops into a chair. "Charlie and another agent are headed to the house—"

Just as Reece is about to speak further, Jax bursts into the room.

He's not even in uniform, only basketball shorts, a T-shirt, socks, and sneakers. His hair is damp from either the shower or sweat, and his chest rises and falls rapidly. His face is twisted with anger.

Until he lays eyes on Aurora.

Then, his expression softens, and his shoulders slump in relief. His palm goes to his heart, and he doubles over, gripping the back of a chair for support.

"Oh my God," he pants as if he sprinted here from the locker room, which wouldn't surprise me at all. "Holy fuck." He blows out a heavy breath. "I thought you were with Patty."

No, he fucking didn't.

Aurora's penetrating gaze connects with mine, her body rigid in my embrace.

I shake my head, but before I can explain, he continues to run his damned mouth.

"She's nowhere to be found either, by the way." He thrusts a hand in the air and huffs. "I may have accidentally broken into her office looking for you."

Aurora climbs off my lap and backs away from me. Her lips are parted, eyes wide.

Heat sears my face and ears. "Don't listen to him. It's not what you think. Patty is a woman from PR—"

"Who wants his dick," Jax finishes, putting considerable emphasis on *dick*.

I jolt to my feet. "No, she doesn't! Shut your fucking mouth for once."

He rolls his eyes and crosses his arms over his chest. "Please. I heard her *giggling*"—he draws out the word, as if it means something far more sinister—"in your office. She's practically begging for it."

That's what this is about? I couldn't wait to get rid of Patty. Reece's text was a godsend. I left right after.

Aurora sucks in a sharp breath and rubs her sternum with her fist.

Forget Hugo. I'm going to murder Jax.

With my hand out, I step toward her, and she steps toward Reece. He smirks and draws her to him.

I drop my arm to my side. "She was showing me pictures from earlier today—of the players holding puppies. She drives a fucking minivan! She probably has kids and a husband."

Maybe she's recently divorced. Maybe she knows I'm divorced. Maybe she's aware of my history—that is her job, after all—but I have no idea why Patty is suddenly interested in me.

"How do you know what she drives?" Aurora's gentle voice is elevated. She's working herself into a panic.

I point a finger in Jackson's direction. "*He* told me!"

"Only because I planned to light it on fire if she continued to flirt with you!"

Reece has the audacity to snicker while Aurora appears horrified.

I glare at Jax and growl, "Why are you like this?" through clenched teeth, attempting to gain some composure. "Please tell me you didn't set her van on fire."

His lip curls and his brows lower in incredulity. "I wouldn't set her van on fire during a game. I'm not an idiot."

"You could've fooled me," I shoot back.

A thought comes out of nowhere. *Is this what he was like with Aurora? When they first started dating?* But I toss it aside—that'd be ridiculous and crazy for him to turn that intensity on me.

And obsessive.

Right up his alley.

"Is she cute, Jax?" Aurora asks, her tone stronger but still apprehensive.

"No. She's not," I cut in. "It doesn't matter. *Nothing* is happening—except for your husband skating laps until his legs break. Or I break them. One or the other."

He shrugs off my threat. "Anyhow. Why are you all meeting without me?" He flops into the chair across from Reece as if he didn't barge in here and provoke Aurora's insecurities.

"No. We're not brushing this aside." With every word I speak, my irritation grows—and here I thought nothing could kill my post-sex vibe. I gesture to Aurora, whose face is tight with worry. "You deliberately upset her to retaliate against me for something that exists solely in your imagination."

He clenches his jaw. His demeanor shifts, becoming rigid and indifferent, but I know him. He's anything but indifferent.

"Whatever. Just tell me what the fuck is going on."

I don't miss the flicker of hurt in his eyes. It stabs at my chest, but I can't allow him to keep using her as his outlet for anger.

Sometimes, I think he acts absurd to lighten the mood or take the heat off others by directing it at himself. Most of the time, his antics are entertaining, but Aurora doesn't find the threat of other women funny.

Unlike with him, she hasn't got my ring on her finger as security. All she can rely on is my word.

And whose fault is that?

With that thought, I drop into my seat and rake my fingers through my hair. I release a heavy sigh and lift my head to meet his gaze. "What did I tell you? If you have a problem, come to me. I'm not stepping out on this family. Ever. I was with Aurora because something happened, and instead of focusing on that, we're focusing on *you*."

"Do I even matter? From the looks of it, you had no intention of including me."

Reece straightens in his seat and adjusts Aurora on his lap. "That's my fault. I asked him to come without you. I didn't want to ruin your game."

He isn't as touchy-feely toward her as Jax and I are, perhaps because we're in the room. She simply sits on his thigh, his hands resting on the arms of the chair.

Seeing her with him doesn't bother me. I don't feel jealous or possessive, but I also don't have that warmth in my chest as I do when she's with Jax.

The announcer comes over the speaker, and I glance at my watch. Fifteen minutes until warm-ups. "Fuck, we have to go. You need to get changed. Did you see Doc?"

My captain gets to his feet. "Yeah, I was leaving his office when I saw you walk out the door…" *With Patty.*

I grab my suit jacket from the back of the couch. "I was coming here. I got a text from Reece."

As I slip it on, he juts his chin at Aurora. Without a word, she comes to him and wraps her arms around his waist.

He cups her face and stares down at her. "What happened?"

She peers over at me, and he redirects her attention.

"Look at me. I'm not leaving until you tell me."

Lips parted, she searches his eyes. "Later, I promise."

His breathing picks up, his chest heaving. This is precisely what I was hoping to prevent.

"Aurora," he snarls, his tone laced with warning. "You hiding shit from me is only making it worse."

Reece rises, fists clenched and muscles bulging. Fucking great. The last thing I need is these two trading blows before Jackson's first home game after his suspension.

I step forward then hesitate, deciding it might not be best to touch him right now. "Can you please take the crazy down a notch? Fuck. We care about you. We're only trying to help." I glance at Reece. "Explain. Quickly."

He maintains his scowl until Jax's grip on Aurora relaxes.

"Hugo followed us to a café in West Hollywood. He didn't do anything. He didn't say much. His intention was to make his presence known and expose me as an agent. My team is reviewing nearby surveillance and traffic cams to pinpoint where his tail began. Charlie is watching the house."

Jackson's focus never wavers from Aurora. He blinks repeatedly, and his Adam's apple bobs. "I'm sorry," he exhales.

She grasps his wrists. "It's okay. I'm fine. Really. I'm only worried about you."

"I had this gut-punch feeling in the locker room. I should've known it was about you and not fucking Patty." He rests his forehead against hers. "I'll take care of it," he says, his voice strained. "What did he say?"

"He called me Mrs. O'Reilly and told me to tell you hello. It rattled me. That's all."

Rising to his full height, he takes a deep breath, his nostrils flaring. "I'll handle it," he repeats with conviction.

"*We'll* handle it," I interrupt, not wanting him to do

something impulsive. "In the meantime, she stays with one of us."

Eerily calm, he nods in agreement and draws Aurora into his arms. "I cleared this suite. Nobody but the caterer should enter." He lifts his chin at Reece. "Thanks for being with her. What did he say to you?"

"He addressed me by my full title and name to prove he knew who I was, something I already considered, based on Kyle's texts. He wanted to taunt us, to send the message he could reach Aurora. He can't. She's safe with me."

"Okay," Jax says before kissing Aurora goodbye. "Don't go anywhere alone."

And that's it. Even in the elevator, he remains oddly mellow, his gaze fixed straight ahead, a faint smile playing on his lips.

With only a few minutes together, I break the awkward silence. "You know I would never touch Patty, right?"

He doesn't so much as glance at me. "You know being overly nice and pretending to be single hurts those who love you, right?"

The doors open, and he exits, leaving me baffled.

I stride after him into the long corridor to the locker room. "I'm not pretending to be single."

He faces me, still wearing that stiff grin. "Really? So it wouldn't feel wrong if it was Aurora sitting outside your office watching your behavior and listening to Patty giggle?"

It would. It *did*. I just didn't know how to respond.

I say nothing, and he continues. "It's you hurting her, not me. What you blamed me for is exactly how she'd react if she saw you. I might be crazy, but at least no one questions my loyalty."

My chest aches, but he's not done driving the knife through my heart.

"What are you going to do? On game days, when your son is here, are you going to ignore him? Pretend he's not there? He'll know you're his dad. He'll be watching you and wanting your attention. How does that not excite you? How are you not dreaming of the day you get to show him off?"

* * *

The walk to the car is quiet, only the sound of our footsteps in the empty parking garage. Jax is still pissed at me. He didn't speak to me the entire night, communicating in grunts and nods.

Reece and Aurora left an hour ago. Jax had a hell of a game, coming close to another hat trick. He ended with two goals and three assists, busting his ass until the very end to secure an overtime win.

The arena was packed and loud with excitement. Robert, the owner, was in attendance and also fired up.

"We have a real chance at the playoffs this year," he said, sitting in my office while Jax took an ice bath in the training room. "Well done."

It didn't feel deserving, and I only mumbled, "Thanks."

"Are you still babysitting him?"

"He doesn't need a babysitter. If you're asking if we're staying together, yes."

He crossed and uncrossed his legs. "Good. It's obviously working. Keeps him out of trouble."

"His father is dead, and he's married to the woman he loves. That keeps him from *relapsing*."

Robert failed to notice my correction. "And she's pregnant, I hear. That's perfect."

A spark ignited within me. That was my chance to disclose our relationship and the baby.

I tapped my pen against the desk. "Robert, there's a reason Jax and I are so close."

"I know." He dismissed me with a wave of his hand. "You don't have to tell me. Actually, I'd prefer you didn't. Not that I'm biased. My grandson is gay, but I'd rather have plausible deniability. Get me?"

Heat radiated from my face, and I knew my skin was bright red. "We're not..." I trailed off. Maybe if I let him believe it, he'd spread the word, and it'd stop Patty from interfering. "It's more complicated than that. His wife is carrying my child. The three of us are together."

His brows nearly hit his hairline, and he blinked several times. "That does complicate things. I'll have to discuss this with legal and PR." He stood and smoothed the front of his dress pants. "You could publicly be the child's godfather or uncle."

I shook my head adamantly. "I won't hide this."

He released a heavy sigh and headed for the door. "We'll work it out. This is the best I've seen the team in over a decade. Give me a few days."

The beep of the car unlocking echoes against the cement walls. Jax and I open our doors simultaneously and settle into our seats. He gazes out the passenger window, and I stare at his profile.

I set the key fob in the cup holder but don't start the ignition. "I fucked up. I'm sorry." I grip the bottom of the steering wheel, the leather squeaking as I rotate my fists. "I didn't know how to respond to Patty. If it was one of you, I would've pushed you aside and told you to get your ass off my desk. I actually hoped you'd come in and do it for me. I figured any minute, you'd barge in and interrupt."

"I should have." He continues to face away from me. "But then, I'd be called crazy for doing so."

"I like you crazy," I blurt.

He side-eyes me, his lips pursed in disbelief.

"It's true. You feel things deeper than I do. You're always one step ahead. I'm emotionally broken."

He scowls, and his mouth twists into a frown. "No, you're not."

"I am. I learned to shut off my feelings a long time ago. You and Aurora are the exception. But you're right. I won't be able to ignore my son, and I don't want to. I'd be miserable."

I reach out, intending to weave my fingers through his hair, but he pulls away. Hurt and irritation hit my stomach in waves, and I clench my jaw.

"Seriously? You're that mad at me?"

He shifts his entire body toward the window. "Let's just go home. I don't wanna say some stupid shit right now."

"Like what?"

He doesn't answer.

I jab the start button, and the car comes to life. I hate being ignored. My mood plummets and I grind my molars.

We leave the arena, and he reclines into the seat and closes his eyes. He's exhausted, and why wouldn't he be? The world is on his shoulders, his demons coming back to haunt him, and he still gave me one hundred percent on the ice tonight.

It's hard to take my eyes off him. He's honestly as beautiful as everyone teases him for being. Pure perfection in male form. Softer than me in appearance and emotion, yet so damn strong.

There's no explanation for our relationship or my draw to him. I've been protective of him since the day Kyle waltzed into my locker room and Jax was outwardly uncomfortable. It's more than that, though. I want him in a way that's unfathomable.

I turn my attention back to the road and let my thoughts wander.

I'm not possessive or protective of Reece. I feel nothing toward him. I'm grateful he protects the two people I love, but I think of him as a business partner with aligning goals and priorities. If something were to happen to him, my only concern would be Aurora's attachment.

My world would be forever altered if anything happened to Jax or Aurora. I doubt I'd want to wake in the morning. Even hockey pales in comparison to how complete I feel with them.

My mouth opens, and words tumble out. "I don't have any tattoos. I think I'm afraid of needles."

His eyes pop open, but I don't acknowledge him. I focus on the highway ahead. "Not needles themselves, but the fear of becoming addicted to them. That sounds silly when I say it out loud, but my mom was an IV drug user."

"No, it doesn't." He shakes his head. "You don't have to—we don't have to get tattoos."

"I know. I would for you, though." I glance at him, allowing him to see the truth in my eyes. "In Montreal, when Aurora was sick, the team wasn't the reason I was aggravated." My heart pounds furiously against my sternum as I recall the day. "That smell. The acidic, putrid smell of vomit has to be my worst memory." I can smell it now just thinking about it. "I was five the first time I remember finding her, my mom, lying in her own vomit. There were mornings I thought she was dead."

Sometimes, I wished she were.

She didn't want to live, not without my father.

My throat constricts at the memories of me screaming

and trying to wake her, and I can't go on. I squeeze the steering wheel until his hand takes mine, and he intertwines our fingers, bringing them to his lap.

"For days after Montreal, I felt horrible. I avoided spending the night together, hating my inability to care for Aurora when she needed me, or you when you relapsed." I should have been there for him.

"I'll take care of her," he says with assurance. "You don't have to."

"I know you will." I shoot him a soft smile. "My point is, long before her heart eventually gave out, I went numb. I used hockey as my escape. I blamed her love for my father, which she never had for me, for ruining her. I never wanted that kind of love or heartbreak." Knowing what I do now, I was probably an unwanted reminder of him. Regardless, I have no example of how to love, none whatsoever. "I don't know what the fuck I'm doing, Jax. All I know is that I can't live without you. So please stop being a little brat and tell me what's wrong so I can fix it."

He releases my hand and rakes his fingers through his hair. "If you're going to pretend there's nothing between us, I want to be traded to another team."

I swerve into the other lane before I catch myself. "No."

"I'm not sitting outside your office listening to someone else flirt with you. Just fucking trade me."

"I'm not trading you."

"Then I'll ask Robert."

"Robert is not trading you!" My voice is nearly a growl. "It'd be a terrible business decision. Besides, I told him we're together."

Jax flounders but quickly recovers. "Good. Then he has reason to trade me."

I scoff. "That will never happen. *I* will never let that happen."

He throws off his seat belt and faces me fully. "Why? You were fine coaching without me last night."

"No. Robert is going to tell Patty—"

"I want *you* to tell Patty. I want *you* to acknowledge you're in a relationship." His jaw tics. "I'm starting to think Reece was right. It'd be nothing for you to put a ring on your finger. If you wanted to, you would."

"Really?" I raise my brows and cock my head to the side. "Is that how you're playing this? If you wanted me to wear one, why didn't you offer?"

"Yes, blame me for your lack of self-control—again."

"Self-control? You're the one who broke into Patty's office because you thought we were fucking."

"Hey." He shrugs. "It's just sex, right? Patty. Aurora. Me. What's the difference?"

"Seriously?" I say with an incredulous chuckle. "You're such a fucking brat. Don't worry. By tomorrow, everyone will think we're sleeping together."

"We *are* sleeping together. Or we were until you started screwing around."

"Oh my fucking God!" I can't help but laugh at his ridiculousness. "I'm gonna get your name tattooed on my dick so you'll shut the fuck up."

"You might wanna go with Aurora. Fewer letters. I doubt mine will fit."

Steering with one hand, I grab his nape and tug him to me. "Why don't you open your mouth and gag on it? Tell me how it fits."

He lays his head in the crook of my neck and adjusts his pants. "Jesus, don't make me hard while I'm mad at you."

I tangle my fingers in his perfectly messy hair. "You're

insatiable, you know that? You have no reason to be mad at me."

He makes a whiny noise that's part disagreement and part pout.

"It doesn't matter who flirts with me. I'm not going anywhere. It means nothing."

"It does to me. It does to Aurora."

"Okay. It won't happen again." I brush my lips over his stupidly soft hair. "Now, please, put your seat belt back on."

42
AURORA

"Gram, should you be without your walker?" I glance back into her apartment at the folded piece of equipment leaning against the wall.

She shuffles a little closer to Reece—if that's even possible—and squeezes his bulging bicep. "And let go of this hulking specimen? I believe not."

He peers down at her, his blue eyes glinting with amusement. "I can see where your granddaughter inherited her flirtatiousness from."

"And her good looks. Don't ya think?" She gives a cheeky wink.

He tips his head back in laughter. Gram can't be five feet tall, and he's well over six. Their height difference only adds to the comedy she's providing.

"Wait until Maryanne sees you," she rambles on while I grab her coat. "She's been bragging nonstop about her granddaughter being an influencer on Instant."

"Instagram," I correct. Since her stroke, she tends to confuse words. I lock her door and drop the key into the day bag the nurses packed for her.

"Insta. Instant. Same thing." She dismisses me with a flick of her wrist. "Anyhow, apparently, she's made *millions* on Only Face. Millions? Bullshit," she answers her own question. "No one is prettier than my princess."

"I agree," Reece says, his voice deep and enticing. He's never been hotter than in this moment, smirking at my grandmother while she eats him right up.

The prospect of bringing her new beau through the parlor has her moving along faster. At this rate, we might make it home in time for Thanksgiving dinner.

We enter the 'Bar and Lounge,' reminiscent of a brightly lit 1920s speakeasy, and she waves as if she's the Queen of England. A woman with fluffy, stark white hair rolls her eyes and purses her lips. That has to be Maryanne. Beside her is an elderly man with a scowl that rivals Ethan's, who's glaring hard at Reece.

Gram stands taller and adds a little pep to her step. "You must come to the Valentine's Day dance," she says for all to hear, patting Reece's forearm. "It's *Great Gatsby* themed."

She's not looking at Reece. Her gaze is fixated on Maryanne and the mystery man. It appears Gram is suspicious of more than Maryanne's granddaughter earning millions on Only Fans.

"Sure thing, darlin'," he drawls and covers her hand with his.

"Oh, wow." I scan my card to exit. "Pulling out the Southern charm for my grandmother. I see how it is."

They head toward Ethan's SUV parked at the curb, and she glances over her shoulder with a teasing smile.

"Aurora Belle Embers, don't be selfish. You have plenty of men to share."

Reece snorts and opens the door for her. He holds her elbow to assist her until she's settled. "Wait until Ethan meets you. He thought his hands were full with Aurora and Jackson. He ain't seen nothing yet."

"Which one is he?" she asks with feigned innocence. "The daddy?"

I roll my eyes. She knows damn well who he is.

Reece matches her mischievous grin. "Exactly."

The journey home passes swiftly. Throughout the ride, she rubs my belly, holds my hand, and beams with such joy, it fills me with a sense of guilt for not devoting more time to her. Hopefully, life will calm down, and she can visit more frequently.

It helps that Reece is a medic and understands the nurse's instructions, even though Gram ignored them. She seemed as irritated as I was by the nurse shamelessly ogling him, and of course, she put up a stink. Who cares about emergency heart meds when you have a tattooed Viking to keep your pulse pumping?

"Your manicure is gorgeous." She lays her hand on top of mine for comparison. "They can't do that acrylic stuff, but I got the gel nails."

Like my own, her nails are painted teal blue, the same color as the hockey team. I don't remember her getting manicures before, and now that I'm noticing, she's wearing a Huskies shirt under her cardigan and matching sneakers. Her hair is perfectly styled in a sleek bob, and her skin is glowing.

With a pointed stare, I arch a brow. "It looks like *someone* has been sending you gifts."

She raises her nose in the air. "The LA Huskies sent me a PR package," she boasts. "And a spa gift certificate."

I grin so hard, my cheeks hurt. "I bet they did."

"Yup. I even watched the game last night in my apartment with Steward." She waggles her brows suggestively. "Your boys did well."

"Yes, they did." I nod. "Were you not able to watch before?"

"I have cable and Nextflix now." She flutters her eyelashes. "As a member of the PR team, I can't go without seeing the games...with all my friends...and snacks."

My eyes connect with Reece's in the rearview mirror. He shakes his head and chuckles, "Poor Ethan."

After the oohs and ahhs over everything from the 'fancy pants gate'—her words—and the 'truly delightful courtyard,' we're finally walking through the door. Turkey, spices, loud voices, and a packed dining table greet us upon entering.

Gram freezes, and her grip tightens on my arm. "Holy shit on a cracker, there's more of them." Her wide eyes, full of awe, find mine. "You have one for every day of the week."

The room erupts with laughter, and my face burns hot enough to fry an egg. "Gram! They don't all belong to me."

Two of them are a complete surprise. I had no idea Desi and Dante were spending the holiday with us. Grant and Charlie were invited, but I wasn't sure they'd be here.

"It's like I always say," Gram pauses for dramatic effect, "we don't slut shame in this household."

My eyes prickle with tears, and I can't help but join the hilarity. "You've literally never said that. Ever. In your life."

* * *

"Wait." My brows rise as I take in the sight before me. "The five of you are going out? Together? That's...dangerous." *And suspicious.*

Reece and I returned home from dropping off Gram to

find Jax, Ethan, Grant, and the twins in the entryway, dressed in jeans and button-ups, reeking of expensive cologne.

"We're introducing the twins to LA," Grant answers a little too quickly.

Jax bends down and pecks my lips. "It's a recon mission. G-man is stalking a girl, and on our way back, I'm grabbing my bike from Kyle's garage."

That gives me pause, and I glance at Ethan.

He lets out an exasperated sigh. "I'll keep him out of trouble."

"You're not meeting Patty, are you?" I tease.

It's Jax who responds. "If PR Patty shows up, I'm cutting her brakes. Fucking stalker."

"Aren't you going to stalk some girl?" I point out.

"I'm not. G is." He smirks. "Rejection has left him devastated."

Grant ignores that snide remark, widens his eyes, and sucks in an audible breath. "I *thought* Patty was getting fresh with Coach. I'm glad I'm not the only one who noticed."

Jax huffs and yanks on his boots with attitude while I stare at Ethan, arms crossed over my chest. He'll never live this down.

The broody man shakes his head and twirls the car keys around his finger. "Don't start. It's absolutely nothing. The idea is ludicrous."

Desi scoffs. "You have a model girlfriend *and* a pro-athlete boyfriend. Whoever she is, she doesn't stand a chance." He shoots me a smile full of dimples and winks.

I peer up at Reece beside me. "You're not going?"

"Someone has to stay with you."

Well, now I feel bad. "You can go. I'll be fine."

He tugs my ponytail. "I'm teasing. I have work to do with Charlie."

As the others pile out the door, Ethan hangs back to give me a lingering kiss. "Read a book. Take a relaxing bath. I got him."

"I know you do." I return his kiss. "Thank you."

Instead of reading, I put on a bikini, grab a towel, and head out to the heated pool for a moonlight swim. I float on my back and gaze up at the stars while the ocean waves crash against the shore and the wind rustles the palm trees.

I'll never forget this night. It was a dream to have my grandmother over and see her so animated. She was the life of the party and loved every minute.

During a lull in conversation, she announced Ethan reminded her of her late husband, my grandfather. Jackson nearly collapsed to the floor with laughter, choking and breathless.

"Aurora stayed home with me," she began. "I worked as a seamstress, and I'd entertain her by teaching her how to sew scraps. She'd help me prepare dinner, but as soon as she heard the rumble of her grandfather's truck, she'd abandon everything and run for the door."

Pain lanced through my heart at the memories, and I set my head on her shoulder.

"She'd jump and twirl to show off the newest outfit we'd crafted," Gram continued. "Then, she'd unlace his work boots, and he'd slip them off. He'd pull her into his arms, and that's where she'd be until bedtime."

"Not much has changed," Reece muttered with a fond smile.

"You can blame my Leon." She patted my cheek. "He was my second husband and had no children. He spoiled Aurora like his own."

He was more of a father than my biological father ever thought of being.

I may have shed a few tears when we brought her back to the nursing home.

"You okay?" Reece's deep voice interrupts my thoughts.

I swim to the side of the pool, where the big guy is frowning down at me. "Yeah, I'm good. All finished?"

"Hardly." Flickering blue-green light reflecting off the water dances across his face.

"Boo." I rest on the pool's ledge with my arms folded and kick my feet. "I was hoping you'd join me."

He crouches, a smirk tugging at his lips. "Were you now?"

I reach for a kiss, and he leans in. Our mouths meet, and I grip his shirt. The fabric bunches in my fist, and with a forceful yank, he loses his balance and topples over with a low growl of my name.

My giggle mingles with the loud splash of his body hitting the water. He breaks the surface and pushes his wet hair away from his face. His black T-shirt clings to the well-defined muscles of his shoulders, chest, and abs, and I bite my lip. Fuck, that's hot.

His eyes, bright with shock and a twinge of mischief, lock with mine. "You little devil. I could've landed on you or kicked you. You're lucky I don't have my phone on me."

I hadn't considered electronic devices. "Oops. I had to do something drastic, or you'd never get into this pool with me."

He creeps closer, and I move away.

"You're being very naughty." He lunges, seizing me by the hips, and pulls me to him.

I don't resist at all. I wrap myself around him and weave my fingers into his hair. "I can be naughtier if you'd like."

Rough palms glide over my ass, and a shiver runs down my spine. My skin erupts with goosebumps. His scorching touch fuels my desire, and my nipples harden.

I slip beneath his shirt and trace the indentations of his muscles.

His lips part, his brows lower, and his pupils dilate. "Charlie is staying tonight."

He flexes his hips. His thick erection presses against my center and drags a whimper from my throat. I'm still a little sore from the other night, but it's a delicious soreness, the kind that only arouses me further.

"Kick him out." I'm kidding. Sort of.

He groans, low and husky. "I wish, princess. We're working on something big."

"I know something big I'd like to work on." I writhe my hips and grind against his hard length to drive my point home.

"Fuck." His fingertips dig into my thighs. "What'd I tell you about teasing?"

I ghost my thumb over his pierced nipple, running my finger along the tiny bar. "What if I'm not teasing?"

He glances at my lips, and without hesitation, our mouths come together in a desperate tangle of tongues and low moans, hands exploring each other for the first time.

Breathless, he breaks the kiss far too soon. "If I fuck you, I'll never leave. It's already hard enough to concentrate on this case."

43
REECE

"Who said anything about fucking? Jeez, cocky much?"

Aurora's tone is teasing, but I don't miss the vulnerability reflected in her eyes. Her soft body feels tense, her hands no longer driving me wild with their touch.

I mean this in the nicest way possible: she's been with the wrong guys. Maybe not wrong per se, but certainly not romantic. Jackson and Ethan are straightforward and open with PDA and sex. She's affectionate, playful, flirtatious, and used to enticing men with her body. To her, my holding back is another rejection.

It's not that I don't want her. Believe me, I do. Badly. Just...not like this. I want her to know she's worth more to me, far more than sex.

Her legs loosen from my waist, and she grips my shoulders, readying to put distance between us, but I refuse to release her.

I support her weight with my forearm and intertwine my fingers in her hair. "I'd prefer our first time not to be in this pool."

She opens her mouth to argue, likely to tell me that wasn't her intention, but I continue.

"Or outside the pool, in secret, in a rush, or where others can watch or hear. I want you to myself, in my bed, for far longer than a few hours."

We're almost there. We're nearly at the point where being together isn't so forbidden.

Her eyes turn glassy. "I wasn't—I'm sorry."

I kiss her forehead and then her nose, then her lips. "There's no hurry, angel. I'm not going anywhere."

She lowers her head. "You should be able to love freely. I'm sorry I pushed you."

I tilt her chin and lift her gaze to mine. "I want you—all of you, not only your body. Sex does not equate to love. You give me a sense of purpose unlike anything else. It doesn't matter if we ever get married, have kids, or have sex, although I fucking hope we do. I'm with you, and that's more than enough. I'm not rushing this."

She puts on a soft smile. "You're too good, Reece—What's your middle name?" she whispers.

"James." I chuckle.

"You're too good, Reece James Abercrombie."

"You're too cute." I peck her lips. "I'm just trying to do this right and not hurt you in the process."

Hello, Jackson, who's likely watching.

It's his reaction I worry about most. If Aurora and I cross that line, he's not keeping her from me.

She releases a heavy sigh. "You said you're leaving?"

"I need to finish this case...and a few other things."

Her fingers thread through my damp hair. "Like what?"

I scrunch my nose. "My sister is getting married."

Truthfully, I'm not excited about attending the wedding

and hope work interferes. I'd invite Aurora as my plus-one, but I doubt that'll go over well with Jackson and Ethan.

A flurry of emotions flashes across her face, giving way to curiosity. Her brows knit together, and she cocks her head. "You have a sister?"

I haven't been in the right headspace to discuss my family with her, not without being negative, and I don't want her to think my parents are terrible. They're not bad people, but they're not exactly accepting either. They'll never approve of this relationship.

Before Aurora, I had no plans to visit my family. I don't feel a connection to my parents other than resentment, but they don't realize that. They believe I'm going through a rebellious phase. They're semi-correct—my tattoos and piercings are my way of defying them, a rebellion against their close-minded views. But this is no phase.

When my sister texted and asked for an RSVP update, I found myself wondering what Aurora would think of them—my sisters. I bet she'd love them.

"Two, yes. One older and one younger. The oldest is already married and has a four-year-old."

Aurora's smile widens. "That explains a few things. I'm sure they miss you."

They miss the person I no longer am.

A thought comes to her, and she gasps. "Do they have blonde hair and blue eyes like you?"

I chuckle at her excitement and nod. "They do."

"I bet they're so pretty. Do you have pictures?"

"How about you get changed and come to my room?"

I drag us out of the pool, my pants full of water and sagging. I unbuckle my belt, let them fall to the cement, and kick them away.

"You got me walking around in wet boxers, you little devil."

I carry her to the door and set her on her feet, then I pull my shirt over my head. Her gaze wanders over my body shamelessly. Our eyes connect, and she bites her lip in a failed attempt to conceal her grin.

"So needy." I playfully slap her ass. "Go get changed."

When I enter my room, Charlie is lounging in front of the dual-sided fireplace separating my bedroom from the sitting area—or whatever rich people call it. His feet are kicked up on the ottoman as he scrolls through his phone. He glances up. "I didn't think you'd want me in the security room."

The *security room* is an impressive setup: fortified walls, a reinforced door, monitors, flatscreens, and plenty of space for us to work. All areas of the property are monitored except the bedrooms and bathrooms.

I take back everything I said about Jax being a stalker—although he is. I'd do the same if I had his enemies. If I were traveling as often as him, I'd sure as fuck want to know if Kyle or Hugo decided to stop by.

"Nothing happened, but thanks."

"I'll admit, I laughed my ass off when you fell in the pool. You're losing your touch, going soft."

I grab my bag and head to the bathroom. "She's coming in, so behave."

An hour later, Charlie and I are reviewing Jackson's list when she graces our presence. She's in tiny sleep shorts, an off-the-shoulder cable-knit sweater, and matching tall sweater socks—is that a thing? Wool socks, maybe? Her dark hair is loosely braided, and she clutches a mug piled high with whipped cream.

I cock my head and glower. "There better not be caffeine or sugar in that; it's after nine."

Lately, she's constantly craving sugar. I'm asking the doctor to check her glucose level at the next appointment.

She disregards me and shifts her attention to my partner. "Charlie, would you like some hot chocolate? I have sprinkles and cookies," she singsongs.

He blushes and caves. "Yes, please. Thank you."

"Reese's Peanut Butter Cup, you want one?" Feigning innocence, she sips her hot chocolate and licks the whipped cream from her lips.

I give her a sharp glare, and a tinkling giggle erupts from her.

"I will spank you." Yeah, right. I doubt I could hurt her, even if she did like it.

My dick argues otherwise.

She giggles harder and spins on her heel. "At least you'd be touching my ass." Always flirtatious.

I watch that ass walk away and sense Charlie's stare burning into the side of my face. "Don't open your mouth."

"Reese's Pea—"

I pick up a pen and hit him square in the forehead. "If you *ever* repeat that, I'll strangle you."

She returns, balancing three mugs of hot chocolate topped with whipped cream and sprinkles and a plate of thick chocolate chip cookies, setting them on the coffee table. The way Jax cooks and eats, I'm destined to gain a hundred pounds. I can't miss a day at the gym.

Charlie grabs a cookie and immediately starts munching. "We should work here all the time."

I guide Aurora onto my lap then grab a blanket from the basket between the chairs and cover her. "I've got a few more hours. You wanna sit with me or lie in my bed?"

"I can leave and let you work."

"That wasn't an option."

She rolls her eyes, but I know she loves it.

"I'll finish my drink, then read in your bed."

For the rest of the night, Charlie and I plan one of LA's largest raids while sipping hot chocolate and eating cookies.

Life ain't so bad.

44

JACKSON

I break my attention from the surveillance video of Aurora in the pool and focus on Grant's crazy-ass story about ambushing Sloane. "So, what happened?"

He sets his bottle of water on the cocktail table harder than necessary. "The fucking dog happened."

I assured him he could drink alcohol, but he insists he wants a clear head. I don't entirely buy it, but I appreciate his support nonetheless.

"The one you *had* to have?" I add with a smug smile.

"Fucking thing started practicing its wolf howl. Don't get me wrong, it was cute, but fuck, my balls are still aching. After that, she came to her senses and kicked me out."

I can't help but laugh at his entire fiasco of stalking this girl and climbing over her fence, only to fall on his ass.

Grant joins in, and our laughter catches Ethan's glower from across the room, where he's lining up a shot at the pool table. He lifts his head, and beneath his thick lashes and signature scowl, his stormy gaze meets mine.

"He's pissed," Grant says, following my line of sight. "We

can leave. I didn't think this through, man. I'm sorry. Honestly—"

"It's fine," I assure him for the hundredth time. I'm okay around alcohol, I am. Before, there was this urgency to consume. Now, the thought of drinking turns my stomach. I'm terrified of anything that'll jeopardize my recovery and family. If it becomes too much, I'll leave. "It's not you. Things have been tense between us."

Ethan fires the shot, and the cue ball collides with the others in a series of sharp cracks. He banks at least two. Of course, he's good at pool, kicking all of our asses, just like everything else he does. The twins aren't bad either.

On second thought, it's only me who sucks. I blame being distracted. Getting a ball in a hole shouldn't be so hard, but I'm neither patient nor gentle.

"Why? The whole Patty thing?" Grant scoffs. "Patty is a meddler. She's in everyone's business."

I rake my fingers through my hair. "Not just Patty. I'm sick of hiding. I lived my entire life playing by someone else's rules. I want to be happy. I fought to be free, fought to be with them, and he's still pretending to be single—or is single. Fuck if I know."

In my heart, I know Ethan is not single, but listening to another woman giggle and flirt with him besides Aurora has torn me up. He laughed at something she said, and jealousy coursed through my veins like wildfire.

If Patty had touched him, I might've broken her fingers. I can't imagine what I would've done if I'd found them alone together. The image is worse than picturing Reece with Aurora.

It's a total mindfuck. I'm infatuated with Ethan. I long to be close to him, joke with him, have him put his arms around me in this bar like he does at home. It's killing me that I can't or that he won't.

I'm not capable of letting shit go. I fixate on my problems, and right now, I've got plenty. I'm coming out of my skin, barely able to contain my madness.

Ethan. Aurora. Reece. *Hugo*. The thought of him near Aurora, speaking to her, *threatening* her, has unresolved guilt and rage eating away at me. I dealt with Kyle for too fucking long, putting her through hell. I refuse to do the same with his partner.

"He doesn't look single," Grant disrupts my misery. "He can't keep his eyes off you."

"Yeah, 'cause he's worried I'll do something stupid." Such as relapse.

"I'm not so sure about that." A shit-eating grin spreads across my best friend's face. "I think he's concerned about me like you're concerned about Patty." He reaches over the table, wiggling his fingers. "Should I play with your hair and see if he breaks my skull?"

I seriously doubt Ethan is jealous of Grant. We've rotated playing the winner, and Ethan avoided me even when we faced off against each other. I'm certain this obsession is one-sided.

Still, Grant's point of view lifts my shitty mood.

I chuckle and swat his hand away. "He won't. He'll punish *me*. That's his MO. Now, what's our plan here?"

"Go interrupt her dinner and introduce myself to the family."

"And if Robert says no, you can't date his baby girl?"

Grant narrows his eyes. "She's far from a baby. He'd better get the fuck over it."

I bring my water bottle to my lips. "That serious, huh?"

"Very," he declares with conviction and no further explanation.

Who am I to judge or argue? I place the drink down. "Well, what are we waiting for?"

We walk past the pool table on our way out. I lift my chin toward Desi, who's nursing a beer and watching the room. "Be right back."

Ethan drops his pool stick onto the felt and straightens to his full height. "Where are you going?"

I smirk. "To see Robert. Wanna come?"

He holds my gaze. "No," he draws out, as if it's obvious.

So that's his problem? He's irritable about being here with Robert, about the possibility of us being seen together outside of hockey?

Disappointment churns in my gut. I shake my head and walk away.

* * *

Ethan clears his throat. "You coming straight home?"

Palms sweaty and heart pounding, I make a noncommittal noise. "I'll see you soon." Then, I exit the car.

I'm finding it hard to compartmentalize, and if I meet his troubled gaze, I'll break. He'll know I'm lying. Grant left with Sloane. The opportunity arose for me to pick up my bike alone, and I'm taking full advantage of it.

I circle the garage and key in the backdoor code. The overhead lights flicker to life as I enter, blinding me, and I shield my eyes.

A car door slams in the driveway, and I curse. He won't let this go. He tried to engage me in conversation throughout the ride to Kyle's, but with the twins in the backseat, he didn't push.

I swiftly kick the door shut and flip the deadbolt. The handle rattles, and I freeze, waiting for what he'll do next.

He doesn't knock, and after a tense moment, I hear the clanking of the iron gate. Despite the guilt gnawing at me, I breathe a shaky sigh of relief.

Boxes rifled through haphazardly by investigators litter the floor, along with sports equipment, tools, and other junk long ago forgotten. The three-car garage remained unused except for storage. Kyle parked under the carport, next to the kitchen entrance. I stashed my bike here in May to keep it hidden, knowing he'd never see it.

I shove aside a tote of decade-old Christmas lights. I guess it'll be my responsibility to toss or donate this shit once Reece gives me permission. He didn't say I couldn't pick up my bike. In fact, he handed me the key.

There's still an unmarked van in the driveway, crime scene notifications on the gate and garage doors. Maybe they're hoping I'll lead them to something they missed, like a secret room or an underground bunker. If Kyle had either of those, which I doubt, he didn't share it with me.

I make a mental note to rent a dumpster...if Ethan doesn't strangle me.

My bike sits gathering dust at the rear of the garage, where a retractable door opens to the backyard. The size of the estate is deceptive. The grounds are covered with dense landscaping and walking trails, and beyond the pool house lies a forest that borders two roads leading outside the subdivision. I've used these woods countless times to enter and exit the property without notice.

The home was built in the 1940s. I have no clue if Kyle chose the place for its obscurity or if my mother owned it before they married. At no point did they reminisce and share stories of how they met or when they moved in together. There weren't any 'good old days' you hear kids with divorced parents talk about. It was hell between them for as long as I can remember.

My mother never sat me down and said, "Hey, your dad is an abusive douchebag, but I have no way of escaping." She also didn't defend or make excuses for him. She shielded me the best she could while I struggled to piece this deranged world together amidst a haze of trauma and drugs.

I recall little of my early childhood, but I remember spending our days in the kitchen or at the beach. I have a vague recollection of her family. In my memories, the meetings were strained, and as I grew older, I wondered if she and Kyle weren't some business arrangement.

It wouldn't surprise me to learn my mother was given to him through blackmail or some shady deal. I can't imagine any woman willingly choosing that monster.

Rocco believed my grandfather ensured his trust was airtight to prevent Kyle from accessing the Vaughn fortune. If true, he knew what type of man Kyle was. Why didn't he help his daughter?

A shady business deal is the best plausible explanation. The worst possibility is that I resulted from him forcing himself on her or drugging her, then he threatened to take me if she ever left.

The thought has bile rising in my throat. Since our talk in the kitchen, it's been difficult to keep from spiraling, to keep a smile on my face, to keep the intrusive thoughts at bay.

And being here isn't helping.

I failed to do anything about Kyle, and it's too late to save my mother, but I'll die before I let Hugo threaten what's mine.

I've waited my entire life for vengeance, and tonight is my chance to take it.

45
ETHAN

Fucking Jackson.

The night is pitch-black. There are no windows, no light filtering outside—only blackness. I can't see a foot in front of me.

Why are there no outdoor lights on?

Jax avoided meeting my eyes the entire drive, his knee bouncing. When I went to talk to him, he slammed the door in my face.

He was adamant about getting his motorcycle tonight, despite having no interest in riding prior. Grant left with a girl, and Jax still wanted his bike.

He's unpredictable, all over the place lately. My fear is he's taking off. He arranged for us to succeed without him—he transferred everything in our names and provided evidence to Reece—and now, he's targeting Hugo.

I edge around the garage in search of another entrance. Thorny bushes snag my clothes and scratch my face, adding to my irritation. When I get my hands on him... I don't know whether I'll wring his neck or plead with him to stay.

Wring his neck and demand he stay—that's more my style.

Maybe Reece is right, and I'm too easy on him.

I inhale deeply, filling my lungs, and will my agitation to calm the fuck down. It's pointless; my chest still aches.

Earlier, I received a text from Robert stating Anaheim offered to buy out Jackson's contract and management was taking the long weekend to consider it. I wanted to rage, but I kept my mouth shut. I wasn't ruining Aurora's Thanksgiving with her grandmother.

It's only an offer, I told myself. *Nothing has been confirmed.* But the longer I stewed, the angrier I became. Then, we ended up at the same bar—which we should've never stepped foot in—as Robert's family?

Bullshit.

So, I watched Jackson tee-hee with Grant, like my world wasn't collapsing, and grew increasingly aggravated.

Even with our relationship, I have a hard time believing management would be foolish enough to trade Jax in the middle of the season. They'd let me go first. He initiated the trade. That's the only explanation.

Anaheim is an hour away; he can still live at home, but does he plan on traveling with Aurora and my baby?

The knife twists deeper in my gut. He wouldn't fucking dare.

The ground suddenly drops behind the building, and I stumble, losing my footing. I instinctively reach out and find the wall to keep from falling. For a moment, I'm disoriented until a rumble breaks the silence, and I jolt.

A garage door. He must be exiting through the back.

I sneak closer, pressed to the cold stucco. A chill runs down my spine, and my arms bristle with goosebumps.

The door retracts, and light from inside illuminates the

property. It's not at all what I envisioned—at least, not compared to the front. The view from the gate was limited, a glimpse of the pristine white mansion blending into the hillside. The shrubbery obscured everything beyond the house and garage.

Before me appears to be a courtyard, but unlike ours, which is breezy and colorful, this is overgrown and eerie, with bare trees reaching into the dark sky. It reminds me of a creepy graveyard. No tombstones, but I wouldn't be surprised to find a few.

Jax guides his bike onto the stone path from the garage, and I hold my breath, remaining as quiet as possible. Gears whine and metal clanks as he parks the bike. He turns away, and I seize the opportunity to jump out and wrap him in a headlock.

"Going somewhere?" I growl.

Without hesitation, he throws his head back, colliding with my mouth.

Sharp pain radiates through my jaw, the metallic taste of blood flooding my tongue. My teeth now have a pulse.

I'm not sure how I expected him to respond to being surprised in the dark, but *fuck*!

I stagger back and spit blood.

Jax spins around, fists raised and poised for a fight. Recognition strikes him, and his harsh façade crumbles. "Ethan? What the fuck?" Horror resonates in his voice, each word becoming more elevated.

This will hurt him as much as me, but I'll heal. Jax will carry this mental torment far longer.

I cup my chin and draw my tongue along the inside of my bottom lip. By chance, my teeth didn't completely break through.

The laceration is bleeding profusely, mixing with

pooling saliva. The pain in my jaw is bone-deep. My mouth pulsates, likely to swell, but none of my teeth are loose—thank fuck.

"Sorry," I rasp and roll my stiff neck to assess the damage. It's not terrible, nothing urgent, but the headache piercing my skull sends waves of nausea through my stomach, and I wince.

Feral green eyes meet mine. "Why?" He clutches his head. "Why would you do that?"

"I..." Why did I sneak up on him? Why did I surprise him in this creepy-ass place? I was seething and acted out of spite. "I wasn't thinking. I was pissed you were taking off."

Blood and saliva fill my mouth once again, and I spit, wiping my chin with the back of my hand. It burns like hell, and when I bring my hand away, it's covered in bright-red blood. Another injury? It's tough to pinpoint when everything hurts.

His intense gaze fixates on the blood. He clenches his jaw, pulls at his hair, and lets out a stifled scream. His anguish is my own, and my chest constricts.

I step forward, seize his wrists, and guide them around my neck. "Stop." I wrap him in my arms and weave my fingers through his hair. "Shh. It looks worse than it is."

He buries his face in the crook of my neck and sucks in shuddering breaths. "I didn't mean to hurt you." His heart pounds violently, and I feel the wetness of his tears on my skin.

Jax puts on a tough exterior, but he feels deeply, loves deeply. The torture it must have been to be him in a world of monsters.

I rest my cheek on his head, resisting the impulse to kiss his temple. It's not like I can without getting blood all over him anyhow. "I'm okay, Jax. This is my fault."

He pulls back, his lashes glistening. "No, you're not." He tips my chin with trembling fingers and grimaces. "I need to take you to the hospital."

"Reece is on his way. I'll have him check it out."

He narrows his eyes and drops his hand. "You called *him*."

I grasp his wrist. "How else were we getting home? Would you rather it be the twins?"

He scowls. "I wasn't going home."

"I know," I snap, once again irritated. "Why do you think I'm out here and Reece is on his way? You're not leaving. We'll handle Hugo."

We glare at each other, neither of us willing to back down. A gust of wind howls through the trees and rustles the leaves, and he shivers. He's only in a T-shirt.

"Where's your button-up?"

"I was going back in for my riding jacket, *Dad*." He twists and jerks his arm.

"Don't." I tighten my hold. "I will tackle you to the ground and sit on you."

The thought makes me smile, and I quickly regret it when pain splinters through my mouth. I glide my tongue over my swollen bottom lip, and the pungent metallic taste of blood churns my stomach.

His gaze traces the movement, and he frowns.

"Is it that bad?" I ask.

"Fucking awful. Aurora is going to flip."

His eyes well with tears, and I draw him into my chest. I find the hem of his shirt and slip my fingers underneath. He doesn't push me away. His muscular arms encircle my torso, and his body melts into me. He rarely shows me this much affection, and I find I like it—a lot.

Maybe I'm too attached. Maybe we *shouldn't* be on the same team.

No, fuck that. I can't imagine Jax playing for anyone else. I'd go mad.

"I'm sorry I hurt you," he whispers.

"I know you are." I trail my fingertips along his spine. "I'm sorry too."

His breath hitches, becoming shallow and rapid.

"What's going on, Jax? Tell me."

He releases a heavy sigh. "Nothing."

"Tell me. Let me fix it."

If it's Hugo, Reece and I can deal with it. If he doesn't want to be on the same team as me...well, too fucking bad.

"Nothing to fix." His forehead drops to my shoulder. "I'm in love with you."

Ice flows through my veins, then lava as his words hit home.

A grin tugs at my lips, causing a sting, yet I can't stop, nor can I suppress the chuckle that vibrates my chest. "I know."

Even though I sensed it, it's still a relief to hear.

"You're such an asshole." He struggles to separate, but I refuse. "Let me go, you big bastard."

I scoff. "Big bastard?" That's fine. I can top that. "I'm loving you right now," I lower my tone and rumble, "*baby boy.*"

He lifts his head to meet my eyes, his pupils dilated. "Do you have a concussion? Did you lose consciousness?"

"Only for a minute," I joke.

Before I can react, his lips press to my neck and his teeth sink into my skin.

A shudder runs through me, and goosebumps erupt over my arms. I fist his hair, not sure what else to do. "We need to talk about this."

"Why? You love me," he says against my throat, a grin clear in his voice. "You should stop fighting it."

Confused, I pull back, brows furrowed. "I'm not."

He cocks his head. "Don't lie. You didn't even want to be seen together tonight."

I open my mouth to argue when footsteps echo off the brick walkway.

"Holy fuck. What happened to you?"

46
REECE

"Both your shirts are covered in blood." I flip my palms upward. "Did you attempt to murder each other?"

Jackson's red-rimmed eyes meet mine. "How'd you get out here?"

If I had to speculate based on the guilt written on his face, he's the reason Ethan appears to have taken a few punches to the mouth.

"The front door—we changed the lock. I walked through the house."

"The twins with Aurora?" He removes his phone from his pocket, likely to put eyes on our girl.

"And Charlie. She's asleep. They installed a PlayStation in the security room to play games on the flatscreens."

He shakes his head in disapproval, but his slight smirk says otherwise. "That's for surveillance."

Charlie programmed the alarm to interrupt whatever is on the screens if there's movement on the property. Don't ask me how; I can barely find ESPN.

"They're waiting for you. Let's settle this shit and get the fuck home." I focus on Ethan, his lips and chin swollen and bloody. "What the hell happened?"

He takes a deep breath and blows it out slowly. "I surprised him, grabbed him from behind. He instinctively tossed his head back. It was my fault."

It's plausible. I doubt Jax would intentionally injure his bestie, but he's impulsive, and Ethan wouldn't hesitate to defend him.

I examine the cut on his chin, the skin split open and raw. "It could use a few stitches."

His nostrils flare, and he sways on his feet. "Nope. I'm good."

"He doesn't like needles," Jackson adds.

It's always the big, tough guys afraid of needles—except me. I'm one of those freaks who enjoys piercings and tattoos. "We can butterfly it. I have skin glue at the house."

Ethan gives a curt nod.

"You need to ice that lip. Has the bleeding slowed?"

"Yeah," he mutters and rolls his neck from side to side.

Jax chews his thumbnail. "Should you get an X-ray?"

"No, I'm just sore."

I suspect Ethan is downplaying his discomfort to protect Jackson's feelings, and I make a mental note to keep an eye on him. Aurora will panic if anything happens to him—to any of us.

Irritation curdles in my stomach, and I face the worst pain in my ass. "Were you seriously taking off? How did you expect Aurora to react when you didn't come home? Or Ethan? Did you think about that? Did you think about how fucking devastated they'd be?"

His eyes narrow to slits. "Did you think about how devastated we'd *all* be if Hugo snatched her? What might happen to her?"

"I *have* thought about it. All I think about is protecting her—even from your idiotic decisions." I shift my attention to Ethan. "This is a fucking mess, and it affects Aurora. We need to straighten this out *tonight*. Lay everything on the table."

Neither of them responds, and it's cold and unnerving out here.

Impatient, I huff. "Clearly, you two are having a lover's spat. What is it? Me? Being a part of this?"

"No," they say in unison, equally annoyed.

At least that's a relief. "Okay... Is it work? Are you still arguing over some chick who doesn't matter?"

Jackson straightens and balls his fists. "It does matter!"

Ethan squares his broad shoulders and crosses his arms over his chest. "Is that why you requested a trade? Because of fucking Patty?"

"What?" Jax recoils, curling his lip. "No."

"Then why did Anaheim offer to buy your contract? Why did you meet with Robert?"

"Wait. Back the fuck up." Jax lifts his hands in surrender. "I know nothing about a trade. I went with Grant to see Sloane, Robert's daughter, the redhead he's infatuated with." He brushes his fingers through his disheveled hair. "Is that what your problem was?" A satisfied grin flickers across his lips. "Aww! I thought you didn't want to be seen together, didn't want Robert to know we're together."

Ethan blinks several times, his brows pinched.

He's probably wondering how he got here, to a place where they're together without question or boundaries, where all the imposed rules are locked in Jackson's mind. Jax is the Hotel California, and even if Ethan doesn't realize it, he's checked in and can never leave, same as Aurora.

Yes, I'm only twenty-nine, but I listened to a lot of classic rock while deployed—Eagles and Journey on repeat.

They continue to argue, but something off in the distance grabs my attention.

Branches breaking.

Sticks snapping underfoot.

"Shh!" I place a finger to my lips.

The three of us freeze, listening. The next sound is all too familiar, one that haunts my nightmares, and, knowing the target, I jump before either of them flinches.

On impulse, my hand goes to my hip, but I'm unarmed.

No gun. No vest.

Although I brace myself, conscious of what's coming, the bullet still steals my breath and knocks me into Jackson.

47

JACKSON

A gunshot splinters through the trees, and I jolt. Reece crashes into me. My knees give out, and the air whooshes from my lungs. I stumble back and catch him under the arms.

He fights to get to his feet. "Fuck," he grunts, the word fragmented and filled with agony.

It all happens so fast, a blur of confusion.

Another gunshot. Terror paralyzes me.

Someone is running—the snapping of twigs and branches echoes through the woods. Are they coming toward us or away? Are there more than one? Two? I'm confident I hear two distinct paces.

There's a pull on my shirt, and Ethan yells, "Move! Move!"

Reece clutches his chest and scrambles to stand. He shields me, putting himself between me and the woods, and crowds me into the garage.

Why? Wouldn't he be happier if I were dead?

I hammer the button to close the overhead door and

follow Ethan's lead to the right, where the walls are lined with shelves, boxes, and totes.

He helps Reece to the floor, yanks his shirt over his head, and presses it to where blood has soaked through Reece's. Behind me, the garage door slams shut with a shudder. The motor cuts off, and there's only the sound of our heavy breaths.

Dazed, I hover over them and rake my fingers through my hair, tugging the strands.

This is a nightmare. It has to be a nightmare.

My heart thunders in my rib cage, its relentless beat muddling Reece and Ethan's hurried words.

Reece is against calling 911. It's not safe to involve the LAPD. We have to wait for backup. Ethan's worried we don't have enough time.

This isn't real. It can't be.

I shake my head, trying to dispel the disbelief, only to realize: *Reece stepped in front of a bullet for me—for Aurora.*

He'd rather risk death and have me around than have her be sad. If that's not love, then I don't know what the fuck is.

"I'm activating my comm." He fights to remove his dog tags from his shirt with a trembling hand. "OIS. Code 30," he rasps, then rattles off the address.

His dog tags are his communicator? His wire? My gaze snags on the dark-red blood covering his fingers. Panic rises and pushes away the shock, and my breaths become rapid and shallow.

"Don't you dare fucking die!" My throat hurts, strained with emotion, and I pace. "Aurora will never forgive me if I injure one of you and the other dies taking a bullet for me." My stinging eyes search for any weapon, landing on a baseball bat. I'm going to kill any motherfucker I get my hands on. "You always gotta show me up, don't you? Both of you. I can't compete with a baby and a fucking bullet to the chest."

I snatch the bat from the floor but feel foolish. What chance does a bat have against a gun?

Still, I grasp the metal like a lifeline and listen for noise.

I glance at the door. It's me they want. I can't stand here, useless, while Reece bleeds out.

"Jax, don't." Ethan's voice is gruff. "Don't fucking think about it. I'll come after you, and that'll mean letting go of Reece. You don't want that."

My stomach clenches painfully, my eyes burn with unshed tears. "They could hurt you next." I step toward the door.

"Jax…" he growls low in warning.

"Jackson, call the twins." The fear in Reece's tone seizes my attention. "Check the video feed. Charlie isn't answering."

My blood runs cold.

No. No. No. Please, anything but that. Anyone but Aurora.

48
AURORA

I jolt awake to raised voices and heavy footsteps outside Reece's bedroom.

"If they break into this house, I'm shooting first and asking questions later."

Desi's snarled words carry down the hall and send a wave of fear through my entire body, pushing aside any remnants of sleep.

"Try not to kill anyone!" Charlie shouts. "Ethan wouldn't want that."

"The fuck he wouldn't," barks Dante from farther away, his voice deeper than his twin's. "He's a Rossi. Ain't nobody touching his family."

Desi throws open the door Reece and Charlie only finished fixing this afternoon, and a beam of light trails behind him. In a hoodie and joggers, he rushes toward me.

I throw off the covers and swing my legs over the edge of the bed. "What's going on?"

"We need to get to the safe room. Men are surrounding the house."

My heart rate skyrockets. "Where's everyone?" If the

twins are home, Jax and Ethan should be home. If not...

"Reece?"

"At Kyle's." He crouches. "I'm going to lift you." He brings my trembling body into his arms and cradles my head. "Tuck in. We have a lot of windows to pass."

Why would Reece be at Kyle's? He wouldn't leave me unless it were urgent—unless there was an issue when Jax went to retrieve his bike.

Now, we're being hit here, which can't be a coincidence. "They wanted me alone? They want to use me against Jax?"

With a forearm under my ass and the other shielding my head, Desi moves into the now silent hallway. "If so, they're in for a big fucking surprise."

Slowly, he approaches the living area. Glass shatters downstairs, a window breaking, and I jolt, letting out a whimper.

"Shh... Dante is down there. He won't let anyone up the stairs."

He presses his back to the wall and peers around the corner at the glass doors leading to the patio and pool. My heartbeat pounds in my throat, and the baby moves, either from adrenaline or from not enjoying the confined space.

I tense, a cold sweat prickling along my skin, and nausea rolls in my gut. It's the oddest thing, but I'm suddenly disturbed by being in someone else's arms—even if it is Desi, and this is an emergency.

Before I can think more of it, he's creeping forward, only to jump back.

"Fuck," he curses under his breath and pivots toward the bedroom. "We won't make it to the safe room. It's gonna have to be the security room."

I point my toes to the floor and stretch out my legs. "Let me go. I'll run there."

He releases me, one hand reaching behind his back. "Lock and barricade the door."

Four gunshots erupt in quick succession, accompanied by an explosion of glass crashing onto the hardwood. The blast is piercing and violent, unlike anything I've ever heard. My breath hitches, and I skid to a halt. I whirl around with my hands firmly clasped over my ears.

Desi blocks the mouth of the hallway, gun raised. He glances over his shoulder. "Go, Aurora!"

Despite the ringing in my ears, I understand him clearly. Sock-footed, I race into the security room and slam the door, my feet nearly sliding from underneath me.

I stare at the keypad, my thoughts fuzzy and in disarray, and for a moment, I'm unsure of what to do.

"Hit the padlock icon, baby!" comes a raspy voice from above.

My quivering fingers locate the button, and the locking mechanism clicks into place.

"Jax!" I gaze at the ceiling, although I can't see him. "We're under attack? All of us?"

"Yes." He lets out a shuddering breath. "Push one of the leather chairs in front of the door and get under the desk."

Hopping from one foot to the other, I pull off my socks for traction and follow his instructions, using all my strength.

Before I climb under the desk, I look up and ask, "Are you alright?"

There's a heavy pause, and my stomach churns, a tear sliding down my cheek.

It's Ethan who answers, his voice raw with restrained emotion. "We're alright, baby girl. Be safe for me. We'll be there soon."

49
ETHAN

"I want a babymoon." Aurora's soft voice resonates in my mind, the memory of us snuggled in bed unexpectedly emerging.

The sun streamed through the sheer curtains, casting rays of light across the hardwood while leaving us in its shadow. Jax was in the gym, putting in an early morning workout, but I was too content to get up just yet.

"Like a light-up moon that hangs in the nursery?" I kiss her forehead and weave my fingers through her long, thick hair. "Order one, and we'll get it installed."

"No." She giggled and gazed at me with those wicked eyes. "Like a honeymoon. A vacation you take before the baby is born to spend time together."

I mentally checked dates but couldn't find availability for a vacation until February. I doubted she'd want to travel during her last month of pregnancy.

"I'm not sure we have time for that, baby girl. We can plan something for this summer. We'll take EJ; we have plenty of help."

"Okay," she whispered and kissed my chest.

I heard the disappointment in her tone and ignored it,

shrugging it off as part of our chaotic lives. I made it up to her with my lips and tongue, but I swear on everything holy, if we make it through this night, I'm taking her on a damn babymoon.

Jax falls to his knees beside me, burying his face in my shoulder, sobbing silently. His arm wraps around the front of me, fingers gripping my neck desperately while his other hand holds the phone in his lap.

I press my head to his. "Be strong for me, just a little longer. Channel that hurt and fear into anger."

He clenches and unclenches his jaw, the muscle furrowing against my clammy skin.

"Come on, baby. I need you to keep us safe. After this, we'll go wherever you wanna go. You wanna go to New York? We'll go to New York. No one will ever hurt us again. I promise you."

"Units are four minutes out. Several more headed to the house," Reece adds, his eyes half-lidded. "This was premeditated. Hugo knew you wouldn't allow him to threaten Aurora. Maybe he was following you. Maybe he came here to cause a distraction, to draw me out, hoping to get Aurora alone. She's their insurance policy—the only way to disrupt the investigation. You just happened to be here, and they took their shot. Either way, they were going to do *something*. It was only a matter of time. We all put protections in place, and they won't expect the twins or Charlie to defend her."

There's a puddle of blood underneath him, and his left arm, the one between us, lies limp. He tried to stand when we connected to the home security app and heard the commotion. Blood dripped steadily from his fingers, and he lost his balance, grabbing the metal shelving before he lowered himself back to the floor.

Jax lifts his head to give him a pained glare. "What if this is your partner's doing?"

"My partner armed the twins. Would he do that if he was involved?" Reece sucks in a labored breath. "Would your father's fan club need to break windows if Charlie was on their side? No, he'd be letting them in the front door."

"Where is he then?" Jax snaps, despair sharp in his tone.

"Take a breath. I saved his life. He'll save mine." Reece's lids droop, and his words become a mumble.

I adjust my posture, coming up on my knees to apply more pressure to his upper chest and relieve my aching shoulders. "I don't give a fuck what he does, as long as he kills them all." On the outside, I'm vacant, my voice emotionless. I can't say I'm numb—far from it. Rage and wrath have suppressed empathy and rationality. I want what's mine, and I want this night to be over. I don't give a fuck about anything or anyone else. "Every. Single. One."

The *pop* of a gunshot brings our attention back to the screen, where it's split between the security room and Reece's hallway. It's grainy in the dim light, and everything moves faster than I can comprehend.

Outside the security room, a masked man dressed in all black aims at the keypad.

Jax trembles against me. "That room is supposed to be impenetrable, fire and smokeproof."

Another *pop*.

I hold my breath.

Nothing. The door remains intact.

Another *pop*. A fine mist bursts from the intruder's head, and he crumbles in a heap on the floor.

Fuck.

Desi enters the frame with his gun drawn, turns toward Reece's bedroom, and fires again. They must be approaching from the beach, breaking in through multiple points at the back of the house.

There's no way the neighbors can't hear this. There's no way the security company hasn't dispatched the police.

"You did good," I tell Jax, my words sluggish and distant.

I don't recognize my own voice. I'm trapped in a hellscape, my mind flashing to an alternative time when I was helpless, a little boy waking up in a roach-infested apartment to another day without food and my mother passed out on the itchy couch.

I vividly remember the fabric. It was covered in rough, abrasive lint balls. Alone, I'd pick at them for hours, but they'd never come off. The threads were bare, and the yellow, spongy cushion pushed through the holes. It smelled of mold and stale cigarette smoke.

Dirt is stuck between my feet and the plywood from where the linoleum is torn and jabbing at my soft soles. I peer down at the drooling woman whose job it is to care for me, and I swear, when I get older, I'll never be powerless again.

Now I'm the caregiver, and what's mine is trembling beside me, bleeding out beneath me, defending my home, and hiding under a desk with my baby inside her.

"Never again."

Jax's bloodshot emerald eyes meet mine.

"Never again do you do something without telling me."

His eyes well up with tears.

"Never again do you take sole responsibility for defending our family. That's *our* job. The three of us work together, communicate better. Do you understand?"

He nods then tilts his head, his ears catching a beeping sound. "The door," he whispers.

"Hit the lights," Reece croaks, pushing himself into a seated position.

"They're motion sensors." Jax scrambles to his feet, snags the bat, and races toward the rear of the garage.

I wipe my bloodied hands on my pants and follow. Fuck, my arms don't want to cooperate, my muscles stiff and my head throbbing.

I nearly trip on a hockey stick and grab it as a weapon. How fitting.

The door creeps open, and Jax hides behind it, bat raised over his shoulder. Black leather-gloved hands clutching a gun appear first, and I press myself against the wall next to Jax.

He lifts his foot and boots the door. *Smart.* It bounces off the person with a resounding thud.

They attempt to shoulder their way in, but Jax repeats the action in quick succession—*kick, kick, kick, kick*—until the individual stumbles forward, collapsing and dropping the gun.

I slide it blindly behind me. Maybe I should've snatched it, but in all honesty, I've never shot a gun.

Jax goes to town, swinging the bat over his head so fast, it blurs in the air. "My wife says hello," he grunts.

With every lift of the bat, blood spatters on the white wall beside me, droplets landing on my cheek and bare chest.

Holy. Fuck. And I thought he had a powerful slap shot...

Movement in the doorway catches my attention. Another motherfucker. Another gun. When will this nightmare end?

"Get down!" Reece shouts as someone else yells, "Drop your weapons!"

I release the hockey stick and get to my knees. What the fuck else am I supposed to do? I'm pretty much useless.

Jax keeps swinging, pulverizing the face and skull of a bald man whose jaw is slack, his teeth strewn across the floor. Are those dentures? Is that an eyeball lying there?

A gunshot resonates through the building. I grab Jax by the belt, yank him down to the floor, and shield him with my body.

SWAT rushes in, screaming their demands. From his knees, Reece asserts authority, and officers hurry to his aid. He says his scapula is fractured along with his humerus; he can't move his arm. He tells them we were protecting him.

Jax gasps for breath underneath me, his tense body shaking, his haunted eyes staring at Hugo's lifeless body.

I sit back on my haunches, draw him into my arms, and brush the sweaty hair from his forehead. "It's over, baby. He'll never touch you again. It's over."

50
REECE

A whirlwind of activity surrounds me like bees swarming an agitated hive, only adding to my confusion.

There's a method to the madness, I assure myself. *Trust the process. You've been on countless raids.*

Only this time, my life is at stake, and I don't mean the likely hollow-point bullet that struck me.

Aurora.

I attempt to rise from my knees, lifting one foot at a time as I battle the dizziness.

A forceful hand clasps my shoulder. A jolt of sharp pain lances through my spine and the back of my skull, and I buckle.

"Lie your ass down. You must have lost a liter of blood already."

Shit, I forgot a member of my team was next to me—an officer-trained medic.

"Mercer?" I croak, asking about Charlie, my throat raw and dry.

She places a knee on my collarbone to reduce blood

loss, and black spots cloud my vision. "Units are approaching." She tears open an IV bag with her teeth.

"Jax..." I fight the agony and turn my head side to side until I find him near the doorway. "Open the gate."

"Tell them to let me fucking go then." His blood-spattered face is twisted in a snarl.

At a murder scene, you can't simply leave. An officer collects evidence from under his fingernails while another takes pictures of his hands. They'll want to bag his clothes too.

There's a prick in the back of my hand, and ice floods my veins.

I close my eyes and ride out a wave of nausea. "He'll snap, and we'll get nothing."

"Hey," my superior yells from behind me. She's a tiny woman, but her voice is shrill and terrifying. "Collect evidence at the hospital. Let's get that gate open and this night over with."

For them, this night is far from over. "That's Police Chief Hugo Isaac on the floor." My speech is garbled, and I swallow thickly. "Execute the other raids."

Blackness becomes solace, and the pain recedes. My body is lifted, but my eyelids remain heavy.

"Jax?" A gentle tone resonates in my sleep.

Aurora. My heart skips a beat then pounds hard.

"Unlock the door for Charlie, babe. He's taking you to the hospital."

Sirens wail in the distance. *She's going to the hospital.*

"With the twins. You don't leave without them," adds a gruff voice.

We have twins. I can't picture them. Am I deployed? Have I met them?

I crack my eyelids to a bright light and the blurred faces

of two men peering down at me. My eyes water, and I blink away the tears. "Angel." It rolls off my thick tongue, slow and slurred.

"Reece? What's wrong?"

Her voice trembles with fear, and I reach for her, only to find my arms entangled and uncooperative. "Give me her."

Fingers wrap around my wrist. "Calm down, Viking. You'll see her soon."

Viking. Is that my new code name?

"What's happening?" she asks, frightened.

My mind goes dark, and I thrash against my bindings. "Give me her. Don't touch them!"

"Shit, he's delusional. Quiet her," demands a woman.

I lunge for the bigger threat, a silhouette of broad shoulders. "Don't touch her!"

He casts a looming shadow, obscuring the bright light. He overpowers me and pins me down. "Easy, Reece. She's safe."

My arms don't work, but my legs do, and I shove the shadow away.

"Sedate him." *Another male, several feet away.*

Aurora calls for me, and I kick out, striking the person nearest to her voice. "Don't fucking touch her."

"Fuck," he grunts. "She's *my* wife."

A deep, rumbling laugh echoes in the cell.

"I'll kill you." It's a weak threat. My head is woozy, and I collapse onto a firm mattress. "She's mine."

"Sharing is caring, Viking."

This time, my kick only connects with metal bars.

"Babe, listen to me. It's okay. We're in the ambulance. He's hopped up on pain meds and well enough to fight. I think he'll live. Jesus, fuck."

Why is that voice torturing me?

51
AURORA

Jittery, I step back into the security room and away from Charlie. "I want the twins." My voice trembles, and my lungs struggle to draw in air. I place my hand on my tight chest, trying to ward off the impending panic attack.

You'll be with the guys soon. You can fall apart then.

Our home has become a war zone, and I don't know who to trust right now except Ethan, Jax, Reece, Desi, and Dante.

Charlie raises his hands in a calming gesture. "It's okay, Aurora. I need to get you to the hospital before Reece is taken into surgery. He'd want to see you."

I want that too, but Reece is out of it. I doubt he'll comprehend I'm there. "He'd want me to be safe."

He nods placatingly. "You *are* safe. He asked me to care for you."

Not believing him, I retreat farther.

Across the house, voices yell out, "Clear!"

On the security feed, officers with guns drawn rush from room to room.

"You don't need to be here for this." He moves closer. "It'll trigger your anxiety."

Um, I'm already triggered.

"She leaves with the twins." Ethan's gruff tone fills the room.

"And I'll know if you don't take her to the hospital," Jax adds. "I'll know the moment you stray off course."

"The twins are being questioned and possibly detained," Charlie argues, his gaze fixed on me as if I were a wounded animal on the verge of fleeing.

My throat constricts. "No." I gasp for breath. "They were protecting me."

Static buzzes through the speakers, Jax's angry voice stifled in the background.

The line clears, and a woman snaps, "Mercer! Get them to the hospital. Now!"

Charlie's posture goes rigid. "Yes, Commander."

He pivots sharply and exits the room, leaving me alone to stare at a figure sprawled outside the doorway oozing blood.

I heard the muffled gunshots while I was hiding under the desk with my hands pressed to my ears, but I didn't know someone got this close to me.

Only a door separated me from a man who intended to kidnap and harm me—intended to use me against Jax and take me from my loved ones.

They might have hurt the baby.

"He's dead." The words pass my quivering lips, barely above a whisper. "He can't hurt us."

The gravity of the situation grips my heart like a vise, and panic takes control.

"Aurora, look away." Ethan's voice is distant, muted by the whooshing in my ears.

"I have to get out of here." I step forward and teeter on my feet. I glance down, as if that'll stop the floor from wobbling, and realize... "I'm not wearing shoes."

I can't go to the hospital, to Ethan, Jax, and Reece, without shoes.

"Aurora," he growls. "Don't move."

But I need to escape. I need to get to them.

Holding the doorjamb and wall, I lift my foot over the lifeless being, careful not to slip on the blood. I tremble, fearing he'll wake and grab me. I know it's not possible—his limbs are bent in unnatural ways.

Reece's door is wide open. In the entryway, another body lies motionless on the floor. Crouched beside it is a man with a gun slung over his back. He peers up at me, face fully concealed by a mask.

Both men, dead and alive, are in the same black tactical gear. There's no telling who is who, and, startled, I take off toward my bedroom.

My darting gaze catches the light glinting off shards of broken glass far too late. Sharp pain slices through the soles of my feet, and I fall to my knees.

"Shit." Charlie hurries over, his boots crunching on the hardwood. "Why does no one listen to me?"

Without hesitation, he reaches for me, and I bat him away.

"Don't touch me." I rise on shaky legs and stumble backward. My eyes cloud with tears, and I blink several times to clear my vision.

He puts his hands out to steady me if needed, careful not to make contact. "You're in shock and bleeding. You need to sit, preferably off the property."

Blood trickles from my knees. Nausea turns my stomach, and I swallow the bile rising in my throat. "Where are the twins?"

"Desmond is getting fingerprinted. Dante is identifying perps he...*encountered*."

He juts his chin to the patio, where multiple individuals are face down on the concrete, three with their wrists and ankles zip-tied, the others unmoving.

Dante stands over them, pointing and talking with an officer.

Beyond the shimmering blue pool lights lies darkness, and in the shadows, Dante's broad shoulders and muscular build bear a resemblance to Ethan's. Comfort and yearning wash over me, and I call out for him.

He glances up, but so does an intruder, holding me in his gaze.

As he walks by, Dante stomps on the man's head, and I almost feel bad—almost.

"Don't look at her, motherfucker," he snarls. He approaches, brows pinched with concern. "What happened?" he asks Charlie, accusation thick in his tone.

"Don't blame me. She stepped on glass. Jesus, y'all are a tight-knit group. You refuse to trust anyone. It's a problem."

"Accurate. Now, get my brother, or you'll find out how much of a problem I can truly be."

Charlie walks away, shaking his head.

"Fuck, I hate cops," Dante mumbles. "We need to clean you up before Ethan strangles me."

Blood runs down my legs, but all I feel is embarrassment and the urgency to leave. "I'm sorry. I just wanna go." My voice breaks, and I curl my toes to relieve the agony and hide my discomfort from him. "I need shoes."

He extends his arms. "Either way, I have to carry you over this glass. I'll take you to your room for shoes and get you cleaned up quick."

In the driver's seat, on the way to the hospital, Charlie mutters about not following procedure and contaminating the crime scene. I rest my forehead against the window and stare off into the night. Despite the anxiety pulsating in my veins, the world around me grows hazy, and my eyelids flutter shut.

52
JACKSON

I wait impatiently outside the emergency department doors. The only reason I'm not pacing is because Ethan's arms are around me from behind, his head resting on my shoulder. I don't blame him for being exhausted, and I'm sure he's hurting, which is my fault.

I've never been this bone-tired in my life. Even my fingers are sore from swinging that bat with everything I had. I put my heart and soul into killing Hugo, and it was worth every ache and pain. I'll dream about his mutilated face and skull. It's far better than the nightmares he's given me.

Despite the fatigue, my body feels lighter, and although I have a world of shit to make up for, I'm not depressed. My mind isn't racing. I worry about the legal ramifications of everything that occurred tonight, but I have faith in Reece.

I know—crazy, right?

The trauma team is currently working on him. They don't believe the bullet hit any major arteries or organs, but he's lost a lot of blood, and the damage to his shoulder and arm is extensive. He'll be taken to surgery once he's stable and the unit is ready.

His commander, Ethan, and I demanded he get the best care—a private room, top surgeons, whatever is necessary. No expense spared.

I owe him my life.

And I don't need Aurora divorcing me because I injured both her boyfriends and destroyed our dream home all in one night.

And put Desi and Dante at risk.

And she could've been kidnapped. Or worse.

Jesus, when I fuck up, I do it in epic proportions.

Regret and guilt overwhelm me. My head spins, and I sway on my feet.

Ethan tightens his embrace. "You alright?"

"I'm sorry I brought this on us. I was going to take care of it myself." I release a shaky exhale and blink the tears away. "I'll fix the house, or we can move. Anything you want."

"I don't give a shit about the house, you know that. I only want us to be safe. We'll figure it out. Let's get through these next few days first." He brushes his lips over my temple. "I have no intention of allowing either of you out of my sight."

"I wish we were always like this." The thought slips past my lips. My weary mind lacks a filter, although I don't have much of one, even on a good day.

"I know." He grows quiet, and just when I think that's all I'm getting from him, he adds, "Me too."

Hope flutters in my stomach like butterflies. "Why can't we?"

"This is really bothering you, isn't it?"

"Yes."

"We can...privately." He yawns and stretches his neck.

"And it's probably something we need to discuss with Aurora."

His yawn is contagious, and I rest against him and close my eyes. "She knows."

He nuzzles the curve of my neck. Something shifts between us. I can't pinpoint it, but I sense it with every fiber of my being.

An agent or officer or whatever they're called gave us *Special Response Team* T-shirts and scrub pants to replace what was confiscated as evidence. The medic patched up Ethan's chin and offered him an ice pack. We washed up the best we could in the bathroom in the private waiting room they put us in.

Now, all we need is Aurora.

As if my thoughts summoned her, the tracker beeps on my phone. "They'll be here soon, thank fuck."

The vehicle comes to a stop, and Dante exits the back seat. "She's injured—not bad, but she won't let anyone touch her."

I round the car before the words are out of his mouth, Ethan behind me.

I'll lose my mind if she's hurt. This is all my fault. These things shouldn't happen to her and wouldn't if she wasn't part of my life.

I pull the door open, and she slumps forward.

Panic shoots through me. I crouch and cup her pale face in my hands. "What's wrong?"

Her eyes slowly focus. "Jackson," she breathes, then her gentle expression crumbles as her forehead falls to mine.

"Baby," I sob, right along with her.

Ethan reaches around me and drags her from the vehicle, setting her on her feet. She whimpers and collapses into him, and he lifts her into his embrace.

"Where are you hurt?" His gravelly voice shakes, and his eyes glisten with tears.

I've never seen Ethan cry, and I come apart at the seams. I'm a fucking mess, leaning into his chest for support while I hold on to Aurora.

Her bottom lip trembles. "Your face—"

He cuts her off with a growl of her name. "Answer me."

"I stepped in glass. I was scared. The men all looked the same... I wanted to get to you."

The men look the same because they are the same—on the outside. LAPD in SWAT gear versus Homeland Security's Special Response Team...in SWAT gear. She would know no difference. *We* would know no difference.

Tears stream down her cheeks, and I brush them away. "It's okay. We're here now. It won't happen again. I swear to you."

I'll quit. I won't leave her side. I'll sell Kyle's properties and investments to fund a war against whoever is left. I'll testify—whatever I have to do to keep us safe.

Ethan's voice softens yet remains stern. "You've been walking around with glass in your feet?"

We saw her take off on the security cam but didn't see where she'd injured herself. Dante helped her to our room, but I lost sight of her after that. Another reason to add cameras to the bedrooms.

"I need you." She buries her face in his neck. "Just hold me. Don't let me go."

She cries, and I cry with her, my heart breaking for all I've put her through.

"I won't," he chokes and hugs us tighter, his head against hers, his fingers in my hair. "I'll never let either of you go."

The three of us cling to one another, releasing the pent-up fear and emotions of the night until Ethan clears his throat.

"We need to check on Reece, baby, and have you examined." He kisses her temple. "And don't tell me no. I haven't forgotten about you not listening to me."

53
ETHAN

My neck and shoulders are on fire, my muscles are rigid, and this headache is piercing, but the fear of losing our family keeps me going. I need to tend to our girl and ensure Jax doesn't snap. He's holding up, but I worry the guilt will become destructive. I have to guarantee Reece gets the best care. He saved the life of someone I can't live without, and Aurora cares deeply for him.

I carry her into the private waiting room, Jackson beside me and the twins following. More people have gathered—agents, given their uniforms—and she stiffens in my arms.

"It's okay. I won't allow anything to happen to you."

I'll never let anyone harm them ever again.

Tears well up. My focus should've been on them, not hockey. I should've protected them better, should've taken Hugo's threats more seriously.

Reece's commander perks up when she sees us enter and hurries over. "The orthopedic surgeon arrived, and they took him straight up. They didn't even inform me. His blood pressure dropped and... He probably wasn't aware anyhow.

He was out of it." She babbles while her keen eyes absorb every detail of our group.

Aurora sniffs, and her soft voice trembles. "It's okay."

"Are you injured? Do you need anything?"

I can't help but notice how accommodating Reece's superior is, especially to our girl, and I plan to take full advantage of it.

"She has glass in her feet," I reply before Aurora can deny it. "And she needs rest—away from the officers who raided our home. No offense."

"None taken. We'll move you to a room. Special Agent Bennett, by the way. If you require anything while I'm gone, ask any agent."

I sit with Aurora nestled in my lap, and she settles into me, her arms wrapped around my neck.

Jax caresses her stomach over her hoodie and peppers her with questions. "Have you felt the baby move?"

"Yes."

"Any cramping?"

"No."

"Are you hungry?"

"Ew, no."

"When did you last eat?"

"We had Thanksgiving dinner, remember?"

That feels like a lifetime ago when, in reality, it was only hours.

While we wait, the team discusses additional raids and the concern of keeping us secluded during and afterward. Jackson gave Reece a list of names and properties involved in the human and drug trafficking ring. Hugo recognized the danger of that knowledge. He and a handful of others risked their lives to silence Jax.

For that reason, we're put in a private suite in the Intensive Care Unit, where Reece will be brought after surgery. Besides the glass wall and the three agents standing guard at the door, it resembles a modern hotel room, with a hospital bed, a couch, and two reclining chairs.

"The only stipulation is that you don't leave." Charlie's critical gaze locks on the twins. "*Any* of you."

"No worries, Sheldon." Desi winks. "The family that murders together, stays together."

Reece's partner stares at him, mouth agape, before shaking his head and storming out.

Dante scoffs. "Did you just reference *The Big Bang Theory* and murder in the same statement?"

Yawning, Desi drops into the chair beside Jax and a sleeping Aurora. "My two favorite subjects."

"Before you fall asleep," I tell him then turn to his brother, "and you sneak out for a smoke, thanks for being here. I—fuck, I don't know what to say." I bury my face in my hands and rub my tired eyes. Lifting my head, I manage, "Thank you for protecting her." I swallow hard. "I hope you killed them all."

Dante stretches his neck to glance out the door. "Tried."

"How many left?" Jackson asks.

"Sheldon apprehended four."

I make a mental note to have Reece keep track of those who aren't dead, although I'm sure he will. The room grows quiet, and I rest my head against the unyielding leather material as I close my eyes.

I'm awakened when a nurse—Brody, according to his badge—steps in. "Hi. Sorry to wake you. Ms. Embers?"

"Hey, baby." Jax wakes Aurora and carries her to the bed. "The nurse is here to examine you."

Her eyelids blink open, and she scoots back on the mattress.

"I was told you have some glass in your feet. Can I take a look?"

Brody extends his hand toward her sneaker, but she withdraws.

She peers over at me, lips pouted and brows furrowed. "Can't you do it?"

As if I'd refuse her.

"How about this?" The nurse weaves his fingers together at his chest. "You remove your socks and shoes, and I'll get the supplies?"

Aurora gives a hesitant nod, and Brody leaves.

Jax positions himself behind her, drawing her between his legs, and lowers his voice. "What is it? Did someone hurt you?"

She shakes her head sharply. "I feel strange." They do that thing where they communicate with their eyes. I sit at the end of the bed and untie her laces but pay close attention.

"It's an echo from the past." He tucks a wayward lock of hair behind her ear. "You were frightened, and your body remembers." He kisses her cheek. "You're safe with us."

His words give me pause, and my gut clenches. I wonder how deep their connection goes, if they're similar in more ways than I thought. The idea of someone hurting them, especially intimately, fills me with such fury and adrenaline, my muscles no longer ache.

By the end of tonight, we'll be inseparable, because I don't know how I'll ever part from them.

54
AURORA

"How could you walk around like this? God-fucking-damn it, Aurora." Ethan carefully removes my shoe. "If you don't start listening to me, I'm sending you to New York."

My blood-soaked sock sticks to the insole. I flinch and attempt to yank my foot away. "No, you won't."

His fingers encircle my ankle, steadying me while he peels off my sock. "Watch me."

"Alright, let's see here." Nurse Brody shines a penlight and ignores our bickering, his chipper tone never wavering. "You've got a few nasty cuts here," he says as he lifts a pair of tweezers.

My heart rate picks up a notch, and I press into Jax behind me. "I picked out a couple of pieces already."

While my adrenaline was high and I was eager to get to the hospital, I sat on the side of the tub and hastily ripped out what chunks of glass I could manage. I whimpered and cried—a lot. It was not my finest moment.

The nurse grasps my foot and digs the tweezers into my inflamed arch.

Hot, searing pain has me trying to pull out of Ethan's firm grip, and I whimper-cry, "Ow!"

My husband tightens his arms around my chest to prevent me from escaping and drops his head to my shoulder. "Fuck, I'm sorry, baby."

I bite my lower lip, and tears wet my eyelashes.

Ethan's stormy gaze meets mine. "In New York, you could work on the loft, design in your studio, and rest. The twins will stay with you, my family will keep you safe." He's serious, his brows pinched in concern.

"I'm not abandoning Reece when he needs us. He'd never leave me, and I'd never leave either of you."

His frown deepens, and he clenches his jaw, the muscle bunching. "There are people who want to hurt you. You *are* hurt. I'd send Jax too, if it wasn't for the case and hockey. We'll hire a nurse—"

"No." A piece of glass is freed, and blood spills from the wound. My frustration boils over, and I shake my head. "Not happening."

"Aurora."

"*Ethan*." I mock his cautionary tone. "We can move into your downtown penthouse. If the twins want to stay, they can take Jax's place. It hasn't sold, and it's only a block from yours. After Reece is discharged, we'll go to Laguna or remain in LA. We're not separating."

Jax lifts his head. "We'll figure it out. Let's not fight. Everyone is tired and cranky."

The nurse switches to the other foot and draws my attention from that icy glare.

"How long is the surgery?" I ask Brody to distract from the pain and the awkward silence.

"Depends on the severity, but about ten hours."

I stare, wide-eyed. "Ten hours?"

"Maybe longer." He concentrates on a stubborn sliver in my heel. "They need to repair damaged blood vessels and nerves, remove bone fragments, and restructure his shoulder and arm with plates and screws." He glances up. "It'll be a long recovery."

My eyes find Ethan's, and he releases a defeated sigh. "You will rest and go *nowhere* alone."

"We'll be here." Desi glances at his brother for confirmation.

"We'll take shifts," Dante agrees. "They can't keep us in this room forever."

Brody bandages my feet and brings some blankets, and I pass out in Jackson's arms.

Multiple times, I'm roused by Ethan brushing my hair from my face and kissing my temple. I catch him doing the same to Jax in between pacing.

I doubt he wants me to go to New York, but he's scared. Tonight's horror has rattled him.

When I wake, I have no idea whether it's night or day, but a new nurse, Kayla, tells us Reece is in recovery.

"We'll need you to vacate so the team can make him comfortable."

Her vague statement churns my stomach, and I have to splash cold water on my face in the bathroom.

"Some orthopedic bigwig was flown in from his vacation in Belize," Charlie rambles while we sit in the waiting room. "The surgery was twelve hours and required seven specialists. When he was shot before, *he* was the specialist. All we had were medics in the desert."

I furrow my brows. "He was shot? In the military?"

"Oh, yeah. In the leg and knifed in the gut, but I should probably shut up."

"Holy shit." Unsure what else to say, I ask, "Is your real name Charlie?"

"No, but that's a story for another day." Despite his words, he takes a breath and continues. "After a bombing, I was the only person left from the Charlie Squadron. Instead of Team Charlie, there was just Charlie."

I gawk at him in astonishment. How freaking sad is that? "I'm sorry."

Jax peers around me with the same stunned expression.

Charlie thrusts his hand in a dismissive gesture. "I don't remember any of it. One minute, I was hacking the enemy's systems; the next, I was lying in the dirt, my skin on fire. If Reece hadn't rescued me, I'd be dead. We've been together since."

Sorrow hits me. I'm the other woman stealing Reece from his partner. No wonder Charlie is critical of me.

"Did Reece ever tell you how he got his nickname?"

I tilt my head. "Ricky? No."

"His is harder to explain. It's a tricky homophone. We were working a makeshift orphanage and wrote our names on tape, thinking the kids could read. They couldn't. One kid sounded out 'Reece' as 'Ricky.' He'd correct them, and they'd laugh hysterically. Finally, he gave up." Charlie averts his gaze, and his voice becomes distant. "It was funny."

His tone is anything but humorous.

"Sheldon," Desi calls out. "Stop making her sad. You really are terrible with women."

Commotion fills the hallway, drawing me from Charlie's grumbles.

I rise and stand in the doorway. A bed is wheeled off the elevator, and I gasp.

The world beneath my feet tilts on its axis.

I comprehend what I'm seeing, but at the same time, *I don't.*

Reece. *My* Reece is pale and lifeless. He lies with his eyes softly closed, his chest rising and falling in an unnatural, mechanical rhythm. Machines and tubes and half a dozen people surround him.

They come closer, and I will his eyelids to open, to show me those ocean blues, to prove to me he's okay.

He doesn't, and I'm left feeling adrift and empty.

55
REECE

Faint, pained groans invade my oblivion.

Whispers slither in the darkness, and an icy dread seeps into my bones.

It's pitch-black, and I try to move, but I'm paralyzed. A jarring alarm rips through the silence, and I fight to control my ragged breathing.

Panic hinders a successful rescue.

I inhale deeply, and the acrid sting of antiseptic fills my nostrils. A rumble vibrates in my chest, my dry throat prickles, and realization hits me—it's me. *I'm* groaning. I urge my eyes to open and my limbs to cooperate, but my fingers only jerk.

A flood of adrenaline intensifies the voices, and my surroundings come into focus. With immense effort, I force my eyelids apart. Everything is blurry. The pull of unconsciousness is relentless, and they fall shut.

"Mr. Abercrombie, do you hear me?"

A presence hovers over me, and I grab it, cloth twisting in my fist.

"Let go, or we'll have to restrain you."

I drag the hissing suspect closer, and he grunts. They're in for a world of hurt if they think they can subdue me.

"You're only agitating him further." *That voice.*

She's here and upset, and my struggles come to a halt.

"A—" Her name lingers in the haze, surfacing only as a hoarse tickle in my throat.

I focus intensely, yearning to hear her. Metal latches on to my wrist, and I swing—or at least try. My muscles are lethargic, and a heavy weight traps my arm.

"You're in the hospital, Reece, and coming out of anesthesia." *Mercer.*

"Let me go," she cries. "He won't hurt me."

The tickle becomes a raw growl, and I grapple to free myself, to reach for her. The alarm sounds again—not an alarm, an incessant beeping—and the cuffs bite into my skin.

"Return to the waiting room."

"Please, Ethan."

Her soft voice fades, engulfed by the fog, and I fight harder.

A hand lands on my chest, and I flinch. "Calm down if you want her."

"Mer..." I swallow thickly. "Mercer." It comes out as a raspy whisper.

"Ethan is a bull right now. He's worried you'll harm her or the baby."

The name resonates in my mind, unable to find its place. "Baby."

"Yes, pregnant, and he's hanging on by a tight thread."

Vague memories flutter behind my eyes like pages falling from a book. My angel asleep on the couch with a tiny baby bump. Modeling flowy, white dresses, black and red lace, pink satin. In a bikini, slightly more rounded, with a brilliant smile on her beautiful face. Aurora talking in the passenger seat next to me while I fret over the seat belt. Her arms around my neck, her fingers in my hair, her lips pressed to mine—the taste of sugar on my tongue.

A soothing warmth washes over me, and my rigid muscles loosen. "I'm calm."

I doubt he hears my mumbles. The commotion diminishes, the silence between the beeps lengthens, and sleep wins.

"*Te amo.*"

A gentle touch glides along my rough jawline, and I stir.

"Charlie, could you take the handcuffs off so I can sit on the bed? There's plenty of room."

"Not a good idea."

The obscurity ebbs, and I recall that bossy tone. *Ethan.*

"But my feet hurt."

I see that adorable pout in my mind's eye, and my mouth twitches.

"You never listen," he grumbles.

The metal unlocks from my wrist. "That's what I said," my partner comments.

"*You* don't get to say."

Another voice, this one provoking, although I'm unsure why.

My hand covers hers, and I settle into her touch, breathing her in. Her sweet, enticing scent drowns out the sharp smell of the hospital, and I weave our fingers together.

I blink my eyes open.

"Hey," she chokes out. Tears stream down her cheeks, and her body shakes with sobs.

"Shh." I attempt to cradle her face, but my other arm is useless, covered in thick bandaging.

"It's okay." Her lips quiver. She struggles to continue. "Stay still. You were shot."

I furrow my brows and peer at the crowd gathered behind her. Most are familiar, a few medical staff.

"The twins went home to rest, to Ethan's place." Aurora draws my attention back to her. "The beach house is now the headquarters for the raid you set up. Do you remember?"

"Our twins?" I wipe away her tears.

Her head tilts. "No..."

Memories emerge, my mind distinguishing reality from dreams. "Desi and Dante came from New York for Thanksgiving."

She nods. "Right. That was yesterday—I think."

"We went swimming." I smirk. "You dragged me into the pool."

Her red-rimmed eyes sparkle. "I was hoping you forgot that part."

"I remember everything before then. After is foggy... There were gunshots at our house. You..." Fear consumes me, and that damn alarm sounds. "They were after you."

I seek Charlie with a questioning stare, wincing at the sharp pain in my temples from the overhead lights.

He steps closer. "We handled it."

A nurse or doctor comes to the other end of the bed to check the annoying beeping. I concentrate until my head is pounding, and I have to close my eyes.

I drift in and out of sleep. People move quietly about the room, chairs creak, doors open and shut, and the entire time, Aurora never leaves my side.

When I wake, I draw her to me. "Lie with me."

She scoots closer. "I don't want to hurt you."

"You won't, and even if you do, it'll be worth it." I lower my voice. "I need to feel you next to me."

Our lips meet in a languid kiss before she rests her head on my shoulder, her body pressed to mine.

"That's disgusting." *Jackson*, his tone sarcastic.

I recall why he aggravates me. He never shuts up. A derisive grin spreads across my face. "You couldn't hold it in, could you?"

"You had to get shot, didn't you?" he snaps back. "I've never met anyone who worked so hard to get laid."

I scoff. "Believe me, I didn't need to get shot to bed your wife."

He turns to his boyfriend and whines, "Ethan, make him stop," like the brat he is.

"You deserve it. Now, find them a blanket. She needs to sleep."

He hops out of the chair. "For that, I'm getting two and making you cuddle with me."

Ethan shakes his head, but the affection in his eyes is unmistakable.

Charlie raises his chin toward me. "I've got your dog tags."

"Hold on to them," I say, my voice leaden with drowsiness. "I won't be returning anytime soon."

"Can we get some? The four of us?" Jax drapes a starched white blanket over Aurora. "They'd be convenient for our family."

I squint my half-lidded eyes. "Of course you want a communicator and tracker on everyone. Stalker."

Wrapped in a blanket, he stretches out on the couch and places his head on Ethan's lap. "I'm just concerned with everyone's safety," he says mockingly.

Ethan's fingers thread through Jackson's sandy-blond

hair and tug to get his attention. "Speaking of which, you wanna explain how you followed a certain someone here without them having their phone?"

I glance down at the massive, smoky diamond on Aurora's finger. I fucking knew it.

Jax sits up. "You wouldn't be growling and pulling my hair if *someone* had disappeared..." He pauses then settles back onto Ethan's lap. "You know what? Forget it. Carry on."

Charlie eyes me strangely, and I raise my brows as a shrug.

We're one big, happy, fucked-up family, and I couldn't imagine being with anyone else.

* * *

"I met him first." Aurora's playful tone whispers through the never-ending fog of sleep.

"And I met you first. So?" Jax asks, equally lighthearted.

"So now *you* get him?"

They must be discussing Ethan.

"And you get Reece," he says matter-of-factly.

"I thought you didn't want me with Reece?"

"Look, we all have to make sacrifices, Aurora."

She bursts into giggles, the sound easing my aching soul. "You really love him."

"Yes, and I love you."

Their conversation lulls, and I nearly drift off again, the heavy medication dragging me under.

Then, she asks, "Are you okay?" with concern.

"I need..." he falters.

"To get out of this room." She finishes his sentence. "You can. I'll be fine."

"I have to hit the gym or ice, you know? Go for a run, anything."

He's getting restless, and the more restless he gets, the more agitated and annoying he becomes. I intend to ask Charlie about the status of the case and when they're permitted to leave. Aurora can't sleep here another night. The hospital bed, no matter how big, can't be comfortable when pregnant.

"Go. Take the twins with you."

"I'm not leaving you, and this is the safest place for you."

"You'll get stir-crazy. See if there's a gym close by." Her tone is gentle, and when he doesn't respond, she asks, "Are *we* okay?"

"We'll always be okay. It's you and me to the end, remember?"

"With Ethan." Once more, she playfully teases, her words woven with a smile.

"With Ethan," he agrees.

"And Reece," adds my girl.

"I guess, since he took a bullet for you."

Memories of the night have resurfaced. I didn't hesitate. I recognized the weapon, knew its target, and acted. I'd do it for any one of them.

It would've sucked if the shot had been a few inches lower, though. I mean, it sucks now, but I'll survive.

"Jackson," she chides. "Not funny."

"I could've taken a bullet, babe—if Reece hadn't stolen the spotlight," he says, loud enough for me to know he intended for me to overhear.

I groan and open my eyelids. "Would you rather trade places?"

He sits beside Aurora on the couch, his knee bouncing, dark circles under his eyes. His hair is a mess and his clothes are rumpled. "God, no. I wouldn't survive Aurora's crying. She'd be distraught."

I straighten in bed and adjust the covers. Nothing more awkward than being practically naked with them and coworkers coming in and out. "Where's your boyfriend?"

He squints, but there's no irritation. "He went to shower and check on the twins."

"Letting him go must have been tough. What if he falls in love with someone else while he's gone?" I give a one-shoulder shrug—at least, I try. "You've yet to get a ring on his finger."

He goes perfectly still. Perhaps if I piss him off enough, he'll burn some energy or take a break.

Aurora, seeming to catch on, bites her bottom lip to hide her smirk. "Do you think he might be meeting with Patty?" She loses the battle and grins.

Jax's sharp gaze darts between us. "You two are horrible. I'm only letting this slide because you're both injured." He removes his phone from his pocket.

56
JACKSON

He answers on the second ring. "Hey, everything okay?"

"Where are you?"

"I haven't even left the parking lot. I had to wait for Charlie and another agent."

"Pick me up out front. These two are ganging up on me. Apparently, they want time alone."

Given the glass wall and staff staring at us, I highly doubt anything indecent is planned.

Still, as I leave, I shout for all the officers to hear, "Good luck getting your dick up with all those pain meds!"

Ethan is quiet and contemplative on the ride, and my edginess reemerges. I center myself by concentrating on how his hand grips the gearstick—it's kind of hot. More and more, Aurora's attraction to him is understandable.

He parks in the underground garage below his apartment and glances in the rearview mirror, checking the location of the agents who followed us. He kills the engine and faces me, but he avoids my gaze.

I can't handle the tension and weave my fingers through his thick hair. "What's wrong?"

He leans against the seat and blows out a breath. "I want to talk to you about something while we're alone, but I don't want to upset you."

Trepidation has my temples pulsating. "Just tell me."

A rosy flush blooms across his cheeks, spreading to his neck and ears. Fuck, it must be bad.

What if I read him all wrong?

No, friends don't touch the way we do, don't connect the way we do.

Maybe the team traded me.

Or maybe Ethan changed his mind about us. Why wouldn't he? I slammed my head into his chin. I destroyed our house and put everyone in danger.

"I'm sorry." I clench my jaw to hold back the tears. "I didn't mean to hurt you. It'll never happen again. I'll—"

He cradles my face, and his eyes meet mine. "Stop. That's not it." His fingers glide into my hair. "I want this with you, but..." He glances away. "I'm not... For you, I can be soft. But if I do something you don't like, I'm worried it'll ruin everything."

He's concerned he'll be too rough and I'll have a flashback or get spooked. He's being overprotective, as usual.

And I leap from the cliff, hoping he doesn't let me free fall—or knock me out.

I fist his shirt, and his eyes widen, his lips parting slightly. I crash my mouth to his, and he freezes, but only for a second.

Holy fucking shit. I'm kissing Ethan.

ABOUT THE AUTHOR

Jessica Lyn is a dark romance author who loves hockey, the mountains, and snow. She lives on the Oregon Coast with her family and a never-ending list of pets. Her stories, initially chart-topping Kindle Vella serials, are influenced by a decade-long career in psych triage. Outside of writing, she's into reading, traveling, crime docs, and a strong cup of tea.

@authorjessicalyn

Printed in Dunstable, United Kingdom